SCORING ZONE
A MM ENFORCER'S HOCKEY ROMANCE

HEATHER LEIGHSON

HL BOOKS CO

CONTENTS

To everyone wrestling with demons and mental health: I see you; I am you.
Don't ever give up, even when your life looks nothing like the one you thought you'd lead.
Pivot and find your joy.

GUIDE ENFORCERS ORGANIZATION

Guide To Enforcers Organization

Ari Dimon - GM

Jayce McKenna - Director of Player Development

Finn - PR Director

Coach - Head Coach

Enforcers Team Roster

Name jersey#-position-country-nickname

Patrik Liska #30-Starting Goalie-Czech Republic-Foxy

Lars Drakenberg #23-Firstline Center-Sweden-Drake or The Dragon

Dylon Felix #7-First line Right Wing-United States-Lucky

Caleb Benz #47-Backup Goalie-United States-Baby Benz

Austin Lapointe #8-Frist line Left Wing-Unites States-Ace

Jamal King #5-Second line Left Wing-United States-Rookie

Mason Griffin #21-Second line Right Wing-Canada-Griff

Chad Richardson #66-Third line Center-Unites States-Not worthy of name

Kenney #18- Defender- United States- trade

Partners

Patrik and Trevor – Truth Zone Prequel

Lars and Dylon –Misconduct Zone

Caleb and Leo – Penalty Zone

Austin (Ace) and Grayson Scoring Zone

Crossover from Unframed Art Series

Shane Reynolds is cousin to Trevor Fox – Shane and Cole MCs of The Truth of Loving You Bk 1

Von Blixt childhood friend of Lars Drakenberg – Von and Alec are MCs of The Truth of Our Past Bk 2

Jayce McKenna is the Enforcers Director of Player Development – Jayce, Emmet & Madyson are MCs of The Truth of Our Secrets Bk 3

ABOUT SCORING ZONE

Scoring Zone is a work of fiction, and I have taken liberties with both hockey rules and mental health guidelines. The suggestions in this book are in no way meant to be used as a substitute for proper mental health care from a licensed caregiver. If you or a loved one is struggling, please contact your primary doctor or for immediate crisis support:

988   Suicide & Crisis Lifeline: Call or text 988 to connect with trained counselors for free, confidential support at any time.

NAMI: https://www.nami.org/support-education/nami-helpline/

Scoring Zone is the third book in the Enforcers MM Hockey Series which includes: best friends to lovers, waking up naked in Vegas, hurt/comfort, found family, self-acceptance, mental health rep.

Love was never the game plan

Grayson

Falling for my straight best friend and waking up naked in Vegas—totally cliché.

Austin helped me through the worst time in my life and is the most important person in my life. He's the family I choose, and I can't lose him.

Not once did I think of him romantically until he kissed me senseless, took me to his room and blew my mind. It was the most incredible night of my life.

Until he ran the next morning.

Austin

Sometimes love demands honesty—even if it breaks everything.

Grayson has been my anchor. He's the only one who sees the real me and expects nothing in return.

That's a lie.

Vegas proved the dark part of me can't be trusted around him. I crossed a line—I kissed him, touched him, and never even asked if it was okay. the guilt is eating me alive. If I tell him the truth, I could lose him. But by staying silent, I already have.

All I know is I've never wanted anymore more, but having him could destroy years of friendship.

Triggers: mental health rep, suppression of feelings, aggression with suppressed feelings, hockey fist fights (one draws blood), parental disapproval which is borderline homophobic (no on-page slurs or confrontations), family drama, and bar fight with legal action.

The dreaded sense of otherness creeps in and begins to take over. I hate it. I'm outside of myself, standing on the edge, observing their fun and their bond of brotherhood forged by long hours together, buckets of sweat, and shared experiences. Things I'm not a part of because I don't truly belong.

My gaze locks on Austin and refuses to look away. His moves are jerky and don't correspond to the beat of the music. It makes me smile, and some of the desolation gripping me fades. He's the type of guy who's so good-looking that bad dancing is more endearing than a turnoff.

I decline a drink and opt for water so my gloominess stays in check.

Leo, a goalie coach, strides into the VIP area like a man on a mission. The gray in his jet-black hair gives him a distinguished air. I understand exactly what his mission is. He told me in confidence he's sleeping with Benz. In our conversation, he gave me the impression it's more than sex. But since Leo's son is on the team and is also Benz's BFF, it's messy.

I wish love could be easy.

I stare at the enormous peacock clock as the countdown to midnight gets closer, and I'm compelled to leave. All the team's significant others are here to celebrate the new year. For me, it's another year without someone special to kiss. It will be chaos, and I can kiss a half dozen drunken people, but it won't mean anything. With my mood, the kisses would taste like sad desperation.

I need to snap out of my self-pity.

I'm lucky to have a friend like Austin. Someone who wouldn't let my injury define me. Without him, I'd be another casualty of the game, working a dead-end job in my hometown and living with my parents. A total loser. He helped me find a purpose to rebuild my life.

Our friends start to couple up, and I have to leave before Austin notices. He'll be fine without me. Security has kept random fans and puck bunnies away, so it's just the team. He doesn't need me.

"Hey, are you partied out for the night?" Austin knocks his shoulder against mine, taking me by surprise.

Too late to escape.

I muster a smile. He can tell when the otherness slips in and always distracts me until I feel a part of whatever is going on.

"Did Benz's superstition get to you?"

"Maybe," I hedge. Benz kept talking about how to manifest love on New Year's Eve by spending it with the person you want to end the year with.

Austin stares at me, and there's a shift. A confusing rush. His piercing blue eyes enthrall me, and I instinctively reach for him. It's as if he's staring into my soul and seeing me from a different perspective. With anyone else, I would assume it's attraction. But Austin is absolutely straight, and instead of cupping his face to ask him what's going on, I slap his shoulder and brush party glitter off his forehead.

It's audacious and presumptuous to allow myself to think of him as more than a friend.

So I don't.

Not until this second with his eyes on my mouth.

He licks his bottom lip, and it takes every ounce of self-restraint not to bite it and work my way down to his prominent Adam's apple. I imagine gripping his short, spiky blond hair and not letting go.

What the fuck is happening?

CHAPTER 2

AUSTIN

Grayson has that look again, and I hop off the table, pushing my way through drunken teammates. He gets this lost expression, as if he doesn't know where he belongs, and tonight I want to fix it.

He assumes he owes me for his job and being a good friend, but the truth is, I couldn't function without him. I don't have to be in charge or pretend to be happy around him. I can just be.

Gray is the light that keeps my darkness locked away where it can't hurt anyone.

I hope to get a smile, but he says he's going back to his room. Tonight, he has seemed distressed ever since Benz talked about starting the year with specific intentions.

The lights play off his long hair, and I've never noticed how shiny it is. It's glossy and loose around his shoulders. Gray has the kindest brown eyes that draw me in and make me feel safe. He's the type of person other people will confess to for forgiveness. But under the compassion, his eyes hold pain.

His usual light is dim, and I long to be the one to relight it.

He reaches for me, but his hands change course, and he swipes my forehead. My skin tingles in the wake of his touch. He hasn't shaved in two days and it accentuates the bow of his upper lip, enticing me.

The seed of temptation bursts from where he touched my head to a full-blown bodily need for him.

The lock on everything I've been holding in breaks free, and my darkness seeps out, morphing into a cavern of endless desire that I don't question because it's Gray.

It consumes me, and the only thing that could possibly fill it is him. I've never been interested in men, but he's all I see. In the past, I've been apathetic about sex, but my body is on fire for him. No one has ever made me feel this way. I thought this level of attraction was movie-made, not based in reality.

My world shifts, and everything becomes clear.

Grayson is mine.

We've always belonged together, but I didn't see it.

His eyebrows scrunch in confusion, and I can tell he's biting the inside of his lip.

The irrational emotions swell inside me. I should be the one biting him, tasting every part of him.

The right thing to do would be to walk away.

I can't do that.

I should ask his permission or consent, but I don't.

All instinct and no thought, I grab the nape of his neck and steer him toward the secluded back-area of the VIP lounge. Unfortunately, I'm not the only one with this idea, but before my patience disintegrates, I find an alcove and shove him against the wall.

The depths of his eyes hold confusion and something else. I take a second to pause, mentally confirming that this is what I truly want and not the alcohol talking. Alcohol or not, my body has never burned for someone else so completely that the thought of walking away is not a feat I can accomplish.

I'm not myself as my fingers twine in his long, brown hair and tug, bringing his mouth to mine to devour. It doesn't matter that I've never kissed a man. My body buzzes with excitement, and his solid chest connects with mine, taking us higher.

Grayson's lips are soft and firm under mine. A slight hesitation, then we kiss as if we've been doing it for years. Licking into each other's mouths and eliciting groans like we already know what turns the other on.

His groan feeds my beast, urging me on. The string of precum calls to me, and I dip my head to taste it. Grayson tastes of relief and home and salty pleasure. But it's not enough.

My brain screams for more.

More.

More.

It's delicious torture. I've never let anyone have this type of power over me. Wave after wave of depraved cravings roll from my mind to every nerve in my body. Countless things I never let myself indulge in, I could do to Gray. He could handle it.

So many firsts for me tonight. Being with Grayson is natural—inevitable. Like I blinded myself to this possibility when I kept the darkness locked away.

But Gray's safe, and I won't hurt him.

As if I need a sign of his strength, he pushes me back on the bed, crawls over me, and drags me up to the pillows. While I'm captivated with him next to me, my clothes disappear.

"Tinny," he murmurs, a nickname he hasn't used in years. A name from a lifetime ago, when we didn't have any responsibilities and hockey was a fun game we played with our friends. When there was no pressure and I won the contest of who could hit the top bar of the goal the most times. It sounds like *tin* when the puck hits it, and it's part of my name. Tin became Tinny.

He spits in his palm and holds it out for me to do the same. When his large, calloused hand closes around our cocks, my eyes roll back, but I don't want to miss this. I'm not sure if it's the way his dick glides along mine with the ridges of our tips catching or the sight of it, but I'm on the edge.

"Let go. I want you to unleash all over me." Gray's watching his hand stroke us furiously.

His words unfurl and surround me. He's talking physically, but I've kept myself leashed for so long it feels like permission to let go. Be who I am.

It's who he wants. Me. Unleashed.

I come with his name on my lips and my soul soaring to the heavens. Our cum mixes together, spilling out of his fist. But he's not done with me.

"I want you." Grayson hugs me close so I'm flush against him. He cups my cheek and lifts up to kiss me.

My cock jumps at the contact, seeking his out for more. That's the word of the night…more.

"Let me explore you, show you how good it can be." His brown eyes beg, and even though the loss of control scares me, I won't say no to him.

His lopsided smile spreads across his face, and he flips us so I'm under him. He nips my jaw, and I can't help myself; I lick his scarred lip. It's smooth but raised from the surrounding skin.

Grayson takes his time, kissing and sucking as he inches toward my throbbing cock. I'm torn between forcing him down and enjoying his attention. His tongue circles my nipple until it's a hard point, and then his teeth graze it as he pinches my other nipple. The shock zings all the way to my balls.

"I might come again before you get near my dick." My hands fist the sheets.

"No, you won't. You'll lie back and let me edge you until you're so far gone you can't help but fuck my face." His eyes lock on to mine as his tongue traces a path down my sternum and into the grooves of my abs.

He places open-mouthed kisses along my V-line, and my dick jumps, hitting his cheek. "Don't worry." He kisses my tip, and lightning zaps me. "I won't forget you."

But he bypasses my length and buries his nose in my pubic hair. Gray inhales and moans. I didn't think it was possible to get hard again so soon after coming.

Tenderly, he cups my balls and licks every inch. When I'm sure I'll explode, he sucks them both in his mouth and I shout at the ceiling. My skin is on fire, heated from the inside out. My brain can't process the insane level of stimulation.

Gray shushes me and laps at my balls. He's at home between my legs, and I cross my ankles behind his back, securing him to me.

Finally.

Finally, he licks from the base of my balls, up the underside of my cock, and around my head. All my muscles go limp as if the strain of holding back is too much, and it's time to give in.

Gray sucks my tip, and my back bows off the bed. I've had blowjobs, but nothing compares to this. His eyes glaze over with need, and I'll do anything to satisfy him.

He swallows me whole, and my life flashes before my eyes, and it's a life filled with him.

"Fuck my face." Gray places my hands on his head and opens his mouth, waiting for me to comply. The sight undoes me, and my hips thrust, ramming my cock into his mouth before I consider the consequences.

He gags and swallows, tightening his throat around me, and it only takes a few pumps before my load floods his mouth. He drinks it all and sighs with satisfaction.

"Gray," I croak, reaching to bring him up so I can reciprocate. I suck him down without hesitation, and his pungent taste spurs me on.

Gray lets out a howl, and his legs shake as he comes down my throat. I'm not prepared for how fast it comes out or how much. He tries to ease back as I sputter, but I love it. I'm so giddy, I'm seeing stars.

He lives on my tongue and inside me.

My fingers on his ass force him to stay in place. In my mouth. Where he belongs.

He collapses, draping himself over me and shivers. He's not cold, but just in case, I roll us back on the pillows, and reach over to wrangle the comforter around us. This...us... unforeseeable, but I love it. I love us together.

We can't stop touching each other, and I lose count of the orgasms. I've never had multiples in one night and attribute it all to him touching me with strength and care. We lose ourselves in each other until I'm drunk on pleasure and close to passing out from exhaustion.

"Tinny?" Grayson tilts back to look into my eyes. The way he says my name asks a hundred questions. Am I all right? Did we go too far? Do I want this? What are we doing?

I'm sure I want him with everything that I am, but since he's not asking specific questions, I don't have to answer him. Rather than speak, I fuse my mouth to his, and we kiss for days.

Gray sighs contentedly in my ear.

"Biggest score of the night," I mumble, floating on air.

We're perfect together.

Until I wake up the next morning and see the harm I've caused him.

CHAPTER 3

AUSTIN

Behind my closed eyelids, the sun burns too bright. Last night is a blur until Grayson shifts beneath me, and it all rushes back. I've got a tight hold, locking him in place. I smile, inhaling his familiar scent that lingers under the layer of menthol and coconut oil from treating players. Beneath it is his comforting smell, warm and inviting, like being wrapped in a blanket of cotton.

Nothing has ever felt so right as Grayson in my arms. I usually like my space, but with him I seek his closeness. It's as if I'm trying to make up for all the times I didn't trust myself to give in to physical touch.

As captain of the team, I have responsibilities today, and as much as I'd like to spend the day in bed with Grayson, I have to get up. A soft groan leaves me as I pry my eyes open to the sun beating through the open curtains, daring us to keep sleeping.

I'm met with a horrific sight.

Gray's sleek hair drapes over my arm, revealing his shoulder, scabbed with my bite mark. His body is covered in bruises from my hands and mouth.

"What the fuck." Bile rises in my throat and I swallow it back down.

Grayson must hate me.

I hate me.

Letting the darkness out was a terrible mistake.

Unforgivable.

It destroys the people I love.

In an effort not to wake him, I ease out of bed. I don't know how to apologize for hurting him or understand how he could let me do that to him. This is exactly why I don't give in to my evil urges. I know better.

"Morning." He stretches, and the sick part of me wants to jump back in bed and leave more marks all over him so he knows who he belongs to. Only a degenerate would think like that.

When he rolls over to look at me, my cock hardens, and I cover it as if doing so will excuse my depravity.

"Oh, hey." The casualness of my words surprises me and leaves me at a loss to say more.

Grayson deserves an apology. He deserves a friend who doesn't fantasize about hurting him more.

I sweat as my panic rises. Saying "I'm sorry" won't make up for what I've done. I can't expect him to forgive me. His body is a mess.

"Hey, it's me. It's fine." Gray sits up against the headboard. The pain of his welts hasn't registered on him yet.

"That didn't happen." I point to the bed to excuse my behavior. Maybe I can leave and collect myself before he knows what I did to him. That's cowardly, but the darkness is cackling with glee, and the rest of my brain is screaming to run.

"Okay." He holds his hands up to calm me down. Grayson is consoling me when I should be falling at his feet and begging him not to hate me.

Instead, I say, "There's nothing to talk about." More evidence that I'm broken. Since I don't see my clothes, I hurry to the bathroom and cover my miscreant dick with a towel.

Dread as thick and black as tar infiltrates every pore. I take deep, calming breaths, but it doesn't work.

Grayson gets out of bed, and I summon the courage to face him and make amends. But my brain short-circuits when I see him in my boxers.

I left them on the bed last night in case I, or a sloppy, drunken teammate, needed clothes.

Carnal hunger washes over me, ridding me of my dread. Grayson should be under me with my cock buried in his ass. This is Vegas; they must deliver supplies to the room.

Shaking my head, I force those thoughts away.

"You're wearing my... Those are mine," I say stupidly, unable to unscramble my brain from wanting him.

"I thought this conversation would require clothes." He bends down and checks under the bed but straightens without more clothes.

"I don't understand. I'm sorry," I say, finally finding words to express my remorse.

"Ace." He uses my team nickname, and it's like a slap.

Last night, he called me Tinny. My favorite nickname from a time when there was no pressure to be anyone other than ourselves. He rarely calls me Ace unless we're with the team.

It's his unconscious way of distancing himself from me. It's the least I deserve.

My phone alarm goes off, reminding me of my duty to the team. I'm supposed to set a good example. I've let everyone down.

"Gray," I beg, but shake my head. He should look in the mirror and see what I've done before I ask for forgiveness. "Fuck." I've ruined us. He's my best friend and the only person I count on. I have to focus on one thing at a time. "I need my phone."

He jumps into action, tearing apart the bed. I try to help him, but I can't be so close to him without wrapping him in my arms. Gray loves hugs and touches, but I can't comfort him when I'm the one who hurt him.

After moving the mattress, he steps away to call my phone, and I find it lying flush against the frame, unseen until it lights up with the incoming call. I clutch it to my chest so I don't reach out and touch him. In the mess of the bedding on the floor, I find my clothes and dress quickly.

We stare at each other. There are too many things to say. I should give him space to process all his wounds before we talk. He seemed to enjoy last night, but he hasn't seen the damage I've done. Surely, he'll look back on last night differently once he knows.

So I do the one thing I thought I'd never do...

Walk out the door and leave him behind.

CHAPTER 4

GRAYSON

As I lie in my bold, gold hotel room bed, my phone blows up with the team's friend chat. They've noticed my absence and relentlessly text until Austin replies to leave me alone, and they do. I should be grateful there's no need to offer any explanation. It means I can wallow in my hotel bed for the foreseeable future.

Austin was so disgusted by what we did, he fled his own room.

The chat is silent, which means they switched to talking to each other in the player's chat. The one I'm not a part of.

I reek of sex but don't want to wash it off because our night together might not feel real.

Everything went from extraordinary to a shitshow within hours, and I can't figure out what happened. One minute I was looking out for Austin, to ensure he didn't have next-morning regret and only hours later, *I* was his next-morning regret.

I knew without a doubt, crossing the line and having sex with Austin would put our friendship at risk yet somehow last night, I convinced myself we were kismet.

My stupid dick gets hard as my fingers graze his bite mark on my shoulder. I've had enthusiastic bed partners, but Austin took it to the next level, and I fucking loved it.

Never in my wildest dreams would Austin and I end up in bed together and crave each other in such a primal way. At first, I purposely let him lead so I didn't push him into anything new or uncomfortable.

Last night he was more than eager, almost possessed. The marks on my body are proof. He acted like he couldn't get enough of me, as if my taste was his new obsession.

And today, it's as if it never happened. He blatantly said it didn't happen.

In the ultimate act of self-pity, I take a picture of my torso to preserve the evidence that I'm not crazy. Austin wanted me last night. At the very least, he wanted my body.

To have his complete attention was more intoxicating than any alcohol we'd consumed. I've always admired his loyalty and devotion as a friend, but knowing what he tastes like is turning my world upside down.

Our physical connection is what I've been searching for but never found. But maybe it's one-sided.

We'd been drinking more than usual, but he was coherent and seemed capable of consent. He wasn't uncoordinated, and his dick rose to the occasion. But maybe I took advantage of him.

I'm privy to Austin's heart, and he's never had a problem with my sexuality or our teammates'. When Lucky came out as bisexual, Austin asked him a few questions but didn't judge Lucky's later-in-life realization.

My reckless belief in a night of fate can't ruin our friendship. I will bury my new attraction to him and never touch him again if we can keep our relationship.

My eyes shut with the memory of his grunts and groans. Shoving those feelings aside seems hopeless, but I'll do anything for him. Deny myself everything, even cut my heart out to keep him with me.

My head pounds along with my heartbeat at the thought of living without him. He's been central to my life since middle school. I can't give that up. We have to figure out a way around last night.

I assumed he'd always be in my life as my friend but for the first time, I let myself wonder if it could be more. I can't ignore the explosive chemistry, but if he can, it doesn't mean a thing.

My stomach grumbles, and I decide to venture out of my room for food. This is Vegas, no one will question why I smell like a brothel. I'll probably get some high-fives.

The Enforcers have reserved a room for brunch/lunch today, but Austin's not there when I peek inside. Of the two of us, he's the talker. I won't pressure him to talk to me before he's ready.

I nod to two of our equipment managers. None of the players are here, so I've timed this perfectly. The team leaves tonight for another away game in Nashville before we go home.

The voice in my head berates me, saying Austin has finally realized I'm holding him back and I'm not good enough for him. Today, it's unusually loud. The voice is an old adversary with a worn-out soundtrack, yet it still rings with a kernel of truth.

That nugget plants itself and immediately sprouts roots.

I've been down this road before and should know better than to let this happen, especially since I went to a therapist after my hockey injury. My depression at the time caused lots of irrational thoughts.

I knew I should've been watching over Austin, and that did not include sticking my tongue down his throat.

He'd had too much to drink, and instead of waiting to talk about his frame of mind when he sobered up, I jumped him.

I fell asleep before checking on him.

In short, I took advantage of my best friend and forced him into a physical relationship.

I smack my forehead with my palm to shut the voice up. Some of those things might be true, and I won't know until I talk to Austin, but I certainly didn't force him into anything.

"Hey, man." Jamal King gives me an up-nod, causing the beads at the end of his zigzag cornrows to click with his movements as he enters with Griff and Kenney. King and Mason Griffin play second-line wingers together. Austin was really worried about King when he joined the team. He's an introvert who has slowly come out of his shell, but Austin was concerned he was being treated differently. As the only Black man on the team, he stands out, and Austin wants to include King but not pressure or bully him into situations King isn't comfortable with. As a fellow introvert, it's a high-wire act to strike the right balance.

"Great job commandeering the brain today." Griff snickers and picks up a plate.

"What?" I cough out my response to this much-needed distraction. The tasteless food is hard to get down.

"You and Ace aren't twinning, and he looks like hell, so it's fair to assume you got the brain today." He turns to Kenney. "You know we joke about them sharing a brain, right?"

"No, but it makes sense," Kenney says seriously. "Did you call or text so you wouldn't dress the same?" he asks me.

"You better hope I've got the brain if you get hurt." I stand and a server takes my plate with the scraps left on it.

"Dude, do not jinx us like that!" Griff slams his plate in horror.

My laugh sounds stilted and too loud.

When I get back to my room, I text Austin.

> **Me: FYI- I got the brain today**

> **Austin: Says who?**

> **Me: Griff**

> **Me: He's telling tales to Kenney**

> **Austin: *angry face emoji* taking a nap**

If last night hadn't happened, we'd be spending the day complaining about getting old and playing video games. But since last night happened and his text reads like he wants to be alone, I go to my room to do the same. He needs his solitude to recharge, and I respect that as part of his personality. Today, his need to be alone comes off as personal, and I should get over that. I ignore the emptiness of solitude. When I lie down, his phantom touches and crisp scent, which remind me of the ice rink and the holidays, linger as if they're real.

Loneliness grips me as tight as a lover as I force thoughts of Austin away.

I've never had butterflies about seeing my best friend. Actually, what's happening feels more like bees than pretty butterflies. My strategy is simple: get on the plane first, sit in my regular seat, and close my eyes. Austin can either sit with me like normal or choose another seat.

Only Austin gets on the plane first, and his carry-on is sitting in my seat. I guess I have my answer. But as I'm walking down the aisle, one of the rookies stows Austin's bag in the overhead compartment for him.

Now I'm unsure what to do. Taking another seat will draw more attention than sitting next to him and ignoring our issue. I slide into my seat.

"Two days in a row," Benz says as he sits next to Griff. I catch him staring longingly at Leo with the other coaches.

"For what?" Austin asks.

"Not dressing the same. I kinda miss it." Benz heaves a big sigh, and Griff elbows him.

Austin side-eyes me and I shrug. No matter how much I dreamed about his hands on me when I took a nap, I'm not projecting my desire onto him.

We don't talk until after takeoff, and no one else is paying attention. He turns as much as he can in his seat to face me.

"There aren't enough words to tell you how sorry I am for hurting you." His sorrowful blue eyes beg for forgiveness.

"I don't need you to be sorry. I'm trying to understand what happened." Our heads are inches apart so no one can hear us. His scent of spicy cloves and vanilla shampoo makes it hard to think.

What hurt the most was him pointing at the bed and declaring that the night we spent together didn't happen. He dismissed the best sex of my life, as if he could will it away.

"I don't know." His eyes cloud with confusion. "All I know is that I hurt you, and I never want to do that again."

It's great that he's taking responsibility for his behavior, but that doesn't give me any clarity about us as more than friends.

"You know you can talk to me. You're not alone in this. I'm here for you to help figure out what upset you." My intention is to offer advice and comfort, but he turns red and his lips pinch together.

"I already said I'm upset about hurting you."

"Yes, but you should consider how you feel about what happened." With the way he's looking at me, I'm sure we're having two entirely different conversations. It's strange to be on a completely different wavelength. Usually, he's easy to read, and his thoughts broadcast straight to me.

"I don't matter when I hurt you." He turns to face forward, and my hope fades that continuing the conversation will be productive.

"As long as we stay friends, that's all that matters." It sounds simple, but the armrest between us could be a steel wall. My best friend might as well be a stranger with the way he's leaning away from me.

"Friends forever." He forces a smile that's detached and unconcerned.

My muscles seize as if I'm about to be attacked, and I painstakingly relax. The voice in my head doesn't believe him, and I can't convince myself it's being a lying bastard.

I rationalize that he needs time to figure out what last night means for him, and then he can deal with what it means for us. I gotta calm my ass down.

If I was smart, I'd take my own advice and think about my wants. But suddenly yearning after my straight best friend isn't good for either of us. Dwelling on how my body is attuned to his every move isn't beneficial. There's a huge possibility that if I examine what I want between us, I'll never be able to settle and go back to being his friend.

He's not as straight as either of us thought, but that doesn't mean he will want to change how he presents himself to the world.

His square jaw is tight, and his blond eyebrows scrunch over his blue eyes so it looks like he doesn't have an upper lid. I don't want to stresses him out.

For all I know, I could've been a one-night experiment gone wrong.

He wouldn't do that.

At least Tinny would not, but I'm here with Ace, the hockey player.

Maybe they don't want the same things.

CHAPTER 5

AUSTIN

The Nashville game is minutes away, and my entire routine is off, which is a bad sign They're a tough team, and my head needs to be in the game. I tune out the locker room noise to mentally prepare.

But I can't understand why Gray is so nonchalant about what I did to him, as if he's more worried about me than himself.

Logically, it makes sense since he has no clue how much I loved marking his skin, and part of me was proud of the horrible red bruises. He doesn't know my dick gets hard every time I imagine sinking my teeth into his shoulder. Or how much I love his long brown hair trailing over my body like silk. How his skin tastes exactly like he smells: warm and sweet with a hint of spice. He doesn't know I dream about doing worse things to his body. That I crave being inside him and being denied might kill me.

There isn't a way to express remorse for those things without confessing them. He can never know how fucked up my brain is. No sane person fantasizes about fucking their best friend so hard it leaves them black and blue.

On the plane, he put his headphones on, cutting off our conversation, and I went to sleep as soon as we got to our hotel. My guilt argues that I avoided the conversation too, but I justify it as necessary for our game.

Hockey always comes first, and Grayson understands that.

Our text conversations are usually a steady stream—now my phone is silent. It'd be easy to text him, but today it feels impossible. My apology didn't cover the depth of my regret, and Grayson has made it clear he doesn't appreciate the word sorry.

Lucky and Benz pester me to dance for our pregame ritual, but I only manage a half-hearted attempt for the team. They claim we can't win if I don't dance. I'm already having trouble concentrating, so I won't mess up their mojo on top of my issues.

"You guys played a helluva game in Vegas, and I expect the same effort tonight. Benz, you up for another goalie goal?" Coach asks rhetorically.

Usually before a game, I stop by Gray's training room for my good luck routine: he claps his palms on my shoulders, taps his forehead against mine, and says "You got this." It's fast and silly, but I miss it. I'm sure he would've done it if I'd gone to him. But I didn't and now I regret it.

The whiff of the ice and roar of the crowd help to get my head in the game.

The puck drops, Drake wins the face-off, and we speed down the ice. It's strange to play with Drake and Lucky now. We've always had great intuition and awareness of each other, but now that they're a couple, they're extra in tune with each other, like they can read each other's minds. It's true opposites attract. Drake looks like the standoffish blond Swede he is, and Lucky is all-American Midwest, dark hair with a dimple inviting a person to share his joke.

That skill has benefited all our playing, but sometimes I can't support them when they're doing their own thing. Lucky feigns a pass to Drake, and the puck lands on my stick instead. Muscle memory takes over and I shoot. The goalie is slightly out of position, not expecting the pass to me. That fraction of a second reorientation from the goalie is all I need, and the lamp lights up.

Lucky wraps me in a hug and smacks my helmet as Drake slaps my back and uses his momentum to steer us toward the bench. The second line goes over the boards, and Gray passes me a water bottle with a smile.

I should stop inventing problems. Gray and I are fine. He's my best friend. All I have to do is focus on my job and forget about how his muscles rippled under my hands. That he woke an insatiable part of me. That, no matter my attempts to find other men attractive, no one compares to him.

Nashville doesn't make the game easy. We have to fight for the puck and every chance to score. One of their defenders trash-talks me and wants to fight. It's not uncommon for hockey fights to be planned, but I'm not a fighter. All the teams know that, and opponents never ask me to throw down.

"Hit up number 23." I point to Drake, who will fight him. Drake never backs down and most often starts unscripted brawls.

"He's not my mark." The Nashville player skates away, and I assume he's going to drop it.

I'm wrong. On our next shift, he drops his gloves and takes a swing at me. I shove him away, but don't take my gloves off or hit him back. That infuriates him, and a second before the buzzer ends the first period, he rips my helmet off and punches me in the face.

The refs immediately descend on us, and his players drag him away.

Coach sends me to the training room with Gray. He points at the exam table and snaps on gloves. I strip off my pads until I'm down to my base layer and sit.

His fingers lightly coast over my cheekbone and eye socket. Gloves are a mandatory part of his job, but I hate the barrier between us. It's irrational, but his gloves add to the distance in our relationship. He has me complete the standard eye test.

"In my professional medical opinion, you're gonna have one beauty of a shiner." He grins at me.

"That's how the professionals talk now?" My shoulders drop inches with the familiarity of his teasing.

"Yupper. That's gotta hurt, eh?" He's looking into my eyes, not at my injury, as his thumb caresses the swollen area.

I blow out a long breath. We rarely slip into Canadian expressions, but I need that connection with him. We grew up together, and whatever is happening won't tear us apart.

"For sure. What's the verdict? Can I keep playing?" I can't let my team down.

"As long as the swelling doesn't affect your vision." He steps away to get an icepack, and I miss his nearness. "Keep this on until the start of the next period.

I'll have new ice ready every time your shift is over, and I'll examine it. But you should be fine."

Grayson pauses and the scar on his lip twitches. "You can fight back. It's okay," he says quietly.

"I can't," I say, harsher than I mean. "You remember why." I hang my head to avoid looking at him. The day still haunts me.

He lifts my chin with his fingers. "One, keep your head elevated for the swelling. Two, that was a long time ago and has nothing to do with a pro hockey fight."

His brown eyes bore into me as if he could either erase the memory or change my mind. Grayson was there, so it's mindboggling how he can say that.

When we were kids, I was aggressive and would fight at the smallest slight. After my twelfth birthday, we went to an away tournament, and a bigger kid kept shoving me into the boards. He blocked one of my shots, and I saw red and attacked him. I must've blacked out for a minute because the next thing I remember is being pulled off him as he screamed and cried. I broke one of his ribs, and he never played hockey again. For the second time in my life, the darkness in me took over and caused serious bodily harm.

The first time was with my sister, and I should've known I'm dangerous. Too violent for Grayson.

"Hey." Grayson removes the latex gloves and places his warm hands on my shoulder. "What happened back then wasn't your fault." I glare at him, but he doesn't relent. "That kid took that hit into the boards and had trouble breathing five minutes before your fight. It might not have been you."

"No twelve-year-old can play with a broken rib." I resist the urge to pull away because his hands on me are an indulgence I can't deny myself.

"If you're going to ignore facts, I'll remind you of his rabid father screaming at him. That kid wouldn't come off the ice unless it was on a stretcher." He flinches at his words because that's exactly what happened. "At least his father shut the hell up."

"You always see the good side of things." I lean forward to rest my forehead on his chest, and his hands curve around my back. Touch is part of his job, and he gives and receives it easily. For me, touch is more of a forbidden fruit. Once I have a little, I'm afraid I'll need it—rely on it.

"And that kid became an oncologist. He makes a ton of money and doesn't put his body at risk. He's fine. If he knew you felt bad, he'd probably send you a basket of syrup and maple cookies." He rubs my sweaty head, and I relish his hands threading through my hair.

"Don't stereotype our people," I grumble. Grayson's right. The guy's a doctor and probably doesn't have to worry about what his father thinks about his career. Any father should be proud of their doctor son.

All the residual tension leaves my body, and I'm ready to play. He always knows how to get me in the right headspace when my mind veers off track.

"Back to my original point. You can participate in a fight and not worry about something bad happening. These guys are tough. They can take it. Just like I can take your aggressive side. You don't need to hide it."

He's being sincere and honest. But he's wrong. New Year's Eve was proof that I can't be trusted. He shouldn't endure pain for my pleasure. That's despicable. He's also forgetting I'm the reason his hockey career ended. I refuse to take more from him with my selfishness. I've done enough harm in his life.

"If you hurry, you can show off your pretty eye to the team before the second period." Gray's crooked smile freezes the air in my lungs, and his thumb stroking my eyebrow while he cups my jaw causes my stomach to flip-flop.

It's a simple gesture from a friend who isn't afraid to touch people.

But for me, it's so much more—an off-limits physical connection with a man I'm desperate for. I'm not safe for him, and I won't harm him again. What I want doesn't matter.

I smack my head, hoping to regain my senses.

"Careful with the precious merchandise." Gray gathers icepacks and other things he'll need for the rest of the game.

I lean into his body, soaking him in as I vow to protect him from me.

CHAPTER 6

GRAYSON

The silence in our apartment echoes as loudly as a blaring alarm. Soundproof windows block out the city noise and traffic. Austin and I live together, but this is a busy part of the season, and we don't have downtime together. Correction, we're not prioritizing each other in our downtime.

We don't have to avoid each other.

I stay late every night to work on players who are wearing down from the toll the game takes on their bodies. By the time I get home, Austin has crashed.

He counsels players before practice and games who are mentally losing their edge. Today he's worried about Kenney and is picking him up to drive him to practice.

I haven't had the headspace to address the situation. Maybe it's me. Maybe there is no situation. Maybe Austin is fine with our wary friendship.

The lack of certainty bothers me.

I've been racking my brain to find evidence that I suppressed my feelings for him. I had noticed how fantastic the Captain America costume looked on him. Maybe I've been lying to myself for years.

I shake my head because it doesn't matter.

I'm a walking cliché, catching feelings for my straight best friend. One night has me tied in knots, thinking it was special, like we were meant to be. Thinking that I could have it all—my best friend as my insatiable lover. It's something I never knew I wanted until I had him.

That's my problem, not his. It's not fair that after one night, I went from happily being Austin's friend to pining for him like a puppy. Now I notice his ass and dick outline in his sweatpants. I blame it on knowing what he looks like naked; lusting for a friend is against bro code.

As his friend, I appreciate his big heart and selflessness, which adds to my new physical attraction. It's official—I'm a mess.

Our two-bedroom apartment is normally a cozy refuge above the city, but every foot represents space between us. As if the view of nondescript skyscrapers conspires to stretch endlessly to the horizon. I've loved the open living room and kitchen, but without Austin, it's lifeless. The large TV is off, and the gaming consoles dangle, waiting to be picked up. The only joyful things in the room are the purple pillows with the team logo that his mom made for us.

Trevor's basic bitches comment comes to mind. I haven't given much thought to decorating and it shows. It's also odorless, without his personal vanilla woodsy smell.

We moved in after I finished my master's degree and got a job offer from the Enforcers. Although we had to sign waivers not to blame the team if anything went wrong when I treated Austin, he introduced me to everyone, got me the internship, and lobbied for me to get the job permanently.

From the living room, I glance at his open bedroom door at the end of the hall past mine. There's no use in fighting the urge to straighten his room. He needs to see everything but leaves a mess to clean that stresses him out. I have five minutes before I should leave, which gives me enough time to clear off his bed and toss his stinky dirty clothes in the washer. Unfortunately for me, the stench of his sweat is a turn on.

The dark navy comforter with gray stripes is balled up on his bed like he got in a fight with it. My comforter is the coordination opposite of his, gray with navy stripes. We thought it was fun to match. But really, we added gray and navy to a basic collection of neutral beiges, whites, and blues.

His room has walls so pale blue they almost look white. I can't help but smile at his wall of sticky notes all lined up like a calendar so he doesn't forget things.

A quick skim and I take down the ones that are irrelevant or have passed. The desk in the corner is covered, but there's no time to straighten it out.

From experience, he won't notice what I've done, but I've always wanted to make his life easier since his body takes such a beating for his job.

The sinister voice starts a rant about how we were never equal friends and it's only a matter of time before our friendship ends. I recognize the intrusive thoughts and practice mindful breathing. The thoughts linger longer than usual.

I should've asked in the group chat if anyone wanted to carpool, but then I wouldn't have a ride back to the city unless my last patient/player gave me a ride. I'm not burdening an injured player with my transportation. No one on the team has an obligation to me.

Music blasts in the car to keep me company.

A few players come to see me before practice, including Liska. His back sprain isn't serious. He needs to rest it, but it's hard for him to accept that getting better means no strenuous activity.

Trevor's with him today. "Don't mind me. I'm here to listen and make sure he follows directions."

I bite back a grin as Liska grumbles. I grill him about his activity and remind him of his weight limits. Trevor gasps in horror.

"You did *not* tell me you couldn't pick me up," he huffs.

"Grayson never said I shouldn't specifically do it." Liska crosses his arms over his chest.

"Semantics." Trevor waves his hand dramatically. "You know I weigh over thirty pounds."

"Now it won't happen again," I say, hoping to end this conversation before they tell me more about their sex life.

"Men." Trevor rolls his eyes.

Austin pops into my head, and I agree a hundred percent.

Once I'm done with Liska, I walk into the defense video room to treat a defender with a sore hip flexor. I crouch to talk to him, but I'm confused when Jamal King, our second-line left winger, walks in.

"King-y, King, King," Benz sings so loudly it echoes. "Join us. Tell us all your secrets."

King's bright aqua eyes sweep the room in confusion, and Drake appears in the doorway to take him to the offense video room.

"One of these days he'll stay and play." Benz sighs.

"He's got his own shit to learn." Liska glares at him.

The defender tells me quietly that King wanders into the wrong room on average once a month. I treat a few more players until it's time for them to practice on the ice, and I get a break since no one needs my services.

I sit with Trevor. He's drinking coffee, but the man doesn't need any more caffeine. He's outspoken on his quiet days.

"Should we continue our conversation?" he asks, peering at me over his to-go cup.

"About Liska lifting you? I'm good." My eyes find Austin, and I watch him play.

"No, about your lack of fashion sense and proclivity to dress like your roommate."

"Now you're trying to impress me with your vocabulary," I say dryly.

He snorts and inhales some coffee, causing a coughing fit. Liska's at the boards in seconds.

"Down, boy. Gray's being funny. Who knew?" Trevor finds a napkin in his bag to wipe his face, and Liska shakes his head as he skates away. After a silence, he says, "I'm sorry about the basic bitch comment. It was rude and uncalled for."

"It's fine." I watch the way Liska moves for a minute to make sure he's doing okay. "I'm not a fashionable guy, and we haven't dressed alike in almost a week." I wasn't offended then or now.

"Why? What's wrong?" he asks quickly.

I swallow the lump flavored with fear. "Nothing. Why would you say that?"

Trevor nudges me with his elbow. "You don't think it means you're out of sync?"

"No." No other words come to mind. It's Benz who believes in universal energy and the law of attraction. I don't disbelieve, but this idea gets me thinking. Looking back, we haven't dressed the same since the night we spent together. It usually happens several times a week. We are totally out of sync, but that's not why we're not dressing the same. That would be weird.

He takes pity on me and asks, "What are you wearing to the gala?"

My gaze snaps to his. "You mean the gala that's weeks away? Why would I plan that now?"

Trevor tuts. "You are part of this organization and are representing the Enforcers at a highly publicized charity event. It's not the time to re-wear one of your old suits." He pointedly raises an eyebrow.

I open my mouth to ask how he knows that, but he probably guessed.

"There isn't time to make you a custom suit. But if you come over, we can look at what I have in stock and tailor it for a Grayson-specific look."

"Thank you?" It's a question since I have no style.

"Don't worry, you will thank me when you turn heads and some people can't keep their hands off you." He hides his sly smile with his coffee mug.

I could splurge on a new suit since I rarely buy things for myself. Austin feels guilty about our salary difference and tries to make up for it by spending money on me or prepaying bills and telling me I can pay next time.

Next time never arrives, and he pays much more than he should.

Austin's generous and takes care of his friends. He's the best guy I know, and I miss the way we were. If I have to pin him down, we're having a conversation about us—tomorrow night, since he'll be at the team hotel tonight.

It's a relief to have a plan because even if he goes out with the team, I can stay up for this conversation.

My high hopes go straight to hell before the game even starts.

CHAPTER 7

AUSTIN

My name being called pulls me awake, but I'm confused and on our plush couch. Gray's doe eyes stare at me with concern, and his hair is pulled back but not all in the band.

"Are you all right? Are you hurt?" He yanks the blanket off me as if he'll see an injury.

"I'm fine," I mutter and stand to hug him. It was a horrible night. "Are you okay?"

"I must look like total shit to get an impromptu hug," he jokes, and I clutch him tighter and inhale his warmth.

As I hit a new low in self-pity, the universe reminds me that life isn't all about me. Before the game, Leo was on the ice to coach Benz and got hit in the face with a puck. Grayson went with him to the hospital, and I tried to wait up but must've dozed off. It's time to let go of him, but my arms won't cooperate. They really fucking think Grayson belongs in them. Look at me, blaming my arms.

"How's Leo?" I ask, holding on as if my life depends on him.

"He'll be fine, had surgery on his broken jaw, and it will be wired shut for a few weeks." He gives me a squeeze of reassurance.

"Tonight was a disaster. I envy how calm you can stay in an emergency because I lost my shit and yelled at Benz and Griff." I sigh when he extracts himself from my hold to sit on the couch where I was sleeping.

"That's the least of their concerns."

"No. Of course. I didn't mean to make it about me. Just saying I'm not good in an emergency like you." I cringe at my words, not even saying what I mean. If a puck can take Leo down in the blink of an eye, it could happen to Gray. He doesn't have protective gear. Maybe I should bring that up with the front office. Everyone on the sidelines should wear protective pads.

Could be genius or an overreaction. But the thought of it happening to Gray guts me.

"You're not making it about you. But I checked the team portal, and it didn't list you as injured, so I got worried seeing you sleeping on the couch."

"I was waiting for you," I admit. Falling asleep on the couch is so rare for me that I can't remember the last time it happened. I like my bed and sleep too much to spend an uncomfortable night in the living room.

"Go to bed. We can talk in the morning." He yawns and his head flops back on the couch.

"If you're too tired..." I won't pressure him to talk if he's not awake, but I'm also afraid I'll lose my nerve. We live together, so it's going to sound ridiculous to admit I miss him. He's right here.

"I'm awake. Being with Benz is like a shot of caffeine. It'll take me a few minutes to get off that high." His head tips to the side to assess me and he frowns. "You're not fine. Tell me what's going on."

All I have to do is open my mouth and tell the truth. But I don't. "If Benz was there, then I should've been there."

"Nope. Benz wasn't there to represent the Enforcers, but that's not my story to tell. Don't change the subject. You've shut me out, and I hate it." He re-situates himself so he's facing me, and his knee bumps my thigh. "Sorry about that."

"It's not good when you apologize for accidentally touching me. Can we go back to how we were before Vegas?" It's the only solution to ensure I don't harm him. He knows what I'm capable of, and I'm shocked he's upset about me keeping my distance. He experienced my violence, and it cost him a career in the NHL. I've already taken too much from him.

"I have too many questions for that. You purposely avoid talking about our night together as if it didn't happen, and I feel terrible. I knew you were drunk and should never have taken advantage of you. Clearly you weren't sober enough for consent, and I'm afraid you'll never forgive me."

The pain in Gray's eyes stops me cold.

"Wait. What?" He shouldn't apologize when I'm the one who left marks on his body. I broke the skin on his shoulder like a demon. Even if he had taken advantage of me, I deserved it for all I'd done to him. "I started it, so you didn't read the situation wrong. And of course it happened."

"Austin, you pointed at the bed and denied what happened. I understand dealing with what we did together might be difficult for you, but we have to be honest if we're going to get past it." He reaches for my arm but lets his hand drop to his lap.

I'm shaking my head as if I disagree, but he thinks I'm upset about what *we* did, not how I hurt him. "I'm so sorry, and I don't remember saying that. You're the last person in the world I would intentionally harm, but I physically hurt you. My life is a mess without you."

Not only is he my best friend, but he takes care of me in a way no one else ever has. He came up with a system for me to drop my keys and wallet in the same place, instead of searching for the random places I leave them. And the man picks up my room. He's a saint.

Grayson snorts a laugh and falls back onto the couch's armrest. "You are Mr. Perfect. You've got a seriously sick job, the team loves and respects you, and you've got the world at your feet. I don't do anything for you."

I clear my throat to tell him he's dead wrong without offending him. "G." He sits up at my use of the nickname and broken tone. "I couldn't do any of this without you." I see he wants to argue, so I take his hand. "From the day we met, you never wanted anything from me. I can be myself with you and not worry about my mood or how I filter my words or needing alone time." The irony that isn't true at this moment isn't lost on me, but protecting him is more important.

"Then don't filter yourself now. Tell me why you're so upset." He laces our fingers and shifts closer so his bent leg rests against mine. The leg contact is incidental, but it goes straight to my groin.

"I told you, I hurt you." I fail to keep the frustration out of my voice.

"This isn't about my feelings—"

"Your feelings!" I throw my hands in the air. "G, I broke your skin and left welts all over your body!" And worse, I recall his flavor on my tongue every single day.

He tilts his head in confusion. "But that was my favorite part. I mean, after you put your mouth on me, and after sliding your dick between my cheeks and after stroking us together and coming all over each other, then it was my fave." His lopsided grin appears and steals my breath.

My mind reels. "How could you like that? I totally disregarded your consent and treated you like...like...I disrespected you." There. That's mostly the truth.

Grayson stares at me for a long time. So long that I have the urge to run away.

"Do you judge men who bottom?" he asks, and I flinch at the abrupt change of subject.

"I think everyone gets to decide for themselves what they want to do. It's not my place to tell anyone what they should or shouldn't do during sex." That seems obvious but whatever.

Grayson raises an eyebrow.

He doesn't say anything.

We gaze at each other expectantly.

He bites the inside of his lip, waiting. Waiting for me to do or say something.

I bury my eyes in the crook of my elbow. "I judged you for what you like."

"Are you or are you judging yourself?" he murmurs.

"I lost control and you know..." I wave my other arm in his direction

"Austin Lapointe," he full-names me in a stern voice. "Look at me when I say this."

I breathe deeply, drop my arm, and meet his gaze.

"I enjoy rough sex. Do you know how hard it is to find a person capable of manhandling me? I'm a big dude, so it ain't easy. I. Love. It." He pokes me in the chest as he says the last three words.

I nod, at a loss, and he lets out an indignant hum.

"Listen, during team dance parties, you must have seen Lucky's body. You can't miss the fact that Drake makes it his mission to cover him in bite marks. Benzy blushes and grins like a fool when we call out his purple bruises. They love how their partners show their possessiveness. It's only a problem if one person likes it and the other doesn't. I loved it." He exposes his shoulder, and the skin that used to be red and raw only has a tint of yellow.

I touch it to make sure it's real and not covered in makeup or something.

"Do you trust me?"

"With my life," I say seriously.

"Then trust me to tell you if you're crossing a boundary. We didn't talk about safe words or anything, but I promise I'll tell you if I don't like something." His shirt covers his shoulder again, and I'm torn.

Part of me hates what I did, and another part is disappointed my teeth marks are gone.

"Tinny, I'm a tough guy. A few marks don't hurt. In fact, they were a huge turn-on. I took a picture to remember it." He shows me his phone, and I recognize the ornate mirror from Vegas.

The tightness in me unravels, hearing him call me Tinny, but looking at his bruises is too much. "But I can't trust myself with you." The truth is dragged from my depths as I expose my shame.

"Don't say that because of me. If you didn't enjoy what we did, that's different. But I would put my life in your hands, and I trust you. If I had asked you to stop, without a doubt, you would've."

I wish I had his confidence. This isn't solely about sex. The darkness in me overrides my rational brain. "I want to believe you."

"Have I ever led you the wrong way?" he asks with a chuckle because, as my copilot, he's gotten us lost several times.

"I don't mind following you, even if it's in the wrong direction." It's nearly dawn and my eyes are heavy, but this is too important to stop talking. "What do we do now?"

Gray opens his mouth but closes it and rolls his lips in. "I'll answer that when I can think of something that isn't about your dick."

"You like my dick?" I ask the stupidest question ever. I blame my brain malfunction on exhaustion from the game, stress, and grogginess from waking up in the middle of the night.

He pumps his eyebrows but then gets serious. "Tinny, New Year's Eve blew my mind, and although I'd hate to walk away from amazing sex, our friendship is more important to me. I will do whatever you want."

"That doesn't seem fair." My eyelids are so heavy my blinks last too long, and I struggle to form a convincing argument.

"I get to decide what's fair for me." He stands. "You're exhausted and not in the right frame of mind to make decisions. We'll talk in the morning." Gray scoops me up in his arms and carries me to my bed.

"It really is kinda hot to be manhandled." I loop my arms around his neck, and he kisses my temple. Suddenly, I'm not so tired, but even more confused about what to do.

No, I have to stay strong and keep Gray safe from me.

CHAPTER 8

GRAYSON

Sometimes the universe conspires against me. The game arena usually feels like home, but not today because I'm detached from everything. The otherness is strong like an antiseptic stinging in my nose.

Until I find a sticky note on the training table, from Austin. My fingers run over the ink as if it holds the answers to what is going on between us. There aren't any. The note reads "Sorry I missed you this morning. A." Sweet yet not informative.

The group chat is rarely used anymore and I don't know if I'm being paranoid or everything is happening in the player chat.

It would stand to reason that Austin and I would have plenty of time together during a stretch of home games, but we haven't had a solid chunk of uninterrupted time to talk.

Driving together to practice and a rookie calls to talk to Austin.

After the morning skate, the medical staff wants a full report on everyone from me, and then Austin took an afternoon nap.

Morning off and an assistant coach needs advice on how to manage a player's expectations.

And he's required to stay in the team hotel. I don't have a reason to go there that isn't pathetic or lovesick. *This isn't love*, I berate myself. This is me needing clarity about where Austin stands on us starting a physical relationship.

It's a risk. A huge risk. One I have to be absolutely sure about.

I shouldn't be ready to dive in because I could lose him. Life is hard enough with his fame. If we fail and fall apart, I'll have to leave my job and start over.

Things aren't as tense, but we're in a weird sort of "more than friends but not" limbo. Since Vegas, I've lost my appetite, and all food has a cardboard like quality.

My phone buzzes, and Austin texts me a book meme about hockey. Apparently, hockey romances are big in the book world, and there are tons of videos set to music with funny captions. This one is of a team's pregame skate from behind the glass, and the caption is about going to the man aquarium. A hilarious take on it, but it's not wrong.

I search for one to return and find a guy warming up his hip flexors. It's sexy as hell, and normally I wouldn't send it to him because it wouldn't hit the same, but I take a chance and send it with no caption or explanation.

He texts back a fire and big-eyes emojis.

One step in the right direction. He thinks it's hot. And it is. And he sent me a direct text meant for my eyes only, not in the chat for everyone.

I wonder how he feels about our night together, and if he can imagine a life with me the way my brain took over and reinvented us as a fairytale couple. I've lost my mind.

The job takes over. Liska's back is much better. Benz is hydrating properly. Griff has no residual soreness in his leg. Austin's black eye is fine. Drake's ribs are sore from a hit, but he's good to play. Kenney needs a finger taped, and suddenly it's game time.

The energy in the arena is electric, and sometimes I wonder how these guys stay grounded. I'm proud when thousands of people chant their names, so I can only imagine how they feel.

I'm so focused on the players that I'm not paying attention to the time or the score.

My hands are cramped from a night of rubbing muscles and diligently taping up guys. If I pack up the supplies for the night, someone will need a treatment, so I head over to the locker room to check.

"Last call for treatment," I holler.

"Grayson, we're going to Skytop tonight. Be there." Lucky's statement is more of a demand than a request. "It's team bonding, and everyone needs to be there. Yes, I'm talking to you, King." Lucky points at Jamal King. He's shy but noticeably more comfortable with the team.

I stand by the door, waiting for someone to say they need me. Going out to a bar and having drinks is the last thing I need. Lucky avoided it for his first year of recovery, but now, he's making it his personal mission for everyone to have fun.

There's no way I can watch Austin having a great time and not touch him. I've imagined myself putting my hands on his hips and showing him how to keep time with the music. And once my hands touch him, my mouth will follow. Then everyone will know. These guys gossip like a bunch of soldiers, swapping stories to get the latest tea. We haven't talked about whether he wants to come out or not.

Being around Austin and alcohol is not allowed until we talk about what we're doing. I'm not involving the team. They already joke we're a couple, and if we break up, they'll choose sides. He's their captain. Of course, they'll choose his side no matter what happens or who's at fault.

I'm getting so ahead of myself. He never once said he's interested in me. I have all these fantasies about the way he tastes and how his cock would ruin me for other men. Yet he has not said or done one thing to give a sign that's what he wants.

Austin was tired when we talked, but he didn't say he wanted to have sex again.

When the team's distracted, I slip out of the locker room, pack up, and go home alone.

> **Austin:** Where are you?

> **Austin:** We called a few cars and they're here

> **Austin:** Not leaving without you

> **Me:** Sorry

> **Me:** Not feeling great

> **Me:** At home. Have fun

Guilt eats at me that I should've texted him first. But he's with his team and doesn't need me.

Tip-toeing around each other isn't good for us. Enough is enough. I'll talk to him as soon as he gets back. He rarely has more than one drink, so he should be sober and awake.

After I've showered and changed, Austin's standing in our living room, pointing the remote at the TV.

"Why are you home?" I cross the room to get a better look at his face. Even with a black eye, he's absurdly gorgeous. Both women and men flock to him. He has the "it" factor that attracts people. I've never been able to bring myself to ask him why he doesn't have a girlfriend. Plenty of beautiful and kind women have shown interest. He's gone on dates but never more than a few with the same woman. Maybe karma's the reason I didn't want to put the idea of him finding his person out into the world so it could become a reality.

He shrugs. "Don't avoid me."

I drag him over to sit on the couch. "I'm not avoiding you." His eyes widen in disbelief. "Not exactly." I'm unsure how to tell him that our night together plays over and over again in my mind, and I want more. That right now, I imagine crawling into his lap and kissing him until dawn. More than just kiss him.

But none of that comes out. "You need time to figure out what you want."

"Bullshit." Austin scowls. "Tell me the real reason."

"You won't like it." If I tell him, it could break our friendship, and if I don't, it could destroy our trust.

"G, talk to me." His blue eyes soften with a pleading expression.

I take the remote from him to have something to fiddle with. "I never thought we'd be more than friends. You accepted my sexuality without question or judgment. That meant and means the world to me. You pulled me through the darkest time of my life." After my career-ending injury, Austin took care of me. He made sure I showered, ate, and he went to all my appointments on top of his schedule in the CHL. Without him, I wouldn't have had a reason to get out of bed. "Our friendship is the most important thing in my life."

Our lives are so intertwined; the thought of him not being around is an ache.

"For me too," he cuts in earnestly.

"I never had a secret crush or wished you were bi because that would complicate things. But now...now things are complicated. You're not just my friend, you're the guy who made me come harder than I ever have. You made me want more." I take a deep breath. "How do I ask for that without risking our friendship?" My heart stops, and my stomach falls to the floor. I hope I didn't make a huge mistake.

Austin's silent, but he stares into my eyes. I swear I see heat flare in them before he abruptly stands and starts pacing.

"I'll do anything for you." He flexes his fingers. "We're friends for life. That night in Vegas was incredible, and you didn't do anything wrong. I made a huge mistake." He has his back to me, and his words slice me open.

"I took what I wanted from you in the moment without thinking ahead. And I can't give you what you want." He keeps pacing, fists clenching and unclenching, refusing to meet my eyes. "I'm so sorry, but friendship is all I can do." His voice oozes sorrow, but it doesn't fix the fact that my internal organs have ceased functioning.

The only sounds are his feet striking the floor and the soft swish of his pants rubbing together as he walks.

Even though I prepared myself for this response, reality shreds me. I did the one thing I swore I would never do. I fell for my straight best friend. And I didn't trip and fall; I fell face-first into passion, with my heart in my hand for him.

"Okay," I say in a steady voice. I pledged not to let that night break us. His friendship in the long term means more than the emptiness that currently occupies me.

"It's not okay," he snaps. "I refuse to hurt you."

"Tinny." I use the nickname he loves to soothe him. "I'm disappointed you don't feel the same, but it's not your fault. You can't force yourself to want me for my benefit. I don't want to be someone else who demands something of you. I can't be a drain on your energy." As much as I hate saying the words, they're true. I'd rather have him be honest than fake his desire for me. If he pretends, I'll get more attached, and it will hurt worse when he ends things.

"This isn't what I wanted to happen."

The urge to hug him is overwhelming, but I hold back. Touch is my source of comfort, not his. "I know that, and I'm not mad at you." Heartsick but not angry. I'm upset with myself for letting my emotions take over and for longing for things he can't give me. I'm the idiot.

"You should be." His hands grip his short hair, and I'm surprised he doesn't pull it out. "You should hate me for what I did. What I'm doing."

"I'll never hate you." It's a sad truth. I can't make him feel better, and I need to end this conversation.

Austin hating himself only hurts me more. Since I asked for more than he can give, it's my responsibility to absolve him of guilt. I stand and step into his path.

"Hey." I wait until he looks at me. His eyes are gray and dull. I did that. "We're fine. Our friendship has survived worse. You can probably meet the guys out and have some fun. I'll be here. I'm not going anywhere," I say, willing it to be true. Eventually I'll get over him, but I deserve the torture of living here in the meantime. He's Austin—Ace—Lapointe, last year's leading scorer for the Enforcers and an All-Star. I'm his middle school friend who managed to hang on into adulthood.

He nods and gives me a one-arm bro hug. I thump his back and tear myself away, retreating to my room. If only I could knock myself unconscious and fall into a peaceful oblivion.

Reality sucks.

Austin's muttering to himself on the other side of our shared wall. We unknowingly arranged our rooms so our beds butt up against each other with a thin wall between them. It's never been a problem since neither of us has ever brought a hookup back here. It never felt right since he pays the majority of the rent. He must have his own reasons for not doing it.

After a few minutes of heavy silence, I hear a soft knock on the wall. We do that to say goodnight sometimes. I return it, hoping it gives him some peace, and roll over to find sleep.

In my dreams, Austin is in my bed.

CHAPTER 9

AUSTIN

Lying is a sin. I grew up hearing that every single day. But not telling Grayson the whole truth is better for him. Or that's my excuse for lying to my best friend and denying us what we both hunger for. He's all I can think about. His coconut scent is everywhere in the apartment. It's embedded in my nose. I even smell it in this arena, which is not possible.

The darkness swirls inside me, loose and unpredictable. I can't let Grayson anywhere near me because my desire for him is too wild, too primal, and I'll cause damage. He's sure I'll stop and won't hurt him because we're the same size, but I lift weights for a living and my darkness isn't rational, and it's capable of horrible things.

I cling to the memory of him hurt on the ice in the CHL, a reminder of the damage I accidentally caused. Never again will he suffer at my hands.

His phony smile is getting on my nerves, but I step into his training room for our pregame ritual. Keeping him safe and mine is a balance I'm learning to manage. But I won't be the one to pull away. I can't. He means too much to me.

I'm selfish. I should let him go to find someone else. Someone who won't drag him into the darkness.

"Hey." I shrug as if to say "I'm here."

The left side of his mouth ticks up with a ghost of a smile as he closes the distance between us. "I got your sticky note. Is that our thing now? Instead of dressing the same, you're gonna leave me notes?"

I shrug again like a dumbass because those stupid notes prevent me from confessing my true feelings and putting him in physical jeopardy.

Gray's steady hands land on my shoulder. "Have a great game. You got this."

I inhale, taking in as much of him as I can—his smell, his breaths, and his surety. His forehead rests on mine, and his hair forms a curtain, hiding our faces from the rest of the world. I close my eyes because if there's a hint of pain in his, it will crush me before I get to the ice.

"Thanks," I murmur, and back away, avoiding his gaze.

At first, I think the team is off because of me, but it becomes clear it isn't our night. Griff's serving his suspension from the game, Benz is flakier than usual, and we're not gelling.

"We're still in this." I stalk the bench. "Let's find the back of the net."

On my next shift, I take my own advice and send Drake a quick pass in front of the net. He flicks his wrist, and I'm sure it's going in, but the goalie gets an arm on it. Lucky's there to tap the deflection in past the stunned goalie.

The three of us meet for a hug, and I smack Lucky's helmet. "Way to get it done."

It wasn't pretty, but we're on the board.

Gray hands me a water bottle as I vault over the boards to the bench. "Way to give'r." When I don't respond, he continues. "No pass, no goal. You started the play, Lucky finished it."

"You bet." I guzzle the water. It wasn't the assist I'd expected, but my stats don't matter as long as the team wins.

King is everywhere on his shift. Defending like a champ, stealing the puck, but his line isn't as effective without Griff. King shoots, but it ricochets off the top bar. Benz grumbles as if the net personally offended him. Goalies are weird about the pipes.

I meet King at the wall with water, and Drake appears next to me.

"It happens to the best of us," he consoles King.

King nods in acknowledgment. "I shoulda had it."

"You'll get it in next time." I truly believe it. He's already a crucial part of this team and will definitely be the future as I get older. I dismiss that thought. I've got years ahead of me. Retirement is too many years off to count.

"Drake, how are the ribs?" Grayson asks.

"All good," he responds and hops over the boards.

After a shift in the third period, Grayson nudges me. "What about you? Any aches or pains to report?"

"Nah, just a bruised ego." I haven't scored, and my team is down by a goal. It's my job to fire the guys up and score.

"You're not a one-man team. Go easy on yourself." He pats my arm as he walks away.

On my next shift, the trash-talking escalates. "I hear you won't fight. Just a momma's boy in a hockey uniform," a defender taunts me.

I'm unfazed, but Lucky pushes his defender off the puck, and it's a good thing the ref missed it. "Are the taunts below the belt?" I ask after the ref blows the whistle.

"Nah, just annoying." Lucky skates into position, and I have to take him at his word. As the captain, it's my job to report slurs and other issues to the refs.

King ties the game up on his next shift, but they score again, putting us behind by one.

I take my position on the line for the face-off and ignore their winger grinning at me. He looks maniacal. Drake steals the face-off, and the play starts as usual. Their winger stays on me instead of a defender picking me up. We're a mismatch and Drake notices.

I skate wide and receive Drake's pass to dish it back to him, and he reroutes it to Lucky. Lucky skates around the net with the puck, and I'm in position, but my legs are taken out from behind.

The whistle blows, but their winger has me pinned down.

"You gonna fight me now?" he growls.

Before I can respond, Drake is there, ripping him off me, and Lucky helps me to my feet. The guy drops his gloves, and Drake strips his off.

The darkness rears up. This is my fight, and I'm not letting Drake possibly get hurt defending me.

It's not a choice; it's instinct. I don't remember taking my gloves off, but they're not on when I'm yanked off the ice and he stays down, curled in a ball.

There's a thin streak of red on the ice, which means everything stops. Drake is pushing me back, but I'm horrified by what I've done. My mind flashes back to breaking my rival's rib. I listen for his breathing and don't hear anything.

"He's not moving?" I panic.

"He's a dramatic asshole. And not the good kind," Lucky jokes. "Hey." He smashes his palms on each side of my face. "He's fine. The bastard's faking, hoping to get you ejected."

"There's blood." I point.

"It's yours," Drake says, and it sounds like he's refraining from calling me stupid.

I glance down at my hands, and my knuckles are bleeding. The darkness is so close to the surface. I let it out by mistake, and an innocent guy paid the consequences. This is what I'm protecting Grayson from—my random violence.

Drake wordlessly enters the penalty box to serve my time while Gray cleans me up. "There's no blood on him. It's on the ice from when you put your hand down for balance."

I glance around for the EMTs, but play has already restarted. "They took him out already?" My head is stuck on how badly he's injured.

Gray looks confused. "He's in the sin bin with Drake. He's got extra time for flopping."

What they were trying to tell me finally sinks in. The guy's fine. It's another day at the office.

"This is going to sting."

He's so gentle as he uses the disinfectant on my ragged skin. I'm used to the sting but inhale sharply. He's so close, and I smell terrible. I've never cared about smelling bad around Gray before.

His fingers caress mine as he binds them with tape to stop the bleeding. He's working slowly, as if we're not in a game and I won't have to play in a couple of minutes. He's touching me as if I'm the most important thing to him.

"Hurry up," I snap, unable to tolerate his caring touch. I don't deserve him and the way he forgave me for the past. I've done nothing but hurt him throughout our friendship.

I don't even remember injuring my knuckles. Even if the guy flopped, he was saved by the rules of the game and our teammates pulling us apart.

No one would be there to save Grayson if I lost control with him.

I'd rather take the blame for damaging our friendship than see the marks I left on him.

I'd rather he hate me than to physically hurt him.

I'd rather die than harm him.

Seeing Grayson fake normalcy every day brings a heaviness to the air and an unseen physical barrier between us so large I can't get around it.

Staying at the team hotel before our home game is a break from that. It's one more thing for me to wallow in guilt over. My alarm will go off soon for the team's breakfast. I shut my eyes, hoping to relax. This hotel is my second home, and I'm grateful it has firm mattresses and soft sheets. But there's not a hint of menthol or coconut oil, so it can't compare to home with Grayson.

For the past few days, we've texted and talked as if nothing is wrong. But everything is wrong. He won't confess that my rejection hurt. I can't stop leaving him notes, and I'm not sure if it's for his benefit or mine. That's a lie. It's for me. Doing it confirms I'm selfish and I deserve the darkness that lurks inside me, waiting for the opportunity to cause harm. It has no conscience and no remorse.

Drake pulled me off the player before I could do any serious damage, but I would've if given the chance.

Tonight's game will be a test of the team's restraint. We're playing Tampa, and our former teammate, Richardson, will be out for blood. Trading him was the best thing for our team, but he's a hoser.

Benz loaned me a crystal for calm and clarity. He swears by their powers, and I need all the help I can get. I've given the team a speech about ignoring Richardson's taunts and taking the high road. It would be very embarrassing to black out and lose my shit in this game.

I clutch the purple amethyst like a lifeline. Benz also gave me a leather band to wear the crystal around my neck. I'll keep it in my pocket until game time and reevaluate then.

I'm always evaluating and reevaluating situations.

My mind wanders back to Grayson, and he steals all of my focus. The crystal heats in my hand, and it's a pleasant sensation.

Clamping the lid on my attraction to Gray is the only viable solution.

We'll get past this. We have to.

I'm going crazy keeping my distance. Part of me wishes our night together had never ended. That reality never set in, and we could live in a bubble of naked bliss. I've held myself back from physical touch, and the ache feeds my darkness. It's hard to be in the same room because I crave his closeness and covet his hands on me again.

I press my palm into my growing cock. The thought of Gray's strong fingers gripping me is enough to get me hard. I'm so pathetic.

Vaguely, I wonder if the crystal can keep my dick in check, but I'm not brave enough to test it out.

Instead, I throw the covers off and decide to rub one out in the shower before breakfast. Hopefully, that will be enough to make my dick behave.

I can't sport a hard-on every time I think of Gray or when I get near him. My mouth might lie, but my cock hasn't mastered that skill.

It's going to be a long day, and letting Gray or my team down isn't an option.

CHAPTER 10

GRAYSON

We all knew that game would be like a moose on black ice, but my guys are more banged up than usual. Once the puck dropped, I didn't have the time to spare a thought about the emotional gap between Austin and me.

It's possible the distance is in my head because he's been leaving me cute as fuck sticky notes all over the apartment. One under his dirty laundry with a thank-you, a heart, and XOXO. He without a doubt knows I pick up after him and appreciates it, but I don't know what to do with that information. I absolutely shouldn't sniff his clothes to get a hit of his woodsy smell.

The home crowd is behind the team, and the familiar cheers and chants steady my nerves. Lucky scores first with a pass from Austin, but Tampa gets on the board minutes later.

In my opinion, we're outplaying Tampa, but the score is one to one as the first period ends.

There are lots of bruises to evaluate and banged-up arms and legs. Liska's grumpy when I check in, but his back seems fine. After talking to Coach, he'll play the second period, and Benz will go in for the third.

We score again in the second period, and our defense foils their attempts. Kenney is unbelievable out there.

The team needs the break to catch their breath by the end of the second. I ensure Benz is ready to take over in goal and Liska has ice for his back.

Benz searches the stands for Leo, then locks in on his job. My eyes automatically find Austin, and I wonder how he'll act when he falls in love. Austin loving someone else sends ice through my veins. I have to pay attention to my job and not be distracted by Austin.

The asshat, Richardson, gets increasingly aggressive, and the only break the team gets from him is when he's in the penalty box. The guy isn't playing the puck; he's trying to hurt people and should be ejected from the game.

Late in the third period, I watch in horror as Richardson takes Benz to the ice and starts beating him. The ref blows the whistle, and I'm over the boards and assessing Benz.

"I'm okay." He uncurls himself from the ball he'd rolled into. His eyes dart around before he whispers, "I'm hoping he gets thrown out of the game. I'm not hurt bad."

I nod and take his vitals. He can't be called for flopping when Richardson was literally on top of him, so it's a good strategy. "Do you want a stretcher?" I ask, willing to help.

"No!" He winces at how his voice projects. "I'm not giving Leo a heart attack."

"Fair." I help him to his feet, and the assistant trainer takes his other arm so we can get him back to the exam room. The crowd is furious and chanting Benz's name in support.

"I knew they'd love me someday," he jokes.

"If you were bleeding, they'd erect a shrine." I guide him down the tunnel.

"I'm so into that." He laughs but has to stop because it steals his breath.

"Let's get you on the table." He's in good shape for how many hits he took.

A few minutes later, we hear someone pounding down the hall. Benz tries to sit up, but I push him back down. "I'll get Leo."

Sure enough, Leo is sprinting toward me, wild-eyed and panicked. My assurance does nothing until he can see Caleb with his own eyes. I have to cajole them apart to finish my exam. The game's over, and I'll have a steady stream of guys to patch up.

I follow them into the strangely tense locker room for a post-game win. Benz struts into the middle of the room and cracks a joke but doesn't get a laugh.

I holler, "Anyone else need treatment?" The room is uncomfortably silent, and I lean against the door.

There's a discussion about sexuality, and I should exit the room and wait for the players to come to me, but I'm curious. Apparently, King answered a reporter's question about sexuality, and it got under a rookie's skin, sparking a debate.

Austin announced he's interested in Leo's opinion on queerness, and I'm riveted by his perception. Benz gets Leo his tablet so he can type. With his jaw wired shut from his injury, it's difficult for him to speak clearly.

If Benz and Leo think they're keeping their affair a secret, they are doing a terrible job. Glancing around the room, the team has caught on that one, Leo is not straight and two, Leo and Benz are too cozy not to be sleeping together.

Austin maintains a stoic face while listening to Benz talk for Leo about the assumption of heterosexuality and the frequency of homophobic slurs in locker rooms. I'm so thankful that has changed. It was hard to pretend it didn't bother me, and I knew better than to come out when I played in the CHL.

"At a young age, boys learn to distance themselves from any thoughts or feelings that aren't straight to avoid being different," Benz reads from Leo's tablet, and I wonder if that's what happened to Austin. He buried his emotions so he wouldn't be different. Unwelcome bitterness bubbles inside me at the thought.

If he felt that way, he couldn't completely accept my sexuality and it burns.

Benz continues to read Leo's praise of the team's bravery. Everyone clocks the fact that Benz calls Leo "Lovie" and kisses his head. But no one interrupts. Liska looks smug, and most of the others stunned. Austin's jaw is hanging open.

Benz summarizes by saying, "Leo's too nice to say it, but if you're fantasizing about kissing a dude or touching a dick, you ain't straight." He leans over to read Leo's next words. "It's a spectrum, not a box."

I watch Austin's face for a reaction. It shouldn't disappoint me that he doesn't have an *aha* moment or epiphany that he's into dicks.

It would be too much to ask that one conversation with the team would change his mind about me, his lifelong friend turned spurned lover. I'm leaning into the dramatics of my heartbreak.

"But what if you're like piss-drunk and do something you wouldn't normally do?" a rookie asks.

"I would argue that being drunk lowers your inhibitions and gives you permission to do something you might be too nervous to do," King says. "It's not my intention to point fingers or out anyone. I was making a general statement to the media. No one has to feel pressured to examine their sexuality. It's a friendly discussion."

I try to catch Austin's eye, but he avoids looking at me. This discussion could legitimately be about our situation, and he won't acknowledge me. Any hope I had for his change of heart dies in the locker room.

The sober deathbed for my heart explodes with roars and disbelief as Benz confirms that he and Leo are sleeping together. My gaze cuts to Griff, who has face-palmed with the declaration, but he doesn't seem angry, so that's a huge win for them.

I'd love a win for me right about now. I'm happy for them as Benz sings Leo loves him, but it hurts not to have that.

As I'm trying to make my escape, Lucky yells, "Hey, Gray. I see you. Don't think you're skipping out on us. Again." I'm surprised he noticed I didn't go last time.

By the time I reach the treatment room, the friend chat has blown up with plans to go out tonight.

I don't have it in me to celebrate and pretend to care that they won the game. I've always cared, but tonight I'm going home and watching porn and maybe re-downloading a dating app.

It's time to face the fact that I've let my relationship with Austin stop me from finding love. It wasn't a conscious decision, but I'd rather spend time with him than with a stranger. But a stranger can't become anything else if I don't make an effort.

This is the kick to find my own happiness and not expect Austin to provide it for me. The prospect of being with someone else turns my stomach. I'm so fucked.

Austin knocks on my bedroom door after 2 a.m., but I don't say anything. My light is on because I couldn't sleep, and I'm frozen as if moving will alert him I'm awake.

"G," he whispers, and knocks again.

I'm in boxers with no shirt on and have a nice big ole empty glass of whiskey. If he comes into my room, there is a hundred percent chance I will jump him. The floor creaks, and I snatch my e-reader off the bedside table and position myself as if I fell asleep reading.

"Gray?" He cracks open my door, and I concentrate on breathing evenly.

Maybe because I've known him most of my life, I knew he'd come in. I've stooped to a new low, faking sleep to escape talking to my best friend. But the last time we'd both been drinking ended in disaster, so I'm calling this self-preservation.

"I'm so sorry, Gray." The bed dips as he sits down. His fingers run through my hair that's haphazardly all over the pillow, and it takes Captain America-level control not to react to his touch. "Your widow's peak has always fascinated me. Before you knew how to tame it, your hair would stick straight up." He chuckles and his fingers ghost down my chest. He sucks in a breath, and his hand trembles.

"I hate lying to you. It's killing me. I didn't know I could want another person so viscerally. You're all I think about. How am I going to stay away from you?" His hot fingers rest on my side. My scalp and individual hairs throb with the echo of his touch. There is not a scientist alive who could convince me that hair can't feel.

My heart races so fast I'm afraid it will give me away. He's not making sense, and I wonder if it's the alcohol talking. It's given him liquid courage, but what will happen in the morning? I can't be his drunken booty call. I have to decide to "wake up" or listen to his confession, knowing he's only saying it because he thinks I'm asleep.

"It's like the sleeping dragon woke up, and the dragon is dangerous. You're the best person in my life, and I have to protect you. Please don't hate me. I know you're mad." His voice cracks and he stands.

It's like he handed me a tennis racket to play hockey. All I have to do is pretend to wake up, and I can ask him. We can talk this through and figure it out together. We can do anything together.

He sets my e-reader aside and covers me with the blanket.

"Love ya, G." He kisses my forehead and sneaks out of my room.

I don't dare breathe. I'm afraid to move. The walls are thin.

I turn my head into my pillow and let out a muffled cry.

My cowardice cost me the chance to ask him what he meant. He said he loves me, not "I love you," but still, and he kissed me.

There's a saying about hope giving the heart wings. I dismiss the feeling in my chest as my bed spins from the whiskey.

I'll be counting the hours until I can pay a visit to his room, and I'll use Leo's locker room talk to start it.

I'm not giving Austin up without a fight if he wants me too.

CHAPTER 11

AUSTIN

King's statement about being queer is all over the internet. His quote has been taken out of context and restated as if he doesn't think the men on the Enforcers understand the concept of queerness.

I'm fighting the urge to text the reporter and chew her ass out. She posted his incomplete answer for the shock value.

Leaning on our kitchen island, I run a hand over my face and text King.

Me: Want me to come over?

King: Nah

King: Finn's here

King: I'll text if I need backup

Me: We have your back

Gray stumbles out of his room with his hair a tangled mess around his shoulders and crease marks on his face from the pillow. He's adorable.

"Hey." He pours himself a cup of coffee. "Did you tuck me in last night? I remember reading, but then I woke up with the lights out and my e-reader on the nightstand."

"King's getting crucified." I change the subject. I had a moment of weakness and spilled my guts to him. No more drinking for me because it makes me forget why I can't have Gray. It's fitting I burned my tongue on the coffee this morning like karma telling me to keep my mouth shut.

Grayson pauses with the mug halfway to his mouth. "He played great."

"The press is saying he's accusing his teammates of being clueless about being gay or bi. Finn's with him." I don't look at Gray because he might see the lust in my eyes. His stance has created an opening in his boxers, and I lick my lips at the thought of tasting him again.

"Finn will calm him down and develop a strategy to change the narrative." He moves closer, and I stand to pace. "Are you going over there?"

"No, King said he'll text if he needs me." I flap my hand as if it's easy for me to stay out of it.

"He won't. Let's take him to dinner later. Or we could invite the guys here and not make it a big deal." Gray looks like he wants to say something else, but he doesn't.

Our phones buzz simultaneously.

Trevor: Dinner at our place

Trevor: 7pm no excuses

Trevor: Bring significant others

Lucky: Daddy Drake loves being my plus one

Benz: No sex talk in the group chat

King: Is this my fault?

Me: Team bonding before we hit the road

Drake: Benzy said no sex talk

Me: *eye roll emoji*

"Looks like Trevor had the same idea." Grayson drains his mug and sets it on the counter with a thunk. "We should talk about what Leo said."

A pit opens in my stomach, threatening to swallow me whole. "Why?"

His mouth falls open. "Really? Are you going to pretend our situation has nothing to do with what he said?" The disappointment in his voice rings clear.

I can't think of a proper response that doesn't give away my feelings for him.

"Tinny." He stands in front of me, with his big brown eyes imploring me to listen while his inviting aroma surrounds me. "Don't you think it's hypocritical to say you accept my sexuality but refuse to accept yours?"

I blink rapidly, digesting his words. "That's not the issue." The words are out before I realize the ramifications.

"No? You spend a night with me, acting like you can't get enough, but then tell me it's not what you want. It seems like you're in denial." Compassion softens the harshness of his words.

I've dug myself a hole, and it's filling in around me. The truth isn't an option. Keeping him away from me for his own good is the only way.

I clear my throat. "You're right. You should be with someone who is proud of their preferences and isn't a hypocrite like me." My chin sticks out to give the illusion of confidence.

"Talk to me," he begs, ignoring my statement.

"There isn't anything to say. You're right, and that's another reason why we're better off as friends." I choke the words out in a rush, hoping I sell the lie.

"You don't mean that," he murmurs, coming closer. I back up and shake my head as he reaches for me. "Hey, it's okay. It's me."

I refuse to make eye contact as if that will ward him off.

One warm hand lands on my hip and the other lifts my chin so I'm forced to see him.

"If you can look me in the eye and honestly tell me you don't want me and only want to be friends, I'll never bring it up again." His eyes are searching mine. Digging for the truth that I can't give.

"G, don't make this harder than it already is." I lower my eyes.

"Harder because you don't feel the same as I do or because you want me as much as I want you?" he asks, still holding my chin.

I don't want to lie anymore.

He deserves so much better than me.

Someone who won't hurt him or drag him into the darkness. Someone who won't cause him bodily harm.

"When we were in the elevator in Vegas on the way to your room, I had to restrain myself from humping you in public. I wanted to rub myself all over you so I'd smell like you and you'd smell like me. The way you kissed me felt like ownership and coming home."

My cock loves his words and has plumped up, hoping for some attention.

"Kissing you was an electric shock and a soft caress. Look at me and tell me you're fine never kissing me again." His voice dares me.

"I can't," I wail, disappointed in myself and petrified I'll let him down.

He slides his hand over to cup my balls, and my dick tents my sweatpants. There's no hiding my arousal.

"This feels like a sign you're dying to put your lips on mine. Or maybe you'd prefer my lips stretched around your cock." It jumps and he chuckles. "You lie with your words, but your body tells a different story. If you tell me no, I'll stop."

I'm weak for him, but with my last shred of sanity, I rip myself out of his grip. "I can't be with you. Ever. It doesn't matter what we want. You're not safe with me." I'm panting, and my chest heaves as if I've been skating for hours.

"Tell me why." He tries to get closer but stops when a broken sound leaves my throat.

I tug at my hair, but the strands are too short to really pull. "Take my word for it," I say in exasperation.

"No." He stares at me unblinkingly.

I flinch, taken aback. "No? You can't say that."

His mouth turns up. "I just did. Here's the thing, I would be a terrible friend if I let this go."

"A terrible friend?" I repeat with my one working brain cell. I should retreat to my room and hope he forgets about this. But he won't, so I stay where I am.

"Yes, we're friends first, and my friend"—his crooked smile makes my heart stutter—"is concerned about causing me harm. A friend wouldn't let you suffer, so I'm offering my help."

"That won't work." I stride away and flop on the couch, wishing I could make him understand.

"How do you know if you don't try? The Austin Lapointe I know would never give up without maximum effort first." He sits close enough for our legs to touch, and his are bare.

"You can't dare me into having sex." I shift away and then back because this is innocent and I'm allowing myself this tiny piece of him. This minimal contact from my forbidden friend.

Gray's laughter spreads over me like honey. "I'm not daring you; I'm stating facts." His smile falls away. "Tinny, you don't trust yourself. It's not like you, and I'll do whatever I can to help you figure this out."

"I trust you," I say. It sounds like a simple statement, but it's not. Trusting someone the way I trust Gray is a once-in-a-lifetime bond. We have years of good and bad times we've been through, depending on each other.

Gray picks up my wrist, and at first, I'm confused, but he holds up his hand and muscle memory takes over as we go through the friendship handshake we thought was so cool when we were eleven.

"Without words, you knew what to do. I trust you the same way you trust me." He cuts me off before I can object. "You've earned that trust. If you're concerned, I'm concerned. We can work through it."

If I tell him about what's inside me, he'll think I'm crazy. We could end up on a reality exorcist show. The taglines for two hockey players trying to find love but who need a quick exorcism are endless: *Darkness puts love on thin ice* or *Ice and hellfire combust, injuring an Enforcer's player.*

"Why are you smiling?" His hand rubs my knee. Lucky knee.

"You'll have me committed to the psych ward if I tell you." My body betrays me, and I lean into him.

"There's nothing you can tell me that will change how I feel about you."

Once, I tried to tell my mom, but she said speaking like that was inviting the devil in. Grayson won't think that.

"I'm guessing whatever is going on isn't going away. You don't need to deal with it alone. If hockey has taught you anything, I hope it's that you're stronger as a team. Let me be on your team." His earnest eyes innocently ask the impossible.

"Compromise," I say slowly, thinking it through. He can't get too close, but if he understands, it might help me deal with it.

"Of course." He scoots closer so the shin of his bent leg rests along my thigh.

I close my eyes and take a long breath in. Trust is one of the hardest things to give.

"I've told you that in the past I've been angry and sort of black out and don't know what I've done." His silence allows me to gather my courage and keep speaking. "It's more than anger. I have this darkness inside me that I keep locked away. Sometimes it comes to the surface, and whenever it does, bad things happen to people I care about."

Gray's facial expression doesn't change, and he doesn't move away.

"And you're afraid of it," he states as a fact, but I am compelled to answer.

"Yes, wouldn't you be?" I snap and regret it.

"I'd never choose something that I thought would hurt people. Tell me more...like the first time and what you remember about the times it's happened."

He's even closer, with our shoulders touching, and it strengthens my resolve to tell him what he wants to know.

"The first time was when my sister broke her arm. She'd been following me around all day, and I was sick of her. I climbed a tree, knowing she wouldn't be able to reach the branches to get to me. She tried anyway, and I laughed at her attempt to keep climbing. I knew she'd get hurt, but this thing in me, this darkness I can't control, wanted to see her hurt. Knew that if she got hurt bad enough, she wouldn't bug me all the time." I hang my head in shame.

"What kind of monster wants to see his little sister get hurt? I was supposed to protect her." My throat tightens, and it's hard to swallow.

Gray tugs me to his chest, and I realize I'm crying.

"That must've been hard to deal with as a kid. You had a role in the family but also wanted some alone time." His hand coasts up and down my spine. "I know from personal experience you need your downtime to recharge. You probably didn't understand that as a kid and didn't have the language to ask for what you needed."

"Don't excuse what I did. I made my sister fall and break her arm."

My chest flutters with his insight. I'd never explored the reasons I needed to get away from her.

"I'm not. It's called perspective."

I don't argue that it wasn't an accident because I knew what would happen. He nudges me to keep talking.

"I can feel it coming out. It winds around my heart, squeezing in and getting pumped throughout the rest of my body. It's black and sinister and wants to consume me and feeds on hurting people." Not seeing his face makes it easier to say.

He tries to let go of me, but I cling to him.

CHAPTER 12

GRAYSON

Austin clutching me on the couch breaks my heart. He's convinced he has something evil inside him and seems terrified of my reaction. I have a completely different interpretation of his issues, but he'll argue, so we'll work around it.

"I'm here. I believe you." My arms tighten around him, and after a minute, I bring my hand to the back of his head to massage his scalp.

He sighs with relief. "You don't think I'm crazy?"

"Yeah, no," I say with a half laugh so he knows I'm serious. "As your best friend, I'm going to help you deal with the darkness in you."

Austin rears back in surprise. "You can't help. How can you help?" His tone goes from disbelieving to hopeful.

That is an excellent question, and I refuse to tell him I have no idea what I'm doing. "We'll start with you telling me when it happens. Maybe we can figure out a trigger and work on it from there," I say, and he deflates against me. My gut tells me he represses big emotions to the point that he can't recognize them and over the years has become fearful of them.

"Okay." He turns and rests his head on my shoulder and my nose fills with his vanilla shampoo.

Austin's parents love him immensely, but he grew up in a house where they didn't express feelings, good or bad. If he was happy, they told him he was too boisterous, and sadness was a waste of time, and he should keep his chin up and anger...anger was unacceptable.

I'm not an expert, but after being in therapy for years, the accidental harm parents can do is astounding.

"What does that mean for us?" he asks in a small voice.

"It means that we continue being best friends and put things like kissing aside until you're ready or decide it's not for you." This isn't the time to be selfish. My belly clenches with the suspicion that he won't be able to handle a serious relationship.

"Thank you." He twists his neck to press his lips on my shoulder, and the quick contact on my shirt is enough to send sparks through my entire body.

Hopefully, my attempt to help doesn't end in disaster.

We're a few minutes late to Liska and Trevor's apartment, and Lucky starts right in.

"Glad you could join us, Gray. Thanks for fitting us into your life that's so busy you ditch us," he quips, and gets an elbow from Drake. "What? It's true."

"I'm surprised you could tear your eyes away from Drake long enough to notice." I slap my palm against Lucky's waiting one. My brain sort of skitters around the fact that he's upset I didn't go out the other night with the team. It's surreal.

Benz and Griff look to be consoling King in the corner while Leo watches.

"It's always something with you nuggets." Finn joins Austin, Drake, Lucky, and me at the kitchen island.

"You love it," Lucky sings, and from Finn's expression, he's right.

I hand Austin a bottle of water, and we walk further into the living room adjacent to the kitchen.

"You know what we need? A dance party to get rid of our stress. And you know, the team that dances—"

A chorus from his teammates cuts Benz off. "—together, wins together."

"Exactly." Benz's head bobs as he puts music on his phone that connects to Liska's speakers.

"How did he do that?" Liska demands.

Trevor shrugs with an innocent smile. He's not innocent at all.

"Since this is all for my benefit." King, uncharacteristically, strides into the middle. "I have a request."

"Shoot." Benz turns the music down.

"We need to teach our captain some rhythm. He's the whitest white boy when he dances." King's words are teasing, but Austin is frozen with a half-smile.

He'll do anything for his teammates, but he doesn't understand his lack of rhythm.

"Music is like skating," King explains, but Austin can't figure out if it's a joke. "Your muscles move in time with the music. Like in warm-ups, you glide. And that's a totally different motion from a burst off the line during a face-off. Find the beat of the music and bend your knees in time with it." He bounces along with the music for Austin.

Trevor has Liska move the coffee table and push the couch back so the team has more room to dance.

Austin blushes bright red, and the team dances around him so he's not like a zoo animal on display.

"See, you got it," King encourages him. "Step side to side with the beat." He faces Austin, clapping and keeping him moving with the song.

"Let's teach him that TikTok dance Samba Whisk," King hollers, and Benz changes the song. "Now we'll add some hips." He sways and rotates his hips when the next song comes on.

Austin loses his rhythm with jerky movements. "I can't do that." He shakes his head, but tries again with zest.

"Ain't nothing holding you back." He looks over Austin's shoulder at me. "Put your hands on your boy's hips to help."

I obey immediately, not because I want to touch Austin. Nope. This is strictly about a dance lesson.

My fingers curl around his hips, and he lets me move him in sync with the music.

"C'mon now, you got it. Add the sidestep with your hips." King waves his arms in the air, and Austin exhales with concentration.

His chest expands with a huge inhale, and he doesn't let it out until I whisper in his ear. "Breathe."

I blanket his back as if we're in a club. I move to the music and guide him to follow along.

I can't help myself. My chin eases onto his shoulder, and I keep one hand on his hip and the other splays across his chest. It's a mistake because my dick wants in on the action as my hips press against his.

"You're feelin' it." King takes his hands and moves his arms while I squash the part that wants to bat King away. "Gimme a backward step like this." King shows him the movement, and I tap the leg I want him to move first. "Nice and easy. Chill movements at first," he encourages.

Austin throws his head back on my shoulder, and we move like we did that night in Vegas. As if we already know what to do with each other. As if we're made for each other.

He pushes his ass back against my erection, and he has all the rhythm of a professional dancer. I curse the team and our clothes and my vow of only friendship.

Suddenly, Austin jerks away, leaving me cold and exposed. He realizes what he's done and grabs King around the waist to dance in the center of the guys, taking attention off of me.

"Thanks for teaching an old guy like me something new. How'd I do? Does this mean our locker room dance parties will lead to more success if I have rhythm?"

The guys chant his name in response.

Austin has his plastic smile plastered on his face, and I'm worried. Without alarming anyone, I drag him down the hall into the office/workout room.

"What's wrong?" I ask, shutting the door.

"The darkness is here." He collapses into Trevor's desk chair.

I kneel before him. "Okay. Tell me what happened."

"It was fun. I was having fun. Although you shoulda told me I can't dance," he deflects with a forced laugh.

"You can dance. It's just that you dance to a different beat." I place my hands on his knees. "It was fun until..." I give him time to finish the sentence.

"I like your hands on me." His eyes fixate on the carpet next to me.

"Is that bad?" My heart forgets how to beat.

"No. Yes. Maybe." He grimaces.

"Do you think you shouldn't like my hands on you?" I ask, and resist the urge to move my hands.

"What do you mean? It's not a matter of should." His eyes meet mine, then drift back to the carpet.

"Tinny..." I pause. "A lot of what you do is because you think it's expected of you and you should do it." It's difficult to express without sounding demeaning or like he did something wrong. "Sometimes it's easy, and it comes naturally. Like when a teammate struggles, you automatically seek them out and try to help. You think you should do it as captain, but you also want to do it as their friend."

Austin finally meets my eyes.

"But sometimes it's harder. Like when you're furious about the ref's calls and think your players are being targeted, but you have to remain upbeat and keep everyone positive. Some days, I know you'd choose to cuss the ref out if you could. But you don't because you shouldn't." I play it safe with hockey references.

"Everyone has to do things like that. It's part of life."

"It is," I agree. "But not everyone has to deal with a darkness that sucks the joy from the room. Tell me what the darkness took from you in that moment." I won't force him to face things he's not ready for, so perhaps this is a compromise.

He stands and paces.

"I just wanted to be normal. That's not too much to ask, is it?"

"Of course not." I scan the room and wish Liska had a punching bag, but I spot a foam roller and scoop it up. We use them to stretch and prevent soreness, but I have another use in mind. "Hit the roller like it's the darkness, and tell it to fuck off." It helps that the foam is black instead of a cheery color.

"What if I break it or hurt you?" He stands by the treadmill, looking lost.

"Worst-case scenario, you break it, and we buy Liska a new one. Or you hit me on accident, and I need to ice my wound and get to tell the guys you beat me up," I tease, and his worry slips away. The best-case scenario is him working off some pent-up tension and regaining control of his feelings. I hope I'm doing the right thing.

"Remember, you asked for this." He gets into a boxing stance.

CHAPTER 13

AUSTIN

Hitting Liska's foam roller seems ridiculous, but Grayson wants to help, and since the darkness deprived me of a fun night with the team, I could use a stress release.

That's a massive understatement.

I got lost in his body behind mine, craving his touch and how we fit together. For a second, I forgot about the team, and it was us, me and Gray. As soon as the thought to spin around and grind on him popped into my head—boom. The darkness closed in.

Gray readies himself as he holds the roller out in front of him.

I bounce on my toes and hit it. This room has the underlying pungent sweat of Liska which keeps my focus off Grayson.

"You hit a puck like that, and you'll never score," he taunts me.

I smash my fist into it hard and grin because it surprises him. The release of tension is a relief, so I do it again and again.

"Pretend this is the darkness. What do you want to say to it?"

"Not today, Satan. Not today." But as the words leave my mouth, the darkness creeps in.

"Nope. Don't back down now. Stay on top of the black gunk ruining your night. Who's in charge? You or it?" Gray's calm tone centers me.

"I'm in charge, you piece of crap." I punch with each of my next words. "Get. Out. Don't. Come. Back!" The effort increases my heart rate and I pant.

Adrenaline courses through me, and I regain my control. The foam breaks on the last hit, but he tosses the smaller piece aside.

"Keep going. Show it who's boss."

"You're good for nothing. A screen door on a submarine. Go suck a Timbits box, ya beauty," I ground out a purely Canadian insult, and Grayson's grin takes over his face.

"You tell 'em."

The foam breaks a couple more times, but Grayson won't let me quit. I'm not even sure what comes out of my mouth as I rage at the darkness within me.

It's not fair.

Every time I let myself think of having Gray again, I'm taken over by terror.

It's like the darkness knows I don't deserve him. And I don't.

Finally worn out, I sink to my knees, out of breath. "Thank you."

Grayson sits cross-legged facing me. "Feel better?"

I take pause, taking stock. There's no filth running through my veins, and there's a lightness I'm grateful for. "Yeah." I have the urge to throw myself into his arms for comfort.

There's a knock at the door. "You okay in there?" Trevor asks.

"Yup. But tell Liska, I'll buy him a new foam roller. After the dance lesson, we had a boxing lesson." Grayson yells through the door but his eyes don't leave mine.

"Not asking questions," Trevor mutters, and walks off.

When we go back to the living room, the dance music has been turned off, and Leo and Benz have left along with Drake and Lucky.

Finn and King are on the couch with Liska, Griff, and a couple of other teammates. King's wide blue-green eyes find mine. "I hope I didn't stress you out."

"Nuh-uh, honey britches." Finn slaps his knee and turns to give us a death glare. "That had nothing to do with you."

I'm unsure what to say, but Grayson slings his arms around my shoulder. "Not you at all, King. We're trying something new for your captain. When he gets mad about something like his favorite backup getting hate online, instead of pretending he isn't mad, he's finding an outlet."

Everyone buys his story because it rings with some truth. After hanging out and making sure King is in a good headspace, we head home.

In the elevator, I say, "Thanks for the cover story. It totally worked."

He gives me a strange look but doesn't speak. It's a quick ride to our apartment. Technically, we could walk, but it's cold as balls out.

Grayson gives my shoulder a squeeze and passes me to enter his room. I'm not ready to let him go yet. My traitorous body aches to be near him. His hand on my shoulder isn't enough. I'll take platonic accidental brushes of our legs because I'm so hungry for him.

"How did you know that would help me?" When he faces me, I plop on the couch, inviting him to join me and he does.

"I mean, I wasn't sure, but the way you described it sounded like it was out of your control, and I tried to give you that control back."

"You knew the moment I thought it might take me over and wouldn't let me stop." I stretch my legs, and my right side tingles when our legs touch. My entire body melts.

"That was the point. I'm not afraid of it or you," he says, and I open my mouth to argue, but he stops me. "Worst-case scenario, remember. For argument's sake, let's say it took you over and you devolved into a blackout rage and attacked me. I'm not helpless. I can defend myself, and don't forget, no one wants their captain to break his fist on his bestie's face." He frames his face with his hands, slow-blinks at me, and smirks.

He's so kissable. I should've noticed before Vegas.

"More like they don't want their captain to beat the crap out of their friend and trainer who patches them up."

"Same difference," he says.

My stomach swoops remembering him pressed against me earlier, and I need that again.

"Will you be in the locker room for the next dance party to ensure my hips are moving in the right direction?" I ask without thinking.

"If your hips move in the wrong direction, that's a huge medical issue." He bites his lip. A lip I'd love to lick. "I'd love to help you keep rhythm but..." He trails off, and I feel stupid.

"No, you're right. You have a job and can't worry about my hips." The heat of my embarrassment creeps up my neck and across my face.

He stands abruptly. "Don't worry, Tinny. I'll always worry about your hips." He winks with a sly smile and strides quickly into his room.

He winked at me.

What does that mean?

All I know is that his hands are capable of magic, and it might kill me if he never touches me again. Every day is harder than the last to do the right thing, especially when Gray isn't afraid of what I might do to him.

CHAPTER 14

GRAYSON

Volunteering at Q Solutions without Austin is a welcome distraction. Benz has been here regularly without the team, so he knows all the workers and most of the kids. We're in the industrial kitchen, and I'm at the steel island, cutting vegetables for a salad as the stew bubbles on the stove, filling the air with spices. Benz said he'd get me a bowl, but he's trapped King in the kitchen's alcove.

Ari Dimon, our GM, started the tradition of the team volunteering here. It's a fantastic organization that helps at-risk queer kids and also has outreach programs to aid individuals experiencing homelessness. As a team, we volunteer outside of the PR days to bring awareness to the incredible things they do for the LGBTQ community. I swear, we get more out of it than the kids. At first, they're excited to meet the players, but the kids quickly realize the guys are normal dudes, and it's humbling.

Thousands of fans tell our players they're amazing, but one pimple-faced kid drags you and it puts life in perspective. The clients here think I'm funny because I tell them they're more likely to achieve a career in my job than become an NHL player. As if simply knowing the team gives them an edge even though they've never played hockey. The staff backs me up, and that gives me smug satisfaction. Teenagers are the best and the worst.

I try to catch King's eye to find out if he needs rescuing, but he doesn't look my way. Benzy is the best, but he can be a lot. The drama over King's statements to the blogger has died down, but there's so much hate on the internet that it's hard to avoid. There have been people who've blamed me for players' injuries, so even I'm not immune to it.

"Hey, need help?" Austin stands beside me and bumps my shoulder.

"I thought you had a thing tonight." My voice cracks with surprise. It's an almost out-of-body experience to suppress my instinct to reach for him. I'm in perpetual purgatory, which I guess is redundant, but I feel it so hard. We've gotten over the awkwardness, but there's an underlying tension. It's sexual tension on my part. I'm so in my head about acting appropriately around him that I can't figure out why he's tense.

"It was canceled, so I came to help out. Did you miss me?" His shy smile should not make my heart skip a beat.

I chastise myself with the reminder that I can look, but I can't touch. The universe gave me a mind-blowing night with my BFF, then determined that's all I get. At this point, I'm not sure if I'd do it again if I'm not guaranteed a happy ending. The one where we sleep together all the time.

"Always." I bump him back. We've spent the last few days sort of flirting, but not doing anything about it. He's so subtle I'm not totally sure if he's teasing or seducing me. He's increasing the number of sticky notes he leaves me. On some he's drawn a funny face with "gotcha" and others say "thinking of you." I'm a masochist who considers the funny verses sweet.

He grabs another knife to help me cut.

My suspicion that his darkness represents his repressed feelings worries me. I'd prefer to ignore the issue and jump into bed for beg-for-it-again sex. But that's shortsighted. It could ruin us both.

Above all, I'm his friend. A friend who desperately wants to change his mind about there being something wrong with him. These issues are beyond my pay grade. In my opinion, he needs a therapist, but he has to come to that decision himself. Forced therapy is a recipe for disaster.

"What's going on over there?" He lifts his chin toward Benz and King.

"Not sure, but King might need a rescue. They could be having a great heart-to-heart, or Benz could be telling him about the benefits of every single crystal in existence." My voice is low, and Austin moves closer. He smells like vanilla, so lickable.

"I'll see what's up." He wanders away.

This can only end badly for me. I've loved Austin like a brother, and wanting more is selfish. He's not in a place for a relationship. Ugh, I've fallen into the age-old complication of unrequited love with my best friend. So cliché.

I mean lust.

I'm not in love with him.

That would be insane.

"Careful." Austin puts his hands on my waist to stop me from backing up into him. My body burns where he touches me, craving more. "They're all good. Gossiping about Pride Night and the gala from what I heard."

I have to curb my feelings. If I don't, I can lose him, my job, and a group of guys who will choose him as their friend. In a twist, this line of thinking only encourages the otherness I hate so much. But I don't belong with Austin or with the team without him. Maintaining separateness is the only way to go.

"Shit."

Austin's comment reminds me I forgot to text Trevor back about getting my measurements for the gala suit. He sent me links to different suits, and I picked a couple. He just needs my size.

"Swearing at yourself or me?" Austin tightens his fingers around my midsection before letting go.

I catch myself before I collide with him to maintain contact. "Me. I forgot to get back to Trevor."

I'm relieved when a volunteer comes over to get the veggies from me. The last thing I need is to slice a finger off because I'm preoccupied with my hot roommate.

"Yikes. Text him now. You don't want to get on his bad side." Austin lifts his foot, and it connects with my shin, not in a kick sort of way, but a footsie sort of way. I'm clearly losing my mind and reading more into the touch.

But he's touching me more, or it seems like more. He's never been a touchy guy, stopping with fist bumps, backslaps, and bro hugs with pads on. He rarely bro-hugs his teammates in street clothes, even though most of the players do it.

I'm seeking out the very thing that will ruin us.

"Truth," I agree, and pull out my phone for something to do before our next assignment.

There's plenty to do to set up for dinner service, so once Trevor and I coordinate a meeting, I don't dwell on Austin, even though I'm hyperaware of his location.

An hour later, we're side by side, serving stew and salad to middle schoolers and teens who are not impressed with the dinner.

"I thought it was lasagna night," says a gangly teen with long limbs he hasn't figured out how to use yet. He snatches his plate away before Austin can put salad on it. "I only eat it if I'm tossing salad. Ya feel me, bro."

"I'm a big fan of this salad. It helps me stay in playing shape," Austin says sincerely, and receives an eye roll. "Why do we like this again? What in the hell does he mean, tossing salad, isn't that what this is?" he asks me under his breath once the kid has walked away.

"Because we're helping the community and the little heathens are so thankful, we can't stay away," I deadpan. "And I have no idea, hang on." Pulling out my phone, I ask the app, "Hey Annie, what's the Urban Dictionary definition of 'tossing salad'?"

The Annie app doesn't speak, which is strange, and when I read it, I understand why. "We're old. It's the new way to say eating ass."

Austin tries to stifle his laugh but snorts instead.

"Who are you again?" A girl with purple hair points a yellow nail at me. "You're not on the roster. Are you even allowed to be here?"

"Hey, Bex. I can't decide if you're face blind or purposely hurting me." I clutch my chest with the hand not serving her stew.

She gives me a slow once-over but then turns to Austin with a blindingly bright smile.

"Hey you." She twirls her hair. "Great game the other night."

"Which night?" he asks, clamping his lips together because she's full of shit. I'm proud he's learned these kids' tricks.

"The night you played the purple-and-black team." She bats her eyelashes.

"For future reference, we're the purple-and-black team," he says, and she huffs. "And extra bread will cost you a toonie."

"What the hell is that?" she snarls in disgust.

"Canadian money." I stifle a laugh, and she storms away.

"And be nice to my roommate," he calls after her.

Bex does a one-eighty and returns to us wide-eyed. "You live together?"

"Yes, as roommates," I confirm, and stress the word.

"Pity. I knew you were a loser. It also explains how you used to plan your matching outfits," she says as she flips her hair over her shoulder and flounces away.

"Ouch." I set the ladle down and stretch. "She is not my biggest fan."

"At least she doesn't pretend to flirt with you to get a loaf of Italian bread." He shakes his head, and his eyes skim my midsection where my shirt has ridden up.

His eyes zero in on my bare skin like a physical touch, and I drop my arms. If he keeps looking at me like that, I'll get a hard-on in front of all these kids. Talk about a loser.

"What time are you leaving?" He meets my gaze, and there's heat in his eyes.

I'm stunned speechless as I dissect the question for a hidden meaning. Am I reading too much into the casual touching and playful comments? Or is he suggesting something more?

Another group of kids enters the dining area, and I pay attention to them and learn their names.

"You could be a coach." Austin pats my back, and I give him a questioning look. "You're good with kids. You tease them, but don't let them cross a line. I bet all the single moms and dads would fall all over themselves to sign up for your team. And you know a ton about hockey."

"I'm pretty sure I let Bex cross a line when I didn't call her out for saying I'm a loser." I mindlessly ladle more stew for a volunteer.

"Bex is tough. If she insults you, she likes you," the volunteer says. "We're almost done, so you guys can grab some food if you're hungry."

"Thanks." I scoop stew into two bowls for Austin and me, and he makes plates of salad and bread for us.

We find seats across from each other with Benz and King, then swap plates so we each have a full meal.

"Aww, cute lovebirds," Bex sings obnoxiously.

"Don't be jelly," Austin says, and I almost choke on my savory stew.

"Did he just say jelly?" King asks.

"All the kids say it." Austin shrugs. Our long legs tangle under the table, and he traps one of mine between his two. But he doesn't look at me or say anything.

When his legs squeeze mine, I cough in surprise, and he raises an eyebrow.

Benz thumps me on the back. "We need you, Gray. Don't have a choking accident."

"Yeah, Gray," Austin taunts.

Either I'm crazy or he is.

This could go either way.

CHAPTER 15

AUSTIN

During the ride home, I panic. I don't know what I'm doing. I do but I don't. Because I'm a logical person with anxiety, I overthink things. I've made a million pros and cons lists of being together. I'm going to make the biggest mistake of my life or the best decision ever. Logic has left the building.

All the reasons not to be with him stand, but his quiet acceptance of whatever I'll give him has worn me down. I have to believe I can be better for him. He deserves someone who will try their best, and I won't give up if he doesn't.

My nerves are a live wire that could power the city tonight.

I've been dropping hints all week, and he hasn't picked up on them. Or he's not interested, but I'm an optimist, and he basically said he wants a repeat of our night in Vegas.

My notes weren't direct enough.

The night Grayson asked me to hit the foam roller switched something inside me. I'd felt like a helpless victim, and he handed me a way to get my control back. I've spoken with a sports psychologist, and I'm not naive and think I'm cured, but she told me to stop being afraid of my wants.

Here I am, desperate for my best friend. The physical distance between us needs to disappear. Forever.

This is me being brave.

I want Gray.

He's clearly confused about why I'm rushing him along, but I can't wait any longer. It's been almost a month since Vegas, and I'd convinced myself I couldn't have him.

But if I'm brave, I can.

We've got all night long because we both have a rare full day off tomorrow. One of us usually has meetings if we don't have practice or a game.

All the way home, I keep my hands to myself and think I deserve a medal for my efforts. After all, his hair is falling out of its band, and I greedily want to tear it out to sink my fingers in it.

"What's happening right now?" Gray asks as I lace our fingers and drag him over to the couch.

"I've been thinking." I climb onto his lap. "You were right."

Gray tilts his head, waiting for me to continue. I sort of hoped he'd fill in the blanks of the conversation by kissing me. His brown eyes dance, and his smile has pulled the scar on his lip tight. When he doesn't wrap his arms around me, I push closer and his pupils widen.

"I was stupid and really want to kiss you again. Can I?" As the silence stretches, my heart's beating triple time.

He licks his lips, and I track his tongue. Gray groans.

"Tinny, I'm worried about you." His hands settle on my hips. The relief of his touch is instantaneous.

"I'm sorry. I shouldn't have told you all that stuff and made you worry." He hasn't consented, and it's killing me. Life won't be the same if I'm wrong about us.

"I'm glad you told me, but I wish you'd told me years ago." He glances down, and I don't understand his sorrow.

"Are you mad at me?" I ask.

"Not at all."

"Did you change your mind?" I shift to the side, exploring whether I'm imagining the bulge in his pants or not. I'm not. Thank God. He's hard and growing larger.

"No. But..." He doesn't say anything else as he trails his fingers along my hairline, around my ear, then cups my jaw.

I remind myself to stay where I am and be brave. I've never been in a position where I wasn't sure of the other person's feelings. Most women make it extremely clear what they want.

"Do you like living with me?" he asks, changing the subject, and I rear back. His large palm splays over my shoulder blades.

"Of course," I answer, unsure why he's asking.

"And you like our life and friendship?"

"G, we won't lose this," I say, bringing our foreheads together. "I promise."

I inhale his hungry laugh. "You can't promise that," he whispers, a hair's breadth away from my lips. My body coils tight, ready for him to say yes and give us what we both want.

"I want to promise you everything," I say seriously. I trust him implicitly, and I've never been in a relationship where I think about the person all the time. Only him. He's constantly on my mind.

"What happens when the darkness comes back?" He rubs his cheek against mine, and the friction of our stubble makes me shiver.

"You showed me I can take my control back." I press a light kiss to his lips, and it's excruciating to hold back from devouring him. He's most likely felt this way for weeks, and I've been the one denying him.

"Tinny, promise to tell me if it happens again. I will help you. Please don't shut me out." His voice breaks.

Grayson grabs my ass and pulls me closer.

"Okay." I lean in to kiss him again, but he tips his head back.

"I'm serious. We can't do this if you don't promise to let me support you."

It's the easiest promise to make. "I will. I do," I say, chuckling because I sound silly, almost like I'm making a wedding vow. "For you, I mean it. It's so exhausting, pretending I don't want you naked and with me every second of the day."

"You want me every second or want me naked every second?" He deepens our kiss, and my heart stops, then gallops to catch up.

"Same difference. When Bex was teasing us, I wanted to tell her to shut her mouth because you're not *just* my roommate," I say in between kisses.

"Then you'll be accused of copying Drake and Lucky's coming out," Gray says. Drake and Lucky did an interview at Q Solutions, and their kiss at the end was their coming out. His hand presses my back so we're chest to chest. "Meanwhile, my depraved mind went to choking on your dick with Benz's comment about choking on your stew."

"My dick will not complain." I reposition us into a reclining position so our cocks rub together.

An inhuman groan rips from my throat. Grayson reacts by flipping us so he's on top. It's as if he can read my mind and knows I need him in control. I wrap my legs around him and force his full weight onto me. My body sings in response.

"If we do this, you can't run from me. You can't act like this didn't happen." Gray runs his tongue along my jaw, and I tip my head back so he has better access to my throat.

"What's going to happen?" I ask as I buck my hips into his.

"As much as you want." He sucks my Adam's apple and I mew.

"Everything," I gush.

Gray chuckles and removes his shirt, so I reach behind me to tear mine off.

"Fuck, that was sexy." Gray stares down at me. "That was a movie-worthy moment I'd love to watch in slo-mo over and over."

"Taking my shirt off?" He's seen me do it thousands of times.

"You severely underestimate the one-handed, behind-the-back grab to reveal these abs." His fingertips dip into my grooves, and they dance in response for him.

Plenty of people have admired and commented on my body, but Gray's words lift my soul so high I'm flying.

His hand moves away, but I trap it under mine. "Please keep touching me." My voice doesn't sound like my own.

Gray massages my pecks and crashes our mouths together. He tastes like spearmint gum and home, and I can't get enough. I undo and drag his zipper down. To get his pants off, I'd need to stop kissing him, so instead, I shove my hands down his back to grip his bare ass.

"Tinny..." He moans my name like an ache, a forbidden promise, and a plea for more. Two syllables convey so much emotion that stars burst behind my eyelids.

"We need to get naked." He leaps up, shedding his pants, then yanks my joggers and boxer briefs down in one motion.

Every part of my body yearns for him. I didn't know it was possible to crave someone on a cellular level. I'm jealous of the air surrounding him because it's not me.

"Someone's happy to see me." His fist closes around my cock, which points at him. It usually doesn't lean left, but it knows where he is, and Gray is all my dick wants.

"So happy," I murmur, and pull him back down, sighing into his mouth. Our naked skin presses together as if we can meld into one.

My dick lurches as he opens his hand to take us both.

"I won't last. Give me more," I plead, my orgasm building in my balls. Right before I get swept away, a dark explosion happens in my mind and threatens to take me over.

"Gray, help," I breathe out, screwing my eyes shut and tensing all my muscles to keep the threat from spreading.

"Shhh. I'm here." He maneuvers me into a sitting position. "Open your eyes, Tinny. Show me your baby blues."

Fear acts like a swift poison, freezing me in place.

"Trust me." His soothing voice counteracts the darkness, and his big doe eyes reassure me. "You failed to mention the cock-blocking aspect of your dark friend." He tries to lighten the mood, but he can't keep the concern out of his tone. Despite the desperation to rid myself of the fear, he's right—it has terrible timing.

"What do I do?" I choke out. With anyone else, I'd leave and never come back. But he made me promise, and I live here. Damn inconvenient. I'm so stupid for believing I could do better. That I could force the darkness away out of sheer will and live in the light with Gray.

"Tell me what's happening, and we can figure it out." He's kneeling between my thighs.

"I was about to come, and it was overwhelmingly brilliant, and then the darkness exploded through me instead of an orgasm." Shame washes over me, and I'm itching to pace.

"Can you sit with that for a minute?" he asks, and I nod. "Has it ever happened in place of an orgasm before?"

"No." That's worse, and I'm concerned he'll think it's his fault. "But it's not you. It's me."

"Maybe it's both of us together. I knew better than to do this with you. I promised myself we'd take our time, and you overrode my sanity." Gray gathers my hands in his. "How's the darkness now?"

I register it looming under the surface, ready to strike again. "It's there but in the background." I'm not okay with him deciding I'm fragile and we need to take our time. But I won't say that out loud and cause a fight.

"Like you're in control?" He brings my hand up to kiss my knuckles, and the sweet gesture unties the knot in my stomach.

"For sure." I concentrate on containing the darkness and shoving it back in a box.

"Could it be triggered by your fear of loss of control?" he asks tentatively, moving to sit in my lap as if my impulse to pace is evident on my face. As I think, he asks another question. "Did you have any other thoughts before things turned in your head?"

I blush at the memory and don't want to say the words out loud.

"I'll take that as a yes." He stands and pulls me up too.

"Where are we going?" He's too understanding about the way I threw myself at him and freaked out. He should be with someone more stable than I am. I'll only disappoint him.

"To bed. Together." Gray leads me to my room.

CHAPTER 16

GRAYSON

As my consciousness pulls me from my dreams, Austin's wrapped around me. His morning wood pokes me in the back as he tries to ease away.

"Don't even try to get out of this bed." I roll over and throw a leg over his hip. "Hi." I search his eyes and see a myriad of emotions.

Embarrassment.

Shame.

Confusion.

Frustration with a case of blue balls.

"Hi," he grumbles back.

"Someone isn't their usual cheery morning self." I can read him well enough to know he's second-guessing a physical relationship with me. As long as he's comfortable, I don't intend to fight fair.

"Should I take care of this for you?" I reach between us and pump his cock.

We're still naked except for our socks since we were too impatient to take them off.

"Ruined our night." Austin's gaze skitters away from mine.

"You didn't. We're experiencing a blip in our reality." I dig my fingers into his spiky hair and scratch his scalp.

"W-w-what?" he stammers.

"Could you imagine how boring we would be if we went from platonic best friends to kissing in Vegas, having a night of passion, and living happily ever after? That kinda stuff is reserved for fairy tales. We've hit a roadblock and have to get over or around it to ride off into the sunset." For emphasis, I wave my hand as if I can see the sunset.

"You're ridiculous," he says, but his body relaxes.

"Guilty." I trace a finger around his nipple, and it peaks for me. "Plan A: naked breakfast in bed, served by me, a talk about last night, and sex. Plan B: also a naked breakfast in bed, sex, and then talk about last night. Which works for your schedule today?"

"The first two-thirds of Plan B followed by round two."

It occurs to me that announcing a talk will create stress and work against us. I do the only sensible thing—I mount him.

"Plans can be revised." I plant my palms on his chest and watch his eyes roll back as we grind together. I'm all for experiments, and maybe if I keep talking, it will stop his subconscious from rearing its ugly cock-blocking head.

"Do you like this better?" I ask, and he moans. "Keep your gorgeous eyes on me."

His lashes flutter, but Austin meets my stare.

"I never noticed the tiny flecks of yellow in your eyes. They're so blue, it doesn't seem possible." Our rhythms sync and our cocks glide along each other. I love the rawness of this.

"You smell so good." I nuzzle into the crook his neck and inhale. "I'm gonna lick you all over. Taste every inch of you."

I rise back up to catch his eyes closed. "Don't hide from me. Show me the exact moment I make you spill your cum all over us. Should I clean you up with my tongue?"

"Yesssss." He's loud, and his eyes widen while his movements become jerky.

All his facial muscles tense, then relax into pure bliss. He's the most beautiful man I've ever laid eyes on. Watching his euphoria sends me over the edge, and I rock us through both our orgasms.

I'm sated but not satisfied. It's a strange combination. My balls are empty, yet my mind races with all the things we could do together.

I collapse, thankful I don't have to worry about squishing him. The mess between us dials up my appetite. The urge to fulfill my promise clears the fog in my head. I kiss my way down his chest and lap up our combined cum.

My tongue licks every crevice. The mixture of us is sensational. Too good not to share. Crawling over him, I plunge my tongue into his mouth so he can taste us.

Austin holds my head to deepen our kiss. His fingers dig into my hair, gripping it like reins. It's intoxicating.

We can't get close enough. I'm desperate to be inside him or have him inside me. I'd live in his skin if I could. He's getting hard again, and I need him in my mouth.

Breaking off our kiss, I take a steadying breath and lay my head on his chest. He's solid below me with a steady heartbeat. Then it kicks up, and I groan.

"Tell that mother-canucking darkness to shut it. We're busy basking in the afterglow." I prop my head on my hand to kiss him.

"How did you know?"

"Your heart rate took off." I lean down to listen. "But you've got it under control. It's almost like you need a disruption in your thought pattern to dissolve it, or whatever happens to it."

"I visualize putting it in a locked box," he says, and I sit up straight.

Alarming him will not help the situation, but I think the box represents his repressed emotions. "Did you do that last night or today?"

"I started to do it last night, but I got distracted, and today I didn't even try."

"But it still went away?" I settle my head on the pillow so we're facing each other.

"It did," he confirms, but his stomach grumbles.

"Time to feed the athlete." I sit up, but he hauls me back.

"More naked time in bed." He nuzzles my neck.

"We've got all day, baby." It's rare we have this much time off during the season, and I'm taking advantage of it.

"How about an all-day naked day? No clothes. Just us." His breathing tickles behind my ears.

"I'm on board for that, but we need to eat." I push my ass back and get another rumble from his stomach. "See, food's important." I'd usually have a smoothie made or something for when he wakes up. He loves to eat healthy but isn't great at planning. It's the least I can do to make his life easier.

"Fine." He lets go of me and flops starfish-style on the bed, exasperated like he's given up in a negotiation.

He's so luscious; it's torture resisting him. "I gotta use the bathroom."

"Use mine. We can shower together."

We soap each other up, and my hands learn each curve of his muscles as I clean him.

"You're more ticklish than I thought." Before he can respond, his phone rings in the bedroom. Austin's face falls. "Hey, we still have all day. Answer it, and we'll make a plan depending on who needs you."

He's conflicted, but I stand him under the spray to rinse him off, then shove him out of the shower with a smack on the ass. If he doesn't answer the call, the thought of letting someone down will eat at him.

I admire that about him. He's selfless and has a huge heart. To prove I'm not upset, I order takeout from his favorite restaurant. We lounged in bed and in the shower for so long that it will be lunchtime when the food gets here.

His closet is open with his housecoat hanging on the back of the door. It's the perfect solution for wearing clothes. There's no reason to terrify the delivery person by opening the door naked.

The blender starts, and a stab of guilt hits me that instead of showing him how much I care, he's feeding himself.

The app says our order will arrive soon. That's one thing going my way. I pause in the hallway before I enter the kitchen to listen in case he's in a private convo.

There's a full glass on the counter. I reflexively wrinkle my nose. Austin loves his healthy drinks in the morning, but I'm not an athlete. There isn't any reason for me to ingest his mix of high-performance ingredients.

His back is to me as he says, "That one's yours."

"You didn't do a double batch?" I sniff the contents of the tumbler.

"No kale or raw eggs in yours, but there are extra raspberries."

I set it down and hug him from behind. "You didn't have to do that for me."

He spins in my arms, all glorious naked skin and sexy chest hair. "When's the last time I made you drink my smoothie?" His arms loop around my neck. "It's not considered doing something nice if I know the other person doesn't like it. That's selfish."

"You're spoiling me," I whisper in his ear, and watch goosebumps appear.

"Nah. But I do what I can." His stomach makes a strange sound, so I back up and let him pour his drink. When he turns to face me, he does a double take. "What's with my robe?" He gestures to it hanging on the island stool.

"You are so American if you're calling a housecoat a robe." I hold up my glass to clink his. "Cheers."

Austin chugs his, not coming up for air, and some dribbles out of the side of his mouth. Without thinking, I lick it up and regret it.

He bursts out laughing. "You look disgusted."

"I thought it would taste better off you?" It's a question because my thought process was getting my mouth on him.

"You like me." He does a little happy dance.

"I more than like you." I palm his hips and join the happy dance. Naked kitchen dancing to no music is my new favorite activity, besides my mouth on him or our dicks sliding together. But it's solidly in the top five. All my favorite things have to do with Austin.

"Who called?" I ask when we stop dancing and sway together.

"King and I are going to text later. He asked if you'll be around because he might want your perspective."

"That sounds ominous." I stop moving.

He opens his mouth, but our buzzer rings. "I'll get it." I snatch his housecoat off the island chair.

"What am I supposed to do?" He covers his dick.

"Stand behind the island or, if you're afraid they'll be too overwhelmed by your abs, duck down." He flips me his middle finger.

I paid online with a generous tip, so it's a quick exchange, and I never open the door all the way.

"What did you do?" Austin pops up from behind the counter.

"It's a naked day with no rules." I set the bag down and pull out the containers.

He instantly recognizes them and gets out silverware for us. "My fave. Have I told you lately that you're the best?"

I'm on the verge of saying I'd do anything for my boyfriend, but I hold back for fear of moving too fast and scaring him.

"You can stroke my ego or whatever you want whenever you want." I hand over his salmon and brown rice stir-fry.

"Island or couch since there are no rules?" He shakes his head when I hesitate. "Don't move."

Austin comes back with a sheet and covers the couch. "We can pretend that on no-rules day, you weren't worried about being naked on the couch."

I huff. That's the thing about working in healthcare—the knowledge of germs everywhere. "You would obsess next time the guys come over about who's sitting in the same spot as where our naked asses and balls were."

"Good thing I found a solution." His enthusiastic sounds as he eats, set off endorphins in my brain.

After we've eaten our fill, I put the leftovers in the fridge and lie down on the sofa with my head in Austin's lap.

He picks up the remote. "Sports, movie, or TV show?"

"Whatever you want on in the background." I smile up at him, and his cock hardens.

His watch beeps, and his expression is strange. He pets my head but stares unseeing at the TV, then clears his throat. "Last night, I had an appointment with the sports psychologist, Victoria, but she had to cancel and we rescheduled for today. In thirty minutes."

"I'm proud of you for reaching out to someone. I'll always back you up." It's tempting to ask more questions, but I'll let him talk first.

Austin's shoulders drop. "You don't think it's stupid?"

"Why would I think that? You know I went to therapy and am a big advocate for everyone getting mental health help when they need it." If anything, I'm greatly relieved because I'm not qualified to really help him. I try when he's in distress, but that's not the same as working on the root cause of the problem.

"My game isn't suffering." He glances down, and I roll onto my back.

"No, but you are. And don't put that out in the universe. I know several of your teammates who would condemn you, and one who would insist on a sage cleansing," I tease, and put his hand back on my head because I love his fingers in my hair.

"I've only had one session, and I mostly talked about my fear of going after what I want and the ramifications. I didn't mention the darkness within me." His brow furrows, creating deep lines.

"Does she know about me?" I ask. We all know each other, and I won't break any confidences.

He looks up at the TV again. "No."

"Hey." I take the hand resting on my chest and kiss his palm. "I'm not pressuring you. Telling her is coming out, and you get to decide that on your timeline."

"But what about us?" His blue eyes cloud over.

"We're best friends who live together, and we're exploring sex. You don't enjoy PDAs, and I don't expect that to change. It's not like you're going to kiss me in the locker room or a bar. I'm not going to feel slighted if we're not out in public. Half the guys probably have bets on how long we've been sleeping together. On the road, we're in and out of each other's rooms all the time." I'm on a tangent and pause. "Unless you want things to change."

He blows out a breath and leans down. I meet him halfway for a kiss, and he supports my head and neck. "Part of me is positive I'm being selfish."

"It's not in your nature." I steel myself for him to reject my next words. "I'm here to help you talk things out if you want. But I highly suggest telling Victoria about your darkness. She's better equipped than I am. And when you're ready to trust her, tell her about adding another gender to your sexcapades." My joke works and he chuckles.

"I don't think she'll understand." He lets me go as I sit up to climb onto his lap.

"My sweet Tinny," I cup his neck. "That woman has probably heard things that would make your toes curl. Not to minimize your experience, but she will believe you, and it might not be the strangest thing she's heard in a month. As for coming out, I know Liska had a few sessions with her, and so did Jayce McKenna. Don't mention my name if you're worried about the organization or privacy. When we tell the team, I won't be allowed to treat you." There's a slim chance I could lose my job, but I push that aside and focus on what he needs.

"Wait! What?" His eyes widen in alarm.

"It's standard in the medical community that you don't treat family or significant others." I play with the tiny hairs on the back of his neck.

"But there's no one I trust more than you."

"We don't need to worry about that yet." I kiss the corner of his mouth. "But will you tell her about the darkness?"

"I will."

A thousand-pound weight lifts from me. Now I can concentrate on more fun things like playing with his body.

CHAPTER 17

AUSTIN

My good fortune has to end soon. With Gray's help, I've been able to contain the darkness and enjoy the morning with him. Gray's the only person I've told who didn't tell me I was either crazy or wrong.

I like Victoria, and she's a professional, but that doesn't make it easy. For her sake, I break my no-clothes rule for the video call. Gray thought I should wear my bathrobe, but that's creepy. My laptop is set up at my desk in the corner of my bedroom, and Victoria's smiling face appears on screen as I decide how to reveal my biggest secret.

We recap our last session, and she asks the million-dollar question. "What led you to seek my help?"

She doesn't say my answer last session was unsatisfactory, but it's implied by asking again.

I tell her about how I hurt the hockey player and how my sister broke her arm, explaining that I felt overtaken and not in control of my decisions or myself.

"Has that happened recently?"

"Yes, and I'm afraid I'll hurt someone again." I'm so relieved she's nonjudgmental that I'm lightheaded.

"Tell me about it."

I freeze. "It wasn't on the ice."

We go back and forth while I figure out how to phrase the experience. "I started a new relationship, and it happened twice while we were intimate."

"And this has never happened while being intimate before?" When I confirm, she asks, "Is there something different about this relationship?"

I wince, but she can't help if she doesn't know. "It's with a man."

"Oh." She lets out a long breath as if she needs to recalibrate. "Any big change could spark it. Were you brought up in a conservative or liberal home? Sometimes we internalize beliefs we don't hold, and feelings about issues take on a life of their own."

"My parents were religious and fairly conservative. But they didn't forbid my being friends with Grayson when he came out," I unnecessarily defend my family, and my mouth drowns in sourness.

"It's interesting that your mind immediately jumped to that. Is that something you were afraid of?"

I nod. My parents aren't overtly bigoted or homophobic, but they speak about the natural order of things and how the Bible defines marriage as between a man and a woman. Their silence about my support of Gray and LGBTQ issues said so much.

She asks me very specific questions about my childhood, accidents, injuries, witnessing others who were seriously hurt or killed, and my exposure to abuse of all forms: physical, sexual, and emotional.

"Austin, honestly, my expertise is in how your experience affects your playing, and you seem to suffer from traumatic guilt. I'm not qualified to do a deep dive into healing trauma."

"Traumatic? It's not trauma." I'm glad I'm sitting down.

"How about this? We'll work on your understanding of the darkness and the root of your fear. Once we find strategies to manage it, I may refer you to another therapist to continue to work on things beyond my expertise. I won't stop seeing you until you're ready or have another therapist."

"I can live with that." She'll see I'm not traumatized. I only need to lock up the darkness successfully, and I'll be fine.

"Before our next session, think about your darkness as a part of you, not something outside of your control. See if you can identify any common circumstances or emotions surrounding the episodes."

We disconnect, and I shed my clothes. We have hours left in our naked day, and I'm not wasting them.

"Gray," I call, and hear him thunder down the hall. My bedroom door bursts open and bounces off the wall. "Hey"—I tackle him onto the bed—"we said no clothes today."

"What's wrong?" His hands and eyes roam over me. "Are you okay?"

"You worry too much. Get my robe off." I wrestle him out of it.

"You yell, I worry." He huffs and lets me fling the robe away. "It got cold out there without you to keep me warm." Gray tugs me on top of him, resting his head on my pillow.

"Sorry," I say sheepishly, though I'm not at all sorry to have his naked skin against mine.

"How did your session go?" He wraps a leg around my back, bringing our groins closer.

"Good. I told her I'm in a relationship with a man." As I dip my head to kiss him, he stops me.

"That's a huge deal. It's your first coming-out. Are you okay with it?"

"Umm." I pause because it didn't seem that big. She's bound by her oath not to talk about our sessions. "Fine?"

Gray groans and smacks the side of my head. "You don't have any regrets?"

"I regret this conversation stopping us from doing other things." I raise my eyebrows suggestively, kicking the covers away from us.

"Who knew going bi would make you a sex maniac?" He strums his fingers down my side, and I can't hold back a laugh. "I'm happy if it truly wasn't hard for you and honestly jealous it was so easy."

"Telling her isn't risky. The hard part will be keeping the darkness locked away." I trace his widow's peak and watch his brown eyes melt for me.

"What if we try something different? Things hiding in the dark have power, and bringing them to light takes away their ability to cause harm." He rolls out from under me and rises while I sit against the headboard, then he straddles my legs.

"How?" I'm embarrassed and ashamed of so many of the things the dark side of me wants.

He bites his lip, and my thumb drags it from his teeth. "We all have deep secret desires. Some doable and some loony." He flushes. "Don't judge me, but I couldn't get close enough to you and wished I could wear you as my skin. So that's like crazy-thought level. For obvious reasons, I can't wear you, but I still crave being close to you."

"I wouldn't mind." I press our lips together and relax into our kiss.

"You say that like it wouldn't be a heinous, gross act because we both know it won't happen. But I also want your teeth marks on me, and that is something that can happen." He stares into my eyes. "I told you my fleeting, insane thought. Now you tell me one of yours." Gray sits back on my thighs, waiting.

My head buzzes, and the memory of sinking my teeth into his skin as I came turns me on and disgusts me in equal measure. But he said he liked it.

"You're overthinking. Tell me one thing you're desperate to do to me."

"I want to redden your ass and fuck you like a rag doll," I blurt out, and recover enough to say, "That's in the loony category."

"How would you make my ass red?" I'm so startled by the question that my mind goes blank, so he clarifies for me. "Would you use your hand, a paddle, a flogger, or something else?"

"I'd hurt you, and I'm not doing it." Wicked thoughts of different possibilities take over, and I can barely breathe. I've never fantasized about using something other than my hand, but the flogger... I shut down my excitement.

"That's a damn shame for both of us. We'd both enjoy it." His forefinger traces the ripples in my abs, and my hard dick swells for attention. "Is this another case of your mouth lying and your body telling me the truth?" he asks slyly.

"I'm hard because you're naked and touching me." My chin lifts with childish defiance.

"Hmmm. Pity. I've never been with someone I trust enough, but a flogger has always interested me." He doesn't look away, and I swear the man can read my mind.

My cock is practically waving at him, following its own rules.

"Are you afraid because you think you'll hurt me?"

I crush my eyes shut. "Yes," I grit out through my clenched jaw.

"I trust you, but what if..." I open my eyes to see him shake his head. "Never mind."

"Tell me," I demand.

"It's a terrible idea and won't help you trust yourself. I was talking without thinking." He smashes his lips into a thin line. "Sorry," he says, the way we'd say it in Canada, "soar-ee."

"If anyone should be sorry, it's me. You made me tell you; now you tell me."

Gray scoots closer and loops his arms around my neck. I'll never get enough of his sweet sensualness. "The classic tactic of using my words against me. Fine." He grins. "What if I do the things to you first and show you what it would feel like, and then you can decide if you want to do it to me? Think of it as a trial before a recommendation. You'd never tell someone to eat a food you've never eaten. We're sampling a menu."

"You've got a sex menu in mind." I slap his ass and love the cracking sound that echoes.

"I could whip one up for you." He uses innuendo with an exaggerated wink to ease my tension.

"It might work. Do you know what you're doing? I've never done anything like that before."

"We have the internet." He leans over for his phone and settles back down on my legs.

"What are you searching?" I'm impressed and also nervous.

"As far as I've seen, neither of us owns a flogger, so I'm searching 'spanking for dummies'." He types away with both thumbs.

"Is that a thing?" I will eat my tongue if it's real.

"No, but the search leads to videos and a book about spanking. You choose the first video. We'll watch two or three for different perspectives." He hands me his phone.

We watch one and learn that some spankings are thuddy and some are sting-y. Learning is good. He starts the next video. I'm so grateful he thought of this. There are so many things that I assumed we'd use guesswork for, but this puts it in really easy terms and ways to communicate.

"Cool." Gray closes the video as if it didn't turn him upside down. "Still interested?"

"Yeah. But I'm unsure about pain levels. You?"

He tosses his phone and kisses me, soft and sweet, then bites my bottom lip. "Did you like the kissing and the bite?"

"Yes." I sit taller so we're chest to chest.

"We don't have to know where our limits are. As long as we check in, we can find them together."

His hard cock leaks on me, and I'm so ready for this. "Less talking. More action."

"Hands and knees, Tinny, and no back talk."

I shudder and get into position.

"You have the best ass I've ever seen." He kneads it with his palms. "Meaty and muscular with soft skin." Gray kisses the base of my spine, then peppers kisses all over my ass. "I'm going to spank you, then you're going to fuck me." He lands a stinging slap, and I jolt forward. On the other side, his hand thuds. "You with me?"

I nod.

"I need your words, Tinny."

"Keep going," I beg.

He varies the blows in both position and strength while taking breaks to caress my heated skin. I never in a million years thought I'd enjoy it. Each strike liberates my mind from worry and overthinking, but it also gives me confidence in our connection.

I'm sure words are coming out of my mouth, but I don't know what I'm saying.

At first, I tense up with anticipation, but my body surrenders and relaxes for Gray. There's nothing to fear from him.

"Pain level?" Gray asks.

"Good," I slur.

He chuckles. "Can you give me a number and if it's close to your limit?"

"Don't stop."

CHAPTER 18

GRAYSON

I've never participated in BDSM, but I've heard about subspace and think Austin is in it. His ass is bright red, and if I leave handprints, the guys will see it when he changes.

"Tinny." I grip his hip and stroke my other hand along his spine. In one of my classes, we studied pheromones and if humans are affected by them. Every breath fills me with his and its exhilarating. "Listen to me."

"You stopped," he accuses, and glares over his shoulder.

"Yes, because there might be marks tomorrow and you undress with the team." I couldn't keep going and have him regret this later.

His head drops to the mattress. "They're not even here and they're messing with us." His voice is forlorn.

"Fuck me before I explode." We both need relief, and I'm not dwelling on spanking. His ass is such a pretty red, and my hand stings. If I continue, I'll probably come untouched.

He flattens onto the bed, nodding. To give him a minute or two to recover, I search for his lube and condoms. There's lube in the bedside table but no condoms, which is surprising since he's a planner. I rub his back and he moans.

"Be right back." I leave the room before he can protest to ready myself and grab condoms from my bathroom.

"Don't leave me," he grumbles when I climb back in bed.

"I had to clean myself up for you." Kissing his shoulder, I drop the strip of condoms next to us. No reason to go back and forth.

Austin turns his head when he hears the bottle pop open. "Let me watch." He turns on his side, and I spread my legs to give him a good view. "I've never done this," he says timidly.

"Wanna help?" I ask, rimming a slick finger around my hole. He seems unsure. "You can watch how I do it and try it next time."

He can't take his eyes off my finger as I breach myself. He moves closer and lays his head on my leg. I'm all business, adding another finger, and he sucks in a breath. His face is too beautiful for words. I need him inside me.

"How did you get ready for me?"

I pause, and it's a relief the question takes me off the edge. I explain the process, and he nods with interest.

"How come straight people don't do that when they have anal sex?"

"I have no idea. It's strange, isn't it?" I never thought about it before, but it's sort of icky that straight men and women don't prepare. "Maybe it's all drunk spur of the moment," I guess.

I add a third finger and whimper at the lust in his eyes. They're blue lasers heating my skin.

"Can I touch you?" He pours lube onto his fingers.

"Yes, but only for a second because I don't want to come until your dick's inside me." I remove my fingers. "Start with two."

He stares for an achingly long second, and I fear this might be too much. "You're open for me." His eyes flick to mine in awe as he reaches to touch me. His fingers are featherlight, but it's extraordinary.

"Please, I won't break," I pant, and cant my hips toward him.

Austin's touches zing, hardening my cock and hitting a pleasure center in my brain that reduces me to base instincts.

He teases my rim, focusing on my puckered skin. Then, he sinks his fingers in and groans. "You're so warm." He slides his fingers in and out, and the zings travel through my entire body. "Do you like this?"

"I love you touching me." There's a war within me to let him explore my body forever and get his leaking length inside me. I grab his shoulders and topple backward so I'm under him. "You can add another finger, but I'm ready for you. Fuck me, Tinny." My head is at the foot of the bed, but I can easily reach the condoms from this position.

It's a feat to tear it open with slippery fingers and roll it down his length.

"I want this, please," he pleads, and I hear the desperation tinged with fear.

Last time, I kept his mind occupied with dirty talk, and I can do it again.

"Yes, get inside me." On his knees, he lines up his tip with my hole. This feels like the first time, and I'll explode as soon as he enters me. My chest heaves, waiting and waiting.

"You're so pretty like this."

"I'm about to become a gremlin if you're not inside me in the next breath." My inner muscles contract in the agony of being empty.

Austin breathes out a laugh and pushes in. An asshole has more resistance than a pussy, so his eyes widen and he freezes. I haven't bottomed in forever, and my inner muscles squeeze him gleefully.

"Keep going. I can take all of your big fat cock. Fill me up with all the cum you made for me." My words ignite him, and my body sucks him deeper. I need to keep his mind on me so it can't wander. He deserves a glorious orgasm without his mind sabotaging him.

"It's so good. Help me." He pushes halfway in.

He asks and I answer by gripping his shoulders and hauling myself up so I'm on his thighs, and I don't give him a chance to object as I impale myself on him, giving my body over as a gift for both of us.

Austin makes a guttural sound, and I swallow it down, plunging my tongue into his mouth. "I'm about to move. Are you ready?" I ask, knowing the first time in an ass is as overwhelming as it is euphoric.

"No, I'm not going to last." His big blue eyes want so badly to please me.

"Sweet Tinny. We live together. If you fill the condom, we'll wait and do it again. Unless you try to lie to me and tell me you have to go home to feed your cat." With my quip, his shoulders relax.

"Guess that excuse is out the window." His hand lands on my neck, bringing me in for a kiss. Our bodies undulate together as if we've done this many times.

"Especially since everyone who knows you would know you're a dog person, not a cat person." I roll my hips, and his eyes disappear into the back of his head.

"Do that again."

My hip circles drag my balls over him, but he gets too close to the edge, and I rise to change the angle. In this moment, I know he's ruined me. "You fit so perfectly inside me."

"We should have been doing this for years," Austin pants as I pick up the pace.

"There was the little issue of your straightness." I'm profoundly full. No one will ever compare to my Austin.

"Not anymore." He picks me up, and in a gymnastic move, turns us so I'm on my back with my head on a pillow and he's still inside me. "Let me fuck you like a rag doll?"

"My body is yours." I lift my arms over my head and cross my wrists as if he's tied them.

He growls and mounts me like a predator, plunging in and out. All the sweetness is gone. He's confident and intent on making us come. I'm his, and he has the power to wreck me in the best and worst ways.

"So good." With my commentary, Austin stays with me, and his darkness doesn't steal this from us.

His face is scrunched up as if he's holding back, and that isn't acceptable. The point of tonight is for him to take what he needs. To show him it's safe to explore his fantasies.

"We're going to shift to the edge of the bed so you can fuck me with the force you're craving." I move too quickly, and he slips out with a furious grunt. "Note to self: plan ahead. Stand next to the bed, Tinny. What to you prefer stomach or back?" I'm his to command.

Austin stands and yanks me to him. "I have to see what I do to you."

I bite my lip to keep from saying something ridiculously sappy. Hooking my hands under my knees, I pull them to my chest, exposing my hole to him. "Make me your rag doll."

He roars and thrusts balls deep, causing the bed to move.

"Yes. Like that. Harder," I pant, holding my sweaty legs with all my might.

The pace is brutal, and he fills me, satisfying every desire I've had. His expression is blissed out, like he's floating on air and not ramming my ass. It's a delicious dichotomy. "Fuck me so hard you leave an imprint in my throat." He's so deep; he's ripping me apart and making me whole.

Austin is the only one for me.

His eyelids flutter closed, but he doesn't pause.

"Right there." I arch my back when he hits my prostate.

"I'm so close. Are you going to come for me?" Austin drives into me, nailing me where I need him as he fists my cock.

His hand demands my cum, and I spill into it with a long groan. Nothing exists but him.

"You're squeezing me so tight." His movements become jerky, and his legs tense as he fills the condom. I wish there wasn't anything between us. I want part of him to live in my body.

Austin collapses on my chest, and I let go of my legs to hook them around his back. I should have water for him when he comes down, but I can't leave his side or he'll crash faster.

"Come here, baby, up to the pillows." He's loose and limp, but I'm able to lay him out on the bed with his head supported. "It's different for everyone, but you might have an adrenaline crash. I'm here, and I won't leave you."

"You always keep your word." He nuzzles into the crook of my neck.

"I'll do anything for you." I hold him close and inhale his sweaty, crisp scent.

"That was... I don't have enough brain function for words. Stup...stup...," He groans a laugh, shaking us both.

"If you say stupid, we have a problem." I massage his neck.

"Stupendous," he mutters.

"Good word. You probably used all your available brain cells. Try to sleep."
I barely have the words out before his breathing evens out and becomes utterly
relaxed.

With Austin sated and sleeping, I close my eyes in contentment. But the feeling of otherness rears its ugly head. Ironically, it's similar to Austin's darkness.
It's doubt.

Austin could be with anyone, and I'm the test guy. The guy he uses to figure
himself out before he moves on and finds "the one."

He would never do it on purpose, but he won't settle for me. I'm the plus
one. I don't add any value to his life.

My breath hitches, and I hug him tighter. He burrows into me and mumbles,
"Don't leave."

I'll never leave him. Even if I cling to him knowing it will end with my heart
in a million pieces, I'm not letting go. Austin's mine until he decides he's done
with me.

CHAPTER 19

AUSTIN

I wake up to my phone buzzing, and I panic, thinking I'm alone.

"Hey." Gray kisses my shoulder. "Your phone's on the nightstand. Should I get it?"

My thoughts are slow and my limbs heavy, but I shake my head and roll over.

"Shit. I forgot about King. He wanted to text, but now he's calling." I fumble to answer but miss the call and jab the buttons to call him back.

Gray eases away, but I fling my arm out to stop him. He probably wants to give me privacy, but I need him next to me.

"Hey, sorry, I fell asleep. But I'm here." I rush to say when King answers.

"Nah, man, you're good. I was just checking in because you've never not answered a text within three seconds of receiving it." His voice is light, and there isn't a hint of stress.

"Yeah, I crashed hard." I scoot back to get closer to Gray.

"Go rest up. We can talk tomorrow."

"Are you sure? I'm available now." My body relaxes when Gray's arm encircles me and his hand splays on my chest.

"All good, captain. See ya tomorrow." King hangs up before I can argue.

"Do you have any idea what that was about?" Gray asks in my ear, sending a shiver through me.

"Not a clue. Should I be worried?" I spin in his arms so we're face-to-face. King is one of our best players, and I'm responsible for keeping him safe. He receives more trash talk than the rest of us simply for the color of his skin, and King won't tell me specifics, so I can't report the players. When he comes out, it will be worse. He's only out to the team and his family.

"No. He's a grown man, and you offered your help. He sounded fine. Actually, more worried about his derelict captain than himself. Find him tomorrow. King will be good tonight."

I'm tempted to call King back, but that would imply he's incapable of advocating for himself.

"Here." He hands me a sports drink full of electrolytes. "You need this. Are you ready to eat yet?"

"Are you babying me, Ward?" I can't decide whether I'm annoyed or like it.

"Oh, the last-naming me hurts." He motions for me to drink. "It won't stop me from taking care of you. You go out of your way to ensure all your players have what they need. Let me spend a few minutes doing something for you."

"You're ruthless," I say with no heat, then chug the drink. "Happy?"

"So happy." He leans in for a kiss, and my stomach swoops like I'm on a rollercoaster.

We kiss while our hands explore each other. It feels right. Like this is how we're supposed to be together.

"Let me see your ass." Gray nudges me and I comply. "Don't kill me, but I left some marks, and it's going to be hard to hide them." He places a chaste kiss on each cheek. "I'm sorry."

"Don't be. I'm not." He's opening me up to things I'd never have the courage to do without him. Because I trust him, I can explore another side of myself. A side I thought I had to keep on a leash or hide completely.

"What are you going to tell the team? You know they aren't going to let it slide. They gossip more than the tabloids."

"I'll come to your treatment room and change into my base layer while you wrap my knuckles. I opened the wound from the other night, and you, being the extra cautious trainer, will bandage me so there's no chance of blood on the ice." It's a solid plan, and of course he agrees.

"Did you like what we did?" he asks timidly.

"Do you understand the meaning of the word stupendous?" I rake my hand over his face, and he kisses my palm.

"An orgasm tends to make people sex-drunk, and I'm specifically asking about the spanking part." He face-rakes me back.

I haul him on top of me and knead his ass. "I did. It surprised me how much. Enough that we should do it again."

"Yeah?" His kiss is slow, like it's the only thing we have to do all night.

I love how his hair drapes over me in this position. I nod, not breaking the kiss.

He speaks directly into my mouth. "Will you spank me another day?"

"You think we should wait?" I'm relieved and disappointed.

"You got spanked and had anal sex for the first time. It's been a big day. We don't have to do all the things today. We can spread out the fun." He grinds on me. "The most important thing is that you're comfortable with it."

"The videos made a huge difference in modeling communication and how to do it. It makes me nervous about losing control, but I'm not uncomfortable." My fingers trace each bump on his spine.

"You didn't seem out of control in a bad way when you were fucking me. But you weren't careful, and I loved it. At any point, were you concerned?"

My brain scratches and replays that he loved it. A sense of pride that I'm not used to when it comes to sex wells in me. I've enjoyed sex, but I loved it with Gray. For once in my life, I have the confidence and courage to try new things.

"Tinny?" He asks with distress since I haven't spoken.

"Sorry," I say, going lax and spreading out my arms and legs. "I was basking in the glow of your praise." I almost say it without laughing, but it bubbles out.

Gray pinches my nipple. "Don't change the subject."

That wasn't my intention, but I've never liked examining my feelings. "I felt wild and on the verge of rutting you like an animal until I passed out, but the darkness stayed away." I cover my eyes with my forearm.

Gray won't let me hide and removes my arm. "That's great."

"Most people don't require coddling after sex," I grumble, hearing the resentment in my tone.

"One, I'm not coddling you, and two, if we're going to do any sort of kink, it's standard practice to check in with each other after the session." Gray boops my nose.

I swat his hand away. "Now you're being an asshole." My grin negates my words.

"Not to brag, but I got the impression that you're kinda sorta obsessed with my asshole." He shimmies his torso, and his thick dark eyebrows draw attention to his sensual eyes.

"Obsessed after one time?" I tut like he's absurd. "Fine. Maybe a little," I concede.

"Perfect. Because I'm hooked on you like heroin."

"Should I be offended?" Being compared to a narcotic isn't something I ever imagined, yet I love it.

"Nope. But back to sex. I trust you. You won't hurt me, and I need you to trust I'll tell you if you ever cross a line. We're in this together, and I won't do something I don't like to spare your feelings. We have years of friendship that would be ruined by lying to you. And I expect the same. Tell me the moment the darkness appears."

Gray is going to challenge me to open up to him, and that scares me.

"I can do that." I swallow hard, making the commitment to him and myself.

He reaches for his phone. "Let's buy a flogger."

I'm dizzy with desire.

CHAPTER 20

GRAYSON

In every arena, the smell of man sweat has been embedded in the rooms like it's soaked into the walls.

I shouldn't ogle Austin's ass as he gets dressed in Minnesota's visitor training room with me. But I'm only a man with zero self-control for him. As much as it pains me, I have to tell him the truth.

"You're healed enough that no one will think you were spanked, so you can change with the team." I watch his glutes ripple as he tugs on his base layer.

He glances at me over his shoulder. "But then I'd be depriving you of your favorite view."

I stalk over and seize his mouth, drowning in vanilla-cinnamon sweetness.

A knock on the door makes us jump apart, and Austin jams his head through his shirt.

Clearing my throat, I call, "Come in."

"Your door is never shut." King surveys the room.

"My fault." Austin flushes. "I must've done it when I walked in. Are you okay? Do you need Grayson? He can re-wrap my knuckles later."

King's gaze goes back and forth between us. "Nah. My hairband broke. Hoping you have something to hold my braids back." His intricate pattern of zigzag braids touches his shoulders.

I cross the room to my duffle and riffle through it to find the hairband bag. Hockey players have specific tastes when it comes to their flow, so I try to keep a variety. I find a note from Austin, and my heart stops. It reads *You complete me*. He's been leaving me famous movie line quotes because he says they got it right. I bury it and act casual.

"Here." I toss King a bag of hair ties. "Pick whatever you want."

"You're a lifesaver." King digs out a cloth-covered band and waves as he exits the room.

"I found your note and want to do bad things to you, but we already almost got caught kissing. I know better than to do something so risky." My hands are in my pockets so I don't reach for him.

"Don't apologize. I've heard no is a complete sentence, and I can say it." His eyes dance with amusement as he holds out his hand for me to bandage. "You can do those things later."

I quickly switch out the bandage since there's no actual reason for it besides his need to change here instead of the locker room.

"Thanks, Sunshine." He pecks my lips, leaving me stunned with both the kiss and the nickname as he saunters away. It will end badly for me if we get caught before telling the team. We might be breaking the rules together, but I'm expendable—he's not.

Pregame treatments are a blur, and before I know it, the team's out on the ice. The Minneapolis fans electrify the stadium and players to a fast-paced start. I can't keep my eyes off Austin. His confidence on the ice is unparalleled. The puck drops, and he's off like a shot, all explosive energy and grace.

Drake loses the face-off, but Austin strips their winger, and our first line is unstoppable. Lucky and Drake seem to read each other's minds and pull all of Minnesota's defense to them, leaving Austin wide-open.

He scores the first goal, and my chest swells with pride.

Watching Austin has never interfered with my job until tonight. Every few minutes, I have to give myself a mental shake to pay attention to the other players on the ice. Track their movements and expressions for tells indicating pain. A hockey player can bleed out and look me dead in the eyes, swearing it's just a scratch and he can play. Half my job is dissecting their play before they complain. If they're complaining, shit is bad.

They play with minor and nagging injuries, and tonight they aren't showing any signs of stress or pain. But I stay vigilant in between staring at the hottest man on the planet playing incredible hockey, earning three points between goals and assists.

Minnesota isn't going down without a fight. Our offense is skating circles around them, but our defense is average at best, which makes it a high-scoring game. We're tied at four in the third period.

This is prime injury time, and I check in with each player after their shift to stare them in the eye, seeing what they won't say out loud. So far so good, but I'm not stupid enough to believe that will take us through the end of the game.

The team wins by one in a nail-biter, and no one has an injury that requires more than my examination and instructions to use ice and heat. We're headed for the playoffs again; I can sense it with the way the team is gelling. Our defense needs improvement, but luckily Liska and Benz can save impossible shots.

It's a fast turnaround, so the guys are drinking in the hotel bar instead of going out. The team has taken over and spread out between the bar and tables. We push together three high tops to stand around.

I purposely put distance between Austin and me to avoid any accidental telltale contact.

King steps up to the top of the tables. "I made a decision, and just want to run it by y'all." His bright eyes laugh at our confusion.

"If you're looking to be traded, the answer is no," Drake says with no inflection.

"Agreed." Austin holds up his half-empty glass.

"Daddy Drake and our captain have laid down the law. Hope it's something else." Lucky nips at Drake's ear.

King clenches his jaw and sighs. "No. It's not a trade."

"Spill it, work husband once removed," Benz says, and Leo growls. "What?" Benz can't pull off the innocent act. "He's Griff's work husband, and I'm Griff's BFF, so he's my work husband once removed."

King shakes his head, and I'm afraid he might leave.

"Ignore them. What's up?" I ask.

He wraps a hand around one of his braids and tugs. "There was so much shit about what I said about being on the queer spectrum, I should walk out onto the ice during Pride Night."

Our group is uncharacteristically silent. Since we have out men and women in our organization, our new tradition is that they take center ice before the game to show solidarity and show representation for fans and the LGBTQ community.

"That's admirable, but you don't owe the public your private life if you're not ready." I round the table and slap him on the back. He's not a touchy-feely person, but it seems important to show my support.

"I'd be letting young guys down who look up to me if I don't take a stand. None of the out players look like me, and representation matters." King cracks his knuckles.

Lucky clears his throat. "Seriously, this is a big decision. You have time to think it over, but your life won't be the same afterward. Drake and I have each other, Liska has Trevor, and Benz has Leo. We all have someone to lean on and experience the uncomfortable and hurtful moments with us. Are you seeing anyone?"

"No. But my parents support my decision."

"Lucky's not implying he doesn't support you. We all do, and we all stand behind you," Drake says, and we nod in agreement. "It can be easier when you have a partner, but that complicates things as well. You've seen me lose it when someone makes a derogatory comment about my man." He grips Lucky around the waist and kisses his temple. "Fortunately, you're on the right team."

"We have your back," Austin says, and his gaze finds mine. His face looks conflicted, and I assume it's because he's undecided whether he wants to talk about himself.

A few minutes later, Austin drags me out of the bar to the elevators with stress vibrating off of him. He winces as Benz rushes to catch the doors before they slide closed, and he and Leo ride up with us.

Leo's holding Benz close, and Benz is practically a mooning pile of goo. We're all on the same floor, and for appearances, I turn toward my room, intending to knock on Austin's door after Leo and Benz disappear into one of their rooms. Leo has stepped down as an official coach, but travels with the team, paying for his own room.

"Gray, I have that thing to show you." Austin's eyes shift nervously, like he's about to commit a crime.

"Is this a sexy thing or boring?" Benz jokes.

"You're the one who always says no kissy-face. We can't give our secrets away." I squash my instinct to slap his ass, knowing Leo might punch me.

"They used to dress alike and be so fun." Benz pulls out his keycard. "Let's leave them to their sports talk, Lovie."

"We're wearing the same sweatpants," Austin says indignantly, as if he's offended. I won't willingly admit I love it when he insists I wear his clothes. Me in his clothes is an aphrodisiac for him so I'll never say no.

Benzy shrugs and there's a thud when the door closes behind them. I'm sure they can't keep their hands off each other.

I catch up with Austin, eager to find out why he's so agitated. He paces as soon as we get into his room, in which he clearly planned for a romantic night. It's a departure from the usual mess, with no dirty clothes in sight, and he brought an air freshener. The king bed is made and turned down to be inviting. On the bedside table is my favorite sports drink and snack—barbecue baked chips, which he doesn't like. His distress stops me from commenting on his thoughtfulness.

"Am I failing them? Should I have said something about myself? I should set an example and walk out with the queer players on Pride Night."

I stop him with my hands on his shoulders. "Slow down. Everything we said to King also applies to you. You don't owe the team details of your personal life. Just because the team lives in each other's pockets doesn't mean you're required to tell them. It's been barely a month since you figured out my dick is your favorite thing. You're allowed time to process that monumental fact." I cup myself for comic relief.

Austin sits on his bed, and I lower myself so we're connected, leg to leg, hip to hip, and shoulder to shoulder. He leans in, nestling his head in the crook of my neck.

"I couldn't do this without you. I mean, literally and emotionally." He sighs a laugh.

"Pride Night is almost two months away. There's plenty of time to decide and figure out if you want to come out. This team has taken very different approaches to coming out, and you're in control of your narrative. Jayce held a press conference, Lucky and Drake kissed for the camera, and Leo and Benz have not confirmed or denied their relationship. Telling the team is vastly different from telling the world." I hug him and tilt us backward until our heads are on the bed while our feet remain on the floor. "There are smaller steps to take than Pride Night."

"It feels like a betrayal of you and their trust." He rubs his sternum.

"It isn't. It took me years to come out, and it wasn't until I gave up my hockey career. Thankfully, times have changed, and it's not career-ending to come out. But that doesn't mean it's easy. King didn't tell the team he's gay until he felt safe, and he's known his entire life. Give yourself some grace."

"Please don't think I'm ashamed of you or us." He throws a leg over me.

"If King came to you yesterday and said he realized last month he's into dudes, what advice would you give him?" My lips twitch as I fight a smile as he glares at me.

"Don't be all logical when I'm full of self-pity!"

"I have some goddamn nerve." I blanket him with my body. "You deserve the same space as everyone else. The guys love you because you care about them. They won't judge you for taking time to come to terms with your newfound sexuality. *I* don't judge you."

"You're too good to me." He holds me tight.

"Not possible. You didn't pressure me when I kept my sexuality a secret, and I'm going to return the courtesy. You don't have to have all the answers, Mr. Perfect." Being on top of him is getting me hard, but I don't want this to be about sex.

"You're not going anywhere." Austin traps me in place as I try to slide off him.

"You got me. What are you going to do with me?" I grind on him.

"Whatever the hell I want."

CHAPTER 21

AUSTIN

I decide to tag along with Gray for his fitting with Trevor. Most of Trevor's sales are online, but he rents a small space to display his clothes with a single dressing room and a workroom in the back. It has rich leather and aged wood vibes.

The shop has exposed brick walls and warm wood floors, which contrast with the sleek black metal racks and modern lighting. The minimalistic black wrought-iron desk has a computer, and I assume it's for cashing customers out.

Each design has only one size, so you shop for the color and cut. Once that's decided, Trevor finds your size in the back or cuts a rough design for you. He's a genius with fabric.

When he custom-made my suit, he told me which fabrics, colors, and suit cuts would fit me best, narrowing down the sheer volume of options. It would've taken me weeks, and I probably wouldn't have picked anything interesting.

"It fits fine the way it is." Gray's voice drifts from behind the curtain of the dressing room.

"I don't tell you how to fix up the players, and you won't tell me when your suit fits." Trevor's stern voice leaves no room for argument.

"He told you, eh?" I call.

Trevor pokes his head out, brown hair a mess from running his hands through it. "Don't worry, you're next. Since you're here, you can try your suit on."

That sobers me. I'm not big on being the center of attention, which is ironic given my career and status on the team. Trevor ducks back into the dressing room.

"No, you're not showing him. He can see you when you walk the red carpet."

"We live together. Is this some sort of surprise?" Gray sounds confused. "And I don't walk the carpet."

"You guys have loose lips and can't be trusted to keep your designs under wraps until the night of. This event is the best free publicity for a soon-to-be-famous designer—me. You're not going to rob me of that by slinking in unnoticed. Not when you look this good. That would be a crime."

Now I really want to see Gray in his suit. He's got an impressive body but rarely dresses up. I adjust myself, thinking of how his ass will look in body-hugging pants. Trevor is a master at fitting suits to make us look fantastic.

I hope to get a glimpse of Gray's suit, but Trevor whisks it away in a black bag. Then it's my turn.

The dressing room is claustrophobic. It's not built for someone my size and another person. The two walls are brick, and one's a mirror opposite a small bench. One of us could easily bring the curtain down in a misstep.

"How do you not murder people with those pins?" I hold my arms up as instructed.

"There's a first time for everything." Trevor raises an eyebrow at me in the mirror as a clear warning not to mess with his process. "You look good enough to eat."

Gray has a coughing fit behind the curtain, and my blush heats my entire body. That's something we haven't done yet, but I'm eager for it. Gray wants to take his time, and we're short on that in the midst of hockey season, even though we've been sleeping in my bed every night possible.

He's inspired me to write a novel of romantic movie quotes on sticky notes for him. So far, he's gotten all the movie references, but I have some old-school ones from *Pride and Prejudice*. The internet is my helpful friend in romancing him.

"This will complete the look." Trevor meticulously arranges a magenta pocket square in my suit coat pocket and has a matching tie. The color is so bold, and that's not how I roll. "The color coordinates with your suit and enhances the blue in your eyes," he assures me.

"If you say so." I won't argue since the suit fits better than anything I've ever worn, and he deserves the acclaim that will come from the team wearing his clothes.

"You're all set. I'm setting the twins loose on the world." Trevor slides the jacket off my shoulders.

"It's not a twinsie day," Gray says from a few feet away. We are wearing the same socks and shoes and sweats but have on different shirts and coats.

"Did you guys do a wardrobe plan to avoid the shit talk? Newsflash: they'll find something else to bust your balls over." Trevor has his back to me as I take my pants off.

We never planned to dress the same, and now we don't. A flutter of unease runs through me, but I dismiss it. We're getting back in sync and back to wearing the same clothes. I'd prefer to see him only wear my clothes, but I don't know how to tell him that without spooking him.

Gray drives us to the practice facility forty minutes away.

"Is everything okay?" he asks.

At the risk of sounding like an insecure asshole, I forge ahead. "Do you think it's strange that we stopped dressing alike? We couldn't stop showing up in the same clothes, and it doesn't happen anymore."

I expect him to laugh or tease me because that's who we are. Instead, he holds my hand and laces our fingers. "We're fine. It is kinda crazy, but things change. We didn't dress the same in the CHL; it sort of evolved. We could consult Benz and his opinion on universal energy, but that would give us away." He brings our joined hands to his mouth to kiss my knuckles.

He always knows what to say to validate my frame of mind and put everything in perspective. "The changes have been stupendous." I clench his hand. "We have to ensure we stay us. You're too important to me."

Gray swallows hard, and my eyes track the rise and fall of his Adam's apple. "I can't imagine my life without you." His voice sounds gravelly, choking with emotion.

"You're my sunshine," I say simply. "My world would be bleak without my Grayson."

His eyes cut to mine, and he leans over the console so our shoulders touch. His body heat is comforting, and we don't need any more words to express our affection.

The ramifications of what we're doing hit me. I've loved him as my best friend, and now I'm falling *in love* with him.

We're rarely apart, and if we don't work out as a couple, our friendship will suffer. It doesn't matter that we have decades of history—heartbreak changes everything.

With every fiber of my being, I know I could never purposely hurt Gray. It's the unintentional that scares me to death. Surviving without him doesn't seem possible.

He makes it a habit of asking me if I'm sure. And I'm sure of him but not sure of myself. I lost the thread of what is at stake if I can't be someone he loves.

I'll do everything in my power to be worthy of him. Much better than a broken best friend who can't admit he's bi.

Once we're in the practice facility, I seek out the one person who will give me solid advice and won't worry about offending me. Patrik Liska.

My pulse races as I figure out how to approach him, but he does it for me in the equipment room.

"Trevor says you and Grayson are all set for the gala. Thank you for vearing his designs." His Czech accent is strongest in words starting with a *W*.

"No need for thanks. He makes us look good." I take a deep breath. "Can I get your advice?"

Liska sets aside his stick, which he was taping up, and gives me his full attention without saying a word.

I rub my neck. "I feel like a fraud because I recently realized I'm not straight, and I haven't told the team."

Grayson's words echo in my mind, but he's biased and puts me first. Liska won't do that.

Liska's brown eyes bore into me. "You are not a fraud for taking care of yourself and protecting your sexuality. I vould not have come out if I didn't fall in love with Trevor."

"I shouldn't have to protect myself." That's cowardly.

"Understanding yourself and how that impacts your life takes time. And it's private. You should protect that until you're ready. Your life vill be picked apart, and your family vill be in the spotlight. All your friends and teammates vill be questioned." He claps my shoulder. "I'm not saying it's not vorth it to live your life authentically, but for your peace of mind, you must decide how to do it."

"I'm not letting everyone down?" I clarify.

"You are always here for us, and ve know you have our backs even vhen we do stupid shit. Ve have your back, and you cannot let us down." Liska smacks my ass. "Velcome to the club, brother."

"Do we have a secret handshake?" I say lamely.

"Once you've had your first scandal, you learn the handshake." He exits the room with no indication he's kidding.

That's a lot to process. My parents' reaction never registered in this equation. It's not that they don't love me, it's that they won't want to be associated with any sort of scandal. My sexuality being broadcast in the press, even if the coverage is positive, would be a scandal in their eyes. Deep down, I fear they'll choose their church's ideals over me.

My mind makes a connection I'm not sure how to handle. My parents taught me that sex is dirty and shameful. No wonder I never enjoyed it until Gray.

I don't understand why people can't love who they love and everyone else minds their own damn business.

CHAPTER 22

GRAYSON

Camera lights flash outside our sleek Lincoln Town Car. "How do you do this?" I swallow hard, regretting my agreement to walk the red carpet at the Enforcers Gala. Even though Austin has a face the camera loves, he doesn't like the attention.

"If it were up to me, I'd sneak in like you." He rests a sure hand on my thigh. "But I wouldn't expect the guys to do something I won't. I'll make it up to you when we get home." His last words are breathy, and his hand slides along my leg.

"Are you sure you'll want company after this?" In the past, after public events, Austin retreated to his room to recover in solitude.

Austin's head rears back. "Company? We are way past that." His smile falls, and he stiffens. "Unless you have other plans."

I bump his shoulder. "What plans could I possibly have? You need your alone time, and I respect that."

His shoulders drop in relief. "You got a package today, so *we* have plans. This will be over before you blink. I've got you."

I don't have time to answer before Finn opens the passenger-side door and pokes his head in. "My handsome twinsies. You'll exit the car from both sides and take your place behind King. Once he clears the step and repeat, it's your turn."

"Step and repeat?" I ask.

My stomach somersaults as I watch Leo, Benz, and Griff in front of the frantic press. Everyone's trying to be the first to report on any relationship between Leo and Caleb. It's none of their damn business.

"Signage for the event. Tootles." Finn shuts the door, silencing the yells from the crowd.

Our car moves up, and since Austin is on the curbside, I have a limited view.

"How mad will Trevor be if I skip the press?" My knuckles turn white as I grip the door handle.

"He won't be mad at all." I breathe a sigh of relief before he continues. "He'll drag your ass right to them with a smile and tell them all about your suit. Then"—he gives me a knowing glance—"he'll complain to Liska."

No one wants to be on Liska's bad side, and insulting Trevor is a capital offense. This idea sounded good in theory, but now that I'm here, it's so ridiculous.

No one cares about me. I'm the trainer, and they'll probably ask me to get out of the picture of Austin. And that's fine. I'm not interested in being in the spotlight.

Austin grabs my hand, and his blue eyes burn with intensity. "All jokes aside. If you don't want to do this. Don't. I'll make an excuse. You can go home in the car right now."

He's serious, and it's my turn to step out of my comfort zone for him. "I'm good."

He pumps my hand twice and lets go. "Smile. Here we go." He pastes on his press face and opens the car door.

I inhale the comfort of his lingering scent and do my best to smile, joining Austin as we make our way to the short line.

Damn, I can't take my eyes off King's suit as he exits the carpet area. No wonder Trevor thought I was boring. King has on a green jacket with purple geometric patterns. Two colors I would not pair, but they work great on him. From shoulder to elbow, there's stitching that looks like vertical pleats until there's a trio of horizontal ones at the elbow. All the stitching discreetly flatters his build. His braids have a new pattern to match his suit with no beads, and he has a rare, genuine smile.

The thought sears my brain like a lightning strike. King belongs on the carpet because he's part of the team. He's a player and a huge part of their success.

I don't belong.

I'm not part of the team.

I'm Austin's roommate and plus one.

This is a terrible idea.

Austin strides up to the press, and Finn pushes me after him.

Austin is answering a question about the last game when I reach his side.

A woman from the crowd, not affiliated with the approved media organizations, yells to Austin. "Who's your date? I'll step in if you need me."

A sports reporter in a long skirt turns to her and fires back. "That's the team's trainer, Grayson Ward. Show some respect."

"Not a date?" the woman asks.

"Actually, my roommate is my date every year, but he avoids all of you," Austin says playfully and shifts so our shoulders touch. He's going to start rumors about us if he's not careful.

"Anything to announce?" someone asks.

I'm frozen with fear. Not only do I have impostor syndrome, we didn't think about people assuming we're a couple. Some reporters know I'm bi, and I'd rather Austin not have to deal with questions he's not ready for.

I take a small step back, but as if he anticipated my action, Austin's foot slides behind mine and I risk tripping if I back up further.

"A new announcement?" He grins and casually hooks his thumb in his pocket in an unusually cheeky move.

The crowd leans forward and hollers encouragement.

"I'm wearing a Trevor Fox original design."

The air whooshes out of my lungs, and my head's dizzy from holding my breath.

Crisis averted.

"Why are you matching?"

Our suits aren't even the same color, so we turn to each other and notice the color of my tie and pocket square matches his shirt.

My mouth hangs open, and even media-savvy Austin is silent.

I turn to Finn to beg for help, but Trevor breezes up in a long luxurious coat like he's ready for a runway show.

"It's the designer's choice." He straightens my lapel and pats my chest. "I finally talked this shy, handsome man into one of my suits. And decided the roommates need to match. It's a running joke on the team. Don't scare him away"—Trevor waves a finger like they're naughty children—"or we'll shut down the team interviews." His voice is light and teasing with a bite behind it as if warning them not to cross him.

I'm mute during the rest of the questions and rush into the hotel ballroom, straight to the bar. Servers are circulating with glasses of champagne, but I need something stronger.

Austin's entrance creates a buzz, and he can't follow me, which is a blessing because I need a minute.

There is no reason for me to be here.

I didn't think this through. Yes, most people know we're childhood friends, but the stakes for both of us will change if they find out we're more. It's the thing I've been ignoring, risking my job.

I've been dreaming of a life with Austin, my Tinny, not Ace Lapointe, the hockey player.

Reality crashes in, and the noise in my head is deafening.

I'm not Trevor or Leo. I can't be the partner of a hockey player.

The team never puts me in the press room unless it's critical. We all know I suck at it. Who am I to think I could handle going to events with Austin as his actual date.

I'd be a PR disaster. Finn would need to hire more staff, or I'd be fired. The choice for the team is easy—starting right winger or trainer. He wins every time, as he should.

The bartender brings me a shot, and I toss it back before he leaves and order another. My palate can't discern between top shelf and well. I'm a basic bitch.

This will only work if we don't tell people. I never imagined myself being the type of guy to hide in the closet, but I won't embarrass Austin. It's the only way to protect him.

Thankfully, he's not ready to come out.

Maybe he'll wait, and I'll have my life with Tinny away from Ace and hockey fame.

The second shot goes down smoother than the first, and my chest loosens. I order a couple of beers for us but remain in the bar area. Austin will find me when he's ready. He always does.

"Are you dancing with us tonight?" Lucky hip-checks me and sets his drink on my high-top table. He's wearing a winter floral pattern suit, and Drake's matches one of the more muted colors.

"I'm not much of a dancer." I sip my beer, wondering why they're wasting their time talking to me.

Drake doesn't need to roll his eyes to express his disapproval.

"Hello, have you seen your roommate dance? Skill isn't required, but you've got it *and* rhythm. Not as much as I do." Lucky shimmies; his suit accentuates the movements. "I'm a bird of paradise with grace and body contortions. You're a Japanese snow monkey, spinning and swaying for social bonding. Our captain...he's more like a seal, clapping off beat."

"Harsh." Austin lifts his knee to the back of Lucky's so it bends. He's rough enough to get his point across but isn't likely to do any damage. I hand him his beer. "Don't be a keener."

"Oh, cap, I didn't see you there," Lucky says, but no one believes him.

"A what?" Drake rumbles unsure if he should be insulted for Lucky.

"In Canada, a keener is someone who tries too hard like a brown-noser," I interject.

"Believe me, I don't need to try, *but* I'm tryin' to get your boy to show us his moves later. It's not fair that he's working during our pregame dance parties."

"G's his own man. He'll dance if he wants to." Austin defends me, but his nudge is tentative as if he's unsure of my response. He's been more protective of me since I left the CHL. When I first moved to New York to live with him and complete my grad work, he was a guard dog, ensuring no one slighted me.

My reaction should be the last thing he's worried about.

I refuse to be the one who ruins his reputation.

CHAPTER 23

AUSTIN

As the streetlights streak by, I wonder if I've done something wrong. Gray's been off all night, and I haven't been able to get him alone.

We share a ride with Drake and Lucky, delaying my ability to get answers. The night was an enormous success since we raised over a million dollars for our charities: The Q Solutions, NYC Food Pantry, and youth hockey leagues.

I had big plans for tonight since practice isn't until the afternoon and we don't have any major injuries that require Gray to go in early. But now I wonder if he's having second thoughts.

Dating a pro hockey player isn't very glamorous, and he knows that. It's more headache than fun.

I rub my eye sockets with my palms. Not having Gray in my life isn't an option, but it's so much more complicated than two people falling in—

I cut off my thought. I'm getting ahead of myself. Of course I love him, but I can't have fallen all the way this fast. I'm so far gone I can't think straight, or not-straight in this case. Being unable to read him is making me crazy. It's too soon to be *in love* in love. Right?

I've hit a new low in a conversation with myself.

"Trevor gave you the toned-down version of matching roommates," Drake says stoically, not a question but a statement out of the blue.

The car pulls up to our building.

"We didn't even realize until someone pointed it out."

The driver releases the automatic locks.

"All the gossip sites will ship you tomorrow so have fun tonight," Drake deadpans, and Lucky cackles like a hyena.

"Sugar, you are not subtle." Lucky falls into Drake's lap, laughing.

Gray's already out of the car, and I hurry after him. "Are you okay?" I ask.

The elevator doors shut, and he turns to me. "Do they know about us?" His voice sounds odd.

"I didn't say anything." All I want to do is reach out and hug him, but he's closed off. The words to ask if it would be so bad die on my tongue.

"If Lucky said something, I'd assume he's busting our balls, but Drake..." He trails off and won't make eye contact.

"What's wrong?" My heart is in my throat, waiting for his answer.

"Nothing."

"Nothing?" The word rattles around my brain with sharp edges slicing through my confidence.

We enter the apartment in silence, and I hate this divide between us. He shrugs out of his jacket and tosses it over to the couch. Gray paces and each step increases my anxiety. I'm the pacer. He's the calm one.

"I'm weighing you down. Tinny, I can't be the person to hurt you or your career." He spins around with glassy eyes.

"Don't say that." I gather him in my arms, holding him like I can prevent him from leaving me. "I need you." My voice comes out thick with emotion. I spent years depriving myself of physical contact because it was a void I couldn't fill. Grayson fills that void, and I can't go back to the way things were.

"You don't need me," he scoffs, and his breath washes over the crook of my neck.

Arguing would be useless, so I hug him until his body relaxes into mine.

"Did someone say something to you?" I untuck his shirt to touch the bare skin on his back. He seemed fine before we left, and nervous when we got there, but nothing extreme enough to change our relationship.

"No. The timing isn't right for us."

"That's bullshit." I step back and grip his shoulders so I can see his face. "Tell me the truth."

He won't get away with lying to my face. Gray's been adamant I confront my issues, so he needs to tell me what's really going on.

Gray sits on the couch with his head in his hands and explains all the ways he isn't the right partner for me and compares himself to the team's significant others.

"Could you picture me in a relationship with Trevor? Or Leo? Or any of the wives like Jayce's Madyson?" Amusement seeps into my voice. "I'd need my alone time, and Trevor would follow me around in fix-it mode. I'd never be able to look Griff in the eye if I slept with his dad. And Madyson makes everyone sing karaoke. I wouldn't survive any of them. I don't want you to be like them, G. You're my Sunshine and know me better than I know myself."

He drops his hands into his lap, but his eyes are haunted. "What about your family?"

It's a gut punch and further proof of how well he knows me. I sink down next to him, and he curls into me.

"I won't let my family come between us. They aren't a big part of my life." My stomach twists as I say it.

Gray laces our fingers together.

"Their disapproval will eat away at you." His quiet voice cuts to the heart of the issue.

They think I should've pursued a more noble career and haven't seen me play in years.

"If it's a choice between you and them, I choose you," I say, and he lifts his head in surprise. "You support me with no strings or conditions. I can't keep chasing their approval. There's a huge chance I'll never get it and lose you. That isn't acceptable."

His brown eyes take me in. "So where does that leave us?"

"Exactly here. Right now. If you're okay with figuring it out as we go. I only know I need you in my life." The truth of my words rings in the air.

"I said I wouldn't pressure you, and I hope you don't think I am. Being on the carpet tonight made me think ahead. And face it, you could do better."

"You are the best person for me. This is my fault." I get up and start pacing. His words are so far from the truth. "All I wanted to do was kiss you, so I stayed away. I wasn't ignoring you."

"It's a good thing you did. What will you do if there are rumors about us tomorrow?"

"I don't care if a few fame mongers think we're together. We'll ignore them, like we always do. They didn't know the truth then, and they don't know it now."

Gray steps into my path. "Promise to tell me if I'm holding you back. If being with me hurts you personally or professionally. I can't"—he cups my face—"bear to hurt you or for you to stay with me out of obligation." He shushes me with a peck on the lips when I try to argue. "You are the most loyal man who takes his responsibilities seriously. Don't make me an obligation instead of a partner."

"Never." I smash our mouths together, pouring all of my love and desire for him into our kiss. Conveying with my lips and tongue that I can't function without him. He's the one person in the world who makes my life easier.

His tense muscles loosen under my touch, and he kisses me back with enthusiasm.

"Did you check your pockets tonight?" I ask, hoping he hasn't.

Gray reaches into his suit pockets, digs out a large, lined sticky note, and reads it. "It was a million tiny little things that, when you added them all up, meant we were supposed to be together." He holds the note to his heart.

"Will you let me decide who I want in my life, as my boyfriend and partner?" I ask, and he slumps against me. "Not only do you accept me for who I am, you bring out the best in me. You challenge me to be better." I kiss the tip of his nose. "Come to bed and tell me all the things you like about me." I wrap my arm around him.

"Smartass," Gray mutters.

But he lets me lead him past his door and into my room to sit on my bed. Kneeling between his legs, I slowly unbutton his shirt, giving him time to stop me if he would rather sleep.

"Was that your way of making us official? Telling me you want me to be your boyfriend, enticing me with a sappy movie quote, and luring me to bed with sex?" His knees squeeze my sides. "Thank you." His bottomless eyes convey his sincerity.

"Depends on if it worked." I sit back on my heels. "Boyfriend sounds so juvenile for the way I feel about you, but it works for me. Does it work for you?" My voice gets high and reveals my trepidation. I won't survive if he doesn't agree.

"It really, really works for me." Gray plants a kiss on my forehead, and his mouth turns up on one side. "Are you trying to torture me? If this weren't an expensive shirt, I'd rip all the buttons off." He rests his palms on my chest.

"Yes, until you whisper mushy things in my ear," I tease. Miraculously, I get his shirt off in seconds and start in on his belt.

The gleam in his eyes is my only hint before he ruffles my hair and leapfrogs over me.

I'm too stunned to stop him but follow him back into the kitchen.

Gray picks up the package from the kitchen island and tosses it in the air.

"Is this what I think it is?" His smile lights up the dim kitchen.

"You tell me. It's unmistakably still sealed." I gesture to the intact box. I won't stop him if he's changing the subject by suggesting we play. We can talk later.

"Let's crack this bad boy open." Gray grabs a knife and slices the tape. He digs through the packing material and pulls out a black plastic bag. His eyes meet mine before he tears it open, and the flogger falls out.

Floggers are different than I imagined them to be. Some fit my mental picture of a whip as long as a riding crop, but we opted for something smaller. My hand has a mind of its own as it reaches for the supple leather strands, tracing up toward the silver-studded neck and butt.

Gray offers it to me, but I don't trust myself yet. "It's soft."

My breath hitches when his fist pushes through the strap and closes around its neck. We did our research and watched several videos. The strands are called falls, tresses, or tails that connect at the neck and are held by the shaft. Totally appropriate naming; someone knew what they were doing.

"You still want me to use it on you?" he asks.

His molten gaze melts me.

Instead of answering, I strip off my jacket and curse the tiny buttons and cufflinks on my shirt. "It's like Trevor is cock-blocking us from home."

Gray's chuckle fills the kitchen and warms my insides. He unfastens my cuffs with one hand and peels my shirt off, leaving me in an undershirt and tented dress pants.

"Hands on the counter." He lets the flogger dangle from his wrist as he removes my T-shirt and turns me to press on my back so I'm leaning forward.

Instinctively, I widen my legs, but I have to adjust my stance for him to get my pants off. A shiver racks my body, and a high-pitched giggle escapes me. I don't giggle.

He kisses my neck and huffs a laugh against my skin. "We can try to be all badass and sexy, but we'll always be just us."

My head drops with his understanding, and I push my ass back. "I guess we're not the romance book hero types, huh?"

"You are in my book." He taps my leg so he can take my sock off. "If anyone saw you like this, they would give a nut or breast to be with you. You're better than a fictional romance hero, you're a hockey god."

My skin flushes red and breaks out in goosebumps at the same time—an impossible feat.

"It's really not fair how good-looking you are." He kisses the knobs down my spine and kneels behind me. "But this"—he rids me of my underwear—"this is a masterpiece. Your ass would shame all those famous sculptures in Europe." He plants a wet kiss on each cheek, and I push back farther.

"Someone is eager." His fingers tickle the hair between my legs, and my cock leaks. I'm hyperaware of his presence, and with each shift, I'm more impatient for the first strike.

"Gray," I whine, tipping my head backward until my spine arches.

"Shhh. I'll give you what you need." He nips my ear and drags the flogger over my arm, across my shoulders, down the other arm, and then over my chest. The falls drape against my cock with no pressure, but the mere thought of it creates a string of precum inches long.

It's hard to decide, as if I have a choice, where will be the most pleasurable to receive hits. If, a month ago, someone had told me I'd want Gray to flog my cock, I'd have assumed they had a break from reality. But there's no denying the ache in my balls and the anticipation building so high I might crack before he hits me.

"You're tense." His warm chest blankets my back. "It's more likely to hurt if you're tight."

"I know." Blowing out a breath, I concentrate on loosening my muscles.

"Lucky for you, I have a solution." His tongue trails over my back, and my dick screams for attention. Gray's knees plunk on the wood floor, and he gently pries my ass cheeks open. "Breathe," he instructs, and I let out another slow breath.

His wet finger traces my rim, and although my cock is pissed off, I lean into his touch, begging for more.

He inhales deeply. "If I could wear your scent as cologne, I would." There's no warning before the tip of his tongue breaches me, and my shout turns into a moan.

He alternates between lapping at my rim and tongue-fucking me. There are nerves I didn't know existed back there, and he's kissing them to life. His tongue is warm and wet and a deadly weapon of pleasure, making my knees go weak. I'm nervous I'll embarrass myself and come before the main event. Although Gray would probably be proud of himself.

When I can't take any more and I'm on the verge of coming, the flogger whooshes and stings the side of my butt cheek. It's enough to pull me back from the brink.

"Color?" he rasps.

"Green." My body's confused between pain and rapture.

Gray removes his face from my ass, and I whimper at the loss. For the next few minutes, the only sounds in our apartment are our heavy breathing, the zing of the flogger through the air, and the snap of it hitting my skin.

Each strike is in a different place, with a different intensity, and has staggered timing to keep me off-balance and prevent me from tensing up. Soon I'm sinking into a jagged rhythm, trusting him to care for me.

I'm jelly, unable to stand without him.

CHAPTER 24

GRAYSON

The taste of him on my tongue is driving me mad. One day we'll have enough time for me to eat his ass until he comes, and I'll swallow that down too. I'm feral for him, wanting to rut and stake my claim.

His skin is pink from the flogger, and his sexy groans and moans are music to my ears. As I pause to check in, he snaps, "Green," and bares his teeth for me to continue. Fuck.

I curse myself for not planning ahead for this. Austin's blissed out, slumping over the counter, and I don't want to stop. But I'm afraid he'll collapse.

He grunts in protest when I pull him up and duck under his arm to lead him to the couch. His eyes are barely open, and he's barely aware of what's going on. It's awkward to lay him down, so I drape him over the back of the couch with his knees on the cushions.

Once I'm out from under his arm, he clutches my wrist.

"More," he pleads, and I tease him with light brushes of the flogger while I take my clothes off.

My cock is rock hard, and I'm craving skin-to-skin contact, but this is about him, giving him what he needs. My leaking dick finds the back of his thigh and he groans.

He's not showing any signs of being overwhelmed, and it's my job to keep him in a positive headspace.

"You're gorgeous with your head hanging down and ass pushed back, pleading for more attention."

He flushes in response to my words.

"I want everything," he whispers.

My heart skids as if I've unexpectedly hit the ice. He should have whatever he desires and I'll spend all my time giving it to him

"I'll give you what you deserve." His whimpering response takes me higher than I've ever been. "Your broad back is the perfect canvas for me. I'll take pictures so you can see how good you are for me." Never in a million years would I take photos and risk them getting stolen, but the thought inflames us both.

"Tinny, you love the soft strokes with a bite at the end." I listen for his sounds to guide me. "Although your back provides the biggest surface, you love it on your ass and balls."

His sac hangs full and heavy between his wide legs. I have no doubt he'll come as soon as the strikes stop. Austin's words become blabbering pleas to never stop and then for me to let him come.

I hold him on a razor's edge until I'm ready to blow.

"You love being at my mercy, but I swear, you're going to love having me under your control more." I'm fighting to keep my orgasm at bay, and his body goes rigid.

"Not yet, my sweet Tinny." I pull his languid body until he's on his back and position myself on the outside of his knees. "Come for me," I murmur, and take his head in my mouth.

He detonates immediately as if all the cum in his body tries to exit at once. He would drown me if I had him deeper in my throat. I swallow and swallow and swallow some more.

One of my hands cups his balls while the other finds his hand, and I thread our fingers together. His release fills me, drowning my insecurities and washing them away.

I deluded myself into thinking I could walk away undamaged. I wouldn't survive without him. Thankfully, he's too stubborn to let me go.

I hold him in my mouth until his last tremor passes and I've milked him dry. He's in no condition to reciprocate, and I want to come all over his spent cock.

Austin's eyes remain closed as I jack myself over him, but he bats my hand away. He grips me solidly, a man used to handling a stick in all sorts of positions and conditions.

I'm ready to tease him, but he barks, "Come!"

My vision goes white, and my brain is pure static as ecstasy rolls through every cell in my body, and I obey him.

My legs can't bear my weight, and I pitch forward onto his chest, and he circles his arms around me. I listen to his erratic heartbeat as we come back to earth. I'm content to burrow into him and never leave this spot.

"You have to promise me something," Austin says, clinging to me.

"Anything," I vow.

His adrenaline is crashing, and I'll be what he needs.

"You can't ever leave me because you think it will be better for me. Don't ever take my choice away." His blue eyes blaze with clarity.

"We're in this together. I swear I won't make a decision about us without you." I kiss him.

He knew exactly what to say to ensure I couldn't break us or our trust. It's a leap of faith for him, and I won't disrespect him by thinking I know better.

"Let me get you some water and something for your skin." I stand, but he won't let go of me. Unshed tears sting my eyes with a hope I haven't allowed myself.

I know Austin would never purposely hurt me. He has an unnatural sense of obligation to everyone, and that supersedes what he wants. He always puts others before himself.

I worry about Austin's decision when that time comes.

It's slightly ironic that he asked me never to leave him. The only way I see this ending is by his choice.

"I can get it myself."

"It's your night to be worshipped like a king, and my penance for being a dumbass and making you worry tonight." The bed is so far away, so we burrow into the couch.

"You being here is enough for me. No penance needed."

He's crucial for me, and I'd rather suffer in hell than hurt him.

But it's hard to convince myself that this is real. I'm living in a fantasy world and can't help but wonder when it's all going to come crashing down.

Not tonight.

I shake off my fear, supervise his fluid intake, and apply arnica gel to his ass. He easily pulls me down, and I grab a blanket off the back of the couch before promptly falling asleep with my head on his chest.

Too soon, I wake up with a crick in my neck and my arm asleep under Austin and decide it's time to cuddle in bed. When I lift my head to rouse him, his huge blue eyes are staring at me.

"Not creepy at all." I yawn and stretch, causing me to lose my balance and tumble onto the floor.

"At least I'm coordinated." Austin squats next to me and picks me up.

"If you hurt yourself, the team will murder me," I complain, but I can't keep the smile off my face.

"They'll understand." He grins and it wakes up the rest of my body.

"Like hell." I'm unceremoniously dumped on his bed.

"No back problems tonight."

"Is it still night?" I ask, propping myself up on my elbows so I get a better view of his ass as he enters the bathroom.

Austin returns with a wet washcloth and cleans us both up.

"I should've done that before we fell asleep," I grumble as he tosses the towel aside.

"Not a chance. I wanted you all over me so you'd live in my skin." His eyes bulge as if he didn't mean to say that out loud. "Now that's creepy." He scrubs a hand over his face.

"It works out well because I happen to be highly attracted to creepy."

"Liar." He thumps my chest and knocks me flat on the bed. "Shut up and be the little spoon." Austin curls himself around me when I roll on my side. "Let's do brunch in the morning. Late morning."

"After you have me for breakfast." I gnaw his forearm.

"Obviously."

***

The universe cooperates, and I wake up to Austin sucking me off after one of the best nights of sleep in my life.

The man grins smugly around my dick like he's won a prize. Newsflash, I'm the winner, especially when he slurps both my balls in his mouth.

"This must be your hidden talent." I stare down my body, at his powerful form, and am in awe that I'm so lucky. Austin Lapointe loves getting me off.

He's chosen me for some ridiculous reason. Part of me wants to shout it from the rooftop because I don't think I can contain my happiness. I'm goddamn giddy.

I'm not an excitable person.

He works me over like a pro, and I shoot down his throat like an amateur, having used up all my restraint last night.

"Breakfast of champions." He licks his lips and joins me on my pillow. I swear he stares into my soul before speaking. "Spend the day with me. Just us."

"Every second together...alone...until afternoon skate," I promise.

"Damn job."

"Yup, a serious downer. You get paid a boatload of money to play the sport you love and hang out with your best friends." I feign irritation. "So tedious."

But his phone buzzes with the team chat, and I shove aside the otherness that barges in unwanted. It's his literal job. "Anything important."

"Nah, same old bullshit." He pins me under him and gathers my wrists above my head.

"What's your plan for me?" I suck his biceps, the only thing I can reach.

"I have some ideas," he says coyly.

"I'm yours to command." My muscles go limp, but my cock is ready to play again.

CHAPTER 25

AUSTIN

My head is in the clouds instead of in the Dallas locker room, and the team notices. Every night, more of Gray's belongings find their way into my room, and I couldn't be happier. I encouraged him by clearing out space in my closet and dresser for his things. Our toiletries are mixed together in my bathroom. It's phenomenal.

But I have to keep my mind off my boyfriend. I have a game to play, and the crowd boos us during pre-skate. The Dallas arena is large, and the crowd is heavily involved with chants and songs. I can't fault the fans. Our points are high enough that even if we lose most of our games, we'll still make the playoffs, but we need every advantage we can get.

Our dance party ritual is winding down, and King has made it his mission to keep me on beat with the music. Gray pretended to get mad, but he had the smile that stretches his lips and scar, a clear sign of his happiness.

We start the game off with a miscommunication, and Dallas scores in the first minute. Their goal song annoys the hell out of me.

"Let's not hear that again." I slap players' pads and encourage everyone on the bench.

King and Griff connect to put us on the board, and that ramps the crowd up even more, rooting for their team.

I vault over the wall with Drake and Lucky, ready for battle. The crowd boos and hisses every time we have possession of the puck. This game is being played in the middle of the ice more than against the boards.

They are chirping and itching to fight. Drake keeps his cool, and our shift ends without a brawl but also no goal. Our defense breaks down again, and I hope we can fix our problems before the playoffs. Kenney stands out as fast and skilled, but he's young, and we need a seasoned player to lead by example. We probably have two of the best goalies in the league, but we can't expect them to save shot after shot.

The first period flies by, and we've kept out of the sin bin, so I'm calling that a win. On my next shift, I'm tripped and eat the ice, slow to get up. It knocked the wind out of me, but the game doesn't stop, I decide not to ask for a sub.

By the time my line exits the ice, Grayson's fury radiates off him as he assesses me.

"Got the wind knocked out of me. All good." I catch his eye, but he frowns. "It's true."

Gray nods and moves down the bench to check in with Lucky and Drake.

During the next intermission, he drags me into the treatment room to inspect my ribs, pressing his fingers in and listening to my breathing.

"See. I'm fine." I pull everything back into place.

"I knew when you went down, it was a bad hit." He bites the scar on his lip.

"Thank you for looking out for me, but don't go soft on me," I joke and punch him in the arm.

Liska looms in the doorway, needing a quick treatment, so I join the team in the locker room. I'm torn between loving Gray's attention and being nervous that he's overreacting. It's not his usual thing, and I didn't see myself fall. Sometimes falls look worse than they are, and sometimes a small trip results in a tear needing surgery. I put his concerns behind me and focus on winning the game.

They're ahead by one with only three minutes left, and Lucky fires me a pass in front of the goal while the tender is turned toward Drake. It's an easy shot to slip in, but it hits the pipe and bounces back. A Dallas player gets his stick on it, and I race down the ice to catch him.

It isn't our night. Dallas penetrates our defenses with precision and always finds our weakest link. We couldn't keep up the retaliation scores and lose by one.

We're still ahead in points, and it's not a huge detriment to our goal of winning The Cup, but we're better than how we played tonight.

Gray slings his arm around me in a buddy hug after the game. His combination of clean cotton and medicinal smell eases my tension. His presence has always calmed me. The worst games were the losses before he lived with me. I had a hard time decompressing. In hindsight, I should've realized he's more than a friend. I foolishly wasted so much time we could've been together.

If I could get away with it, I'd skip the team dinner. It's one of those nights I'd prefer solitude with Gray. My body's sore, and I played a shit game. And as if he reads my mind, he tells the team I need recovery time to play in LA and can't attend the team dinner.

I'm so grateful, I zone out and let Gray call us a ride share back to the hotel. Having my best friend here is a luxury I don't take for granted.

When Gray holds out his hand palm up, I'm not sure what he wants until I notice we're standing outside of my room. I fish out the keycard and slide it into his hand. He grins, knowing I could easily open the door, but I'm letting him take charge.

The door closes behind us. "You're only one man on the team. There were lots of missed shots. In fact, the team missed thirty-two shots, which is an all-time high for this season." He cups my face so I have to look him in the eyes. "The loss was not your fault, and even if you had made that shot, it was not a guaranteed win." He walks me backward to the bed and nudges me to sit.

"Get out of my head." I wrestle him onto the bed next to me.

"You like me here." He knocks on my head. "What do you need?" Gray searches my eyes.

"I need my Sunshine," I say, and although it's the truth, I'm unsure how to get back in a positive headspace.

"I'm here. You up for a little play? I have an idea."

I'm suddenly invigorated. Without a word, Gray undresses me and examines my torso and extremities to double-check I'm fine for whatever he has planned. I watch him undress and rifle through my duffel. I'm shocked when he comes to bed with the flogger.

"I snuck it in your bag," he answers my unasked question. "You are in no condition to receive blows, but it's the perfect way to get you out of your head and make me come my brains out. You in?"

I swallow my nerves and take his mouth. He tastes of peppermint and home. "So in."

"If you haven't noticed, it turns me on when you're unrestrained, unleashed, and out of your head. How do you want me?" He leans back to search my eyes and then gives me an encouraging kiss on my forehead.

"Hands and knees. But I'm starting slow." My words are more for me than him. Gray somehow takes away my fear before I know it's there. The man in pure perfection. He presents his glorious ass to me, and I drag the flogger over his curves. He shudders and pushes his ass back. My hand follows the flogger.

"Do you remember how much you loved the sting? Will you let me experience it too?" He gasps as he speaks.

His questions change my mindset. I'm not doing this for my pleasure; I'm doing it for him. The bonus is I'll love it too. The sound of the first crack scares me until Gray moans so loud, I'm glad the team is out and can't hear us.

After a few more strikes, I ask his color.

"Fucking green, green, green."

He sets me free to unleash brutal slaps to his ass and back. We fall into a rhythm, and my cock leaks all over him. Gray shoves his face into a pillow to muffle his sounds, but I'm tempted to tear it away to hear them.

His sounds create an image of me that's ten feet tall and invincible. Gray has given himself to me, and the power is going to my head. I could do anything to him, and he'd thank me. I'm in complete control.

I don't know how Gray held on for so long when he did this to me. It takes extreme concentration not to blow my load all over him and rub it into his skin as if I'm claiming him.

The swishes and corresponding thuds on him become a symphony I could listen to all day, every day.

I drag the tails over his balls, giving them a soft strike.

"Red," he moans, and I fling the flogger across the room and turn him over.

"What do you need? Are you hurt? Did I hit you too hard?" I ask frantically, searching his eyes.

"You are exactly what I need." He cups my face and hauls me down on top of him to kiss me wildly.

"But—"

He cuts me off. "I was on the verge of coming, and I am not ready for this to end, *and* I need to prove to you that you'll always stop if I need it."

"You scared me," I growl.

"Sorry. Take a breath." He inhales and expects me to do the same, then exhales. "Tell me two things: were you ready to stop, and did any part of you hesitate when I said the safe word?"

The questions take me off guard, but I answer honestly. "No and no." I'd been totally preoccupied with getting him off, but when he spoke, I stopped and ditched the flogger. "You think you're so smart." I snake my arm between us so I can gather both our dicks in my hand. "Just because you're always right. Now I'm in charge of when you come." My voice exudes confidence, but I'm shaken by the sudden switch.

I've never held the power. Even though he's made himself vulnerable to me, he's held all the power in our session.

That takes my breath away and immediately puts me on the brink of an orgasm.

"Tinny," he moans in my mouth as his cock swells, and he comes all over my dick and hand. Seeing the ecstasy on his face tips me over the edge, and there's a bucket of cum between us.

Gray grabs my hand and licks my palm with our combined releases. It ignites me, and because he can read my mind, he saves some and brings my hand to my mouth to taste.

"Fuck, what are you doing to me? I thought I was a vanilla guy, and you keep offering me tastes of the rainbow. It blows my mind." I cannot get enough of Gray, and I love it, but it scares me too.

"Let me tell you all the reasons we belong together." He presses our foreheads together.

"Yeah?" I twirl his hair around my finger.

"Yeah. You know me so well and kicked my doubts to the curb like trash. You are the heart and soul of the team. I don't understand why you decided I'm the one, but I'll do my best to deserve you and put you first." Gray's words wrap around me, anchoring me to him.

"You make my life better, and it's my turn to take care of you," I say. I fetch him water and apply the same gel he used on me.

Exhaustion pulls at me when I snuggle up next to him. No one else would put up with my darkness and help me through it. Tonight, there wasn't any sign of the darkness, and he's building my confidence that I won't hurt him.

"Go to sleep, Tinny. I'll be here in the morning."

"But...I'll miss you." My voice gets softer with each word.

"Don't worry. I'll miss you too. You can dream about me."

"Okay." I fling my arm out, and he tucks himself into my side with his hand on my stomach. In my dreams, I'm brave enough to claim him as mine, and we take an extended vacation to Greece.

I decide to wrap his shoulder, not because he needs it medically, but because I think it will help him mentally. On his next shift, he's more aggressive, and I give myself another pat on the back. It's so much easier to figure out what other people need.

Lucky passes to Austin, who shoots right through the goalie's five-hole and scores. Lucky jumps on him, forgetting all about his shoulder pain. LA gives it their best shot, but we win and team spirit is high.

No major injuries, but lots of bumps and bruises that need to be examined and iced.

Ari Dimon, the GM, congratulates the team and asks if they want a night out in LA or to fly back as scheduled. I'm surprised when the team votes to fly home. There were tons of celebrities at the game, and some of the players received invites to exclusive parties.

I want my man behind closed doors and not worrying that his teammates in the next room can hear us. After we board the plane, he falls asleep on my shoulder.

Because of the time difference, it's the middle of the night when we get home, and Coach tells the team they'll have a short afternoon skate tomorrow. Which will leave us time in the morning for each other.

But going by the way Austin's eye-fucking me, he has other ideas. The nap on the plane gave him a second wind.

"I thought I was never going to get you alone." He tosses his hockey bag in the closet and pins me to our door.

His lips are unhurried and gentle. He kisses me like we have a lifetime ahead of us, so there's no rush. Kisses me like it's his only intention. Kisses me like I'm his.

My heart crashes in my chest, wanting that so badly. To be his.

"Tonight, I'm all yours. Tell me what you want."

I don't hesitate. "You inside me and holding me all night long." We talked about him spanking me and getting other toys, but all of that pales in comparison to the soft press of his lips and his powerful arms around me.

He scoops me up, and I let out a high-pitched squeak. "I love it when you manhandle me," I say, nuzzling his neck.

"I know." He smirks. Austin lowers me onto his bed as if I'm made of fragile glass.

"You won't hurt me." I pull him on top and grind against him.

"But you deserve to be treated like my precious ray of sunshine."

"Except I'm more tangible than that. You can own me." It's important for me to reassure him if he's struggling with dark thoughts.

"Stop being so serious." He yanks off my socks and nips the inside of my ankle. "I'm tangible," he mocks me with a grin. "Like fucking sunshine would be something I would try." He lets my foot fall onto the bed. "Gimme some credit for basic physics." Austin rips my sweats down with my boxer briefs. "I might not have an advanced college degree like some people." My shirt is next to go. "But fucking you is way more satisfying than a beam of light."

"Noted." My mind blanks out on a retort as his eyes roam my skin, creating heat in their wake. My dick jumps at the attention, and there's no doubt who it belongs to.

Austin takes his time stripping for me. Each button needs two hands working in slo-mo to reveal his line of chest hair. It takes as much time to get to his happy trail as it does for a pond to solidly freeze over.

He spins around, and I expect him to discard his shirt properly, but he lowers it, exposing his broad shoulders and ripped back. Austin shimmies with a playful glance over his shoulder and raises his eyebrows suggestively.

I wolf-whistle and get the shirt thrown on top of my head. Before I untangle myself, he's naked and glorious. Every muscle has definition, creating curves and dips and angles that must be licked and sucked.

"I will never get enough of looking at you." My mouth waters as I reach for him.

"You'd better not. Not even when I'm old and wrinkly." He takes two steps and launches himself at me, landing on my chest.

"Oof," I groan and trap him in place with my legs. "Someone woke up with sex on the brain."

"I dreamed about all the things I'm going to do to you." He sucks the skin over my heart, and I hope it leaves a mark.

"Do it all." I go limp and let my limbs rest spread eagle on the bed. We've been tested and agreed to sex without condoms. "I'm yours to take however you want."

Austin's eyes cloud over, and his headshake is almost imperceptible before his expression clears. "I want you to come on my cock so I can use it as lube to fuck you with."

His surety sets me aflame. "Lie down and I'll jerk off on you and then ride your cock."

He shudders and gives me a bossy expression. "I like the way you think. But you're not touching your cock, I am."

He's so sexy as he stretches out, and I straddle his thighs. "You drive a hard"—I motion to my dick—"bargain, but if it's what you want, I won't stop you."

He spits on his hand and envelops me. I let out a loud sound of approval because he loves hearing me. "Watching you spit on your hand should not be so unbelievably sexy." I rock, witnessing his smile light up the night sky.

"Nothing is better than the sight of you grinding on me." Austin holds up two fingers. "Suck."

I drench his fingers with my mouth, and he teases my hole, pressing in to work me open. My body greedily sucks him in, and his dick jumps, leaking precum.

Our thighs rub together, and the hair on his legs scrapes mine, ratcheting up my desire. Up on my knees, I'm not riding his dick, but even the friction of the air has me on edge.

"I'm close," I pant out, losing my rhythm.

He finds my prostate and issues a command. "Come all over me, and I'll fuck you the way you're craving."

Jets of my cum land on his balls, dick, and lower stomach.

"Yes," I rasp, spreading my release over his cock. I position myself over him and sink down, making us both groan.

He pulls me down for a frantic kiss. "I won't last, but in my dream, I fucked you so good you came again."

I need to see his cock disappear into me, so I lean back on his shins. The visual is nearly enough to make me come again.

"How did I live without this?" he asks in awe. We've synced our thrusts so he can fuck up into me without throwing me off-balance. "You feel incredible."

"Your dick was made to fuck me. I'm all in as long as you're in." Sweat drips down my temple, and I dream of the life we could have together if he wasn't famous.

He shivers. "So sensitive."

"Too much?" I ask.

"Too much...not enough... It's melting my brain."

"No literal melting." I trail my middle finger along his chest. "We need to do this over and over." I wave my hands in the air and, to show my devotion, yell, "Amen."

"Sunshine," he whispers, and his mouth meets mine.

I flatten myself on top of him, and the full-body connection is so deep it's as if I'm melting into him.

He's babbling, calling me his Sunshine and telling me everything he loves about my body as he empties his balls into me. The warmth of his release sends me over the edge in white-hot bliss.

He moans, the sound reverberating from his chest to mine. "How?" he asks, with eyes wide as pools.

I bury my head in his neck. "You filling my ass really does it for me."

"Should I be more impressed by me or you." He kisses my sweaty hair.

"It was you. I was along for the ride." I'm full of him and sated in a way I've never felt before.

"You did all the work," he murmurs in my ear.

CHAPTER 27

AUSTIN

I get lost in Grayson's warm eyes, and I say the words in my head that I haven't had the courage to say out loud, "I love you." I think it again and again as we're connecting in the most intimate way.

"Dirty sex with you is a divine experience," he says, pupils wide.

"Divine?" I choke on a laugh. The church I grew up in would not appreciate the analogy. "Back in the day, they'd have burned us at the stake."

"Nah, we're not witches." He circles his hips, and his cheeks rub my balls. "We'd keep it on the down-low."

"I'd never be able to keep you a secret," I confess.

"We can fight about this or sleep." He yawns. "Some of us didn't nap."

"I'll get a cloth to clean you up." Before I shift him off me, he's shaking his head.

"Stay inside me as long as possible and let me sleep covered in you."

I pet his hair and down his back, more than happy to sleep with his cum stuck to me. It only takes a minute for his breathing to even out and a soft snore to escape his throat.

His weight grounds me as I listen to him breathe and faintly feel his heartbeat. This is heaven.

When I wake up, he's no longer on top of me. Missing his weight, I'm driven to tug him back, but I'll wake him if I do. I settle for being the big spoon and wrapping myself around his body.

"Love waking up with you." He kisses my forearm. "I hate it when we can't sleep together."

"Me too. Damn rules. Maybe I'll sneak you into my home game hotel room." I nibble on his ear.

"Mr. Perfect Rule Follower breaking the rules? I'll believe it when I see it," he scoffs.

"I'd do anything for you." My voice is rough with emotion. It's true, but the darkness still lives in me and I could let him down even if I don't physically hurt him.

"I know," he says and rolls to face me. "You're my person."

Morning breath be damned, I kiss him.

"Talk to me, Tinny." We share my pillow. I could pretend not to know what he's talking about, but I won't lie to him.

"How can you be so sure of me when I'm not?" It's frustrating to crave him and stress out that it will trigger something terrible.

"In some ways, we know each other better than we know ourselves. Sometimes we have to fake it until we make it." He bites his lip and reaches for his phone. "It's easier said than done. I started using an app to help me." He shows me an app for anxiety and intrusive thoughts. He hits play on an acronym for overcoming fear. "This is one tool, or you could use journaling, affirmations, or meditation. I wish you could see yourself the way I see you."

"Do you use it for the guy's sexy accent?" I ask to change the subject.

Gray glances away and clears his throat. "I've never told you this before, but my mind tells me I don't fit in. Most of the time, I feel like I'm an outsider tagging along in your life."

"Sunshine." I cup his cheek and force him to look at me. "You're my rock. I'm a disorganized disaster if left to my own devices. You are the only person in my life who makes it easy for me to just be myself and relax. I don't have to pretend to be someone I'm not. And that is invaluable to me." My thumb strokes under his jaw.

"I love being that for you. That you trust me to be here and catch you if you fall or bring you back if you're overwhelmed."

"You are."

We lie in silence and listen to the voice explain how to invite your fear in and accept it. It reminds me of Gray telling me to bring things into the light to take away their power.

It's a short audio file, and we stare at the screen until it ends. Gray flips his phone over, and I internalize the words, and they make me brave enough to trust Grayson.

"I chose the flogger the night before last because it's not as loud or as personal as a spanking." He runs his knuckles over my stubble. "Let me show you how trustworthy you are."

I need our physical expression of love to match our emotional connection. Once again, those three words are on the tip of my tongue, but I don't say them. I'm not sure if he means to show me now or in general. I lose myself in him, swept away with love and longing.

I'm not rushing this. It's my turn to worship him.

As I kiss each knob on his spine, goosebumps appear on his arms, which makes me smile. He's taken by surprise when my hand cracks his ass.

"Yesss," he hisses, speaking into the app on his phone. "Hey Annie, set another timer for five minutes."

"Tell me if you want to stop before the alarm." I knead his pink flesh.

"I would've set it for fifteen minutes but thought you might get twitchy." He wiggles his lower half.

"Twitchy." I tap his balls. "We'll see who's twitchy."

"Me. Pick me." His laugh morphs into a groan as my caress becomes a thunk.

"I'll always pick you, Sunshine. You'll never have to worry about where you stand with me. You're mine." My goal is to show him with my words and actions that he's the center of my world. It kills me that he hasn't realized that without him, I'm nothing.

I take in the expanse of his back and the round curve of his ass, needing to take my time to get started. I've watched the spanking video several times on my own and follow its instructions as his skin turns pink. "Do you like the strikes or the thuds better?"

"Both. All. Don't stop."

I'm mesmerized by the way his body undulates under me, seeking my hand. The fear of my darkness hasn't left, but I trust Gray if I lose control. I search my mind and body for any of the telltale signs it's going to make an appearance and find nothing.

I'm consumed by him, and there's no room for anything else.

His skin's on fire, and the pink has turned to red. I catalog the intensity of every sound coming from him to decipher the patterns he likes best. His favorite seems to be a caress, and a thunk, followed by two sharp strikes in the middle of his cheek.

Gray has opened up an entirely new world for me. I'm high from touching his skin, the sting on my hand, and the rush of lust flooding me. My head has gone floaty, and I tingle all over.

"Tinny, please," he pleads. "I need to come."

He's so pretty as my fist circles his cock.

I barely notice his release in my hand until he whimpers with more pain than pleasure.

"Sorry." I rest my forehead on his spine to catch my breath.

Removing my hand from his cock, I bring it to my mouth and savor his release. He watches me over his shoulder with hooded eyes.

"Good?" he asks.

"The best." I dip so my tongue swipes his cock.

He swings a leg over my head so he can sit up facing me. "Now it's your turn." His mouth swallows my desperate length.

Gray sucks once and I explode, no longer able to hold back. He drinks me down, suckling me after I finish.

We collapse into each other's arms and make our way up to the pillows.

"How was that?" He searches my eyes. "Did the darkness creep in?"

The grin that takes over my face makes him laugh. "I like our system of checking in." I palm his ass. "Seriously, thank you. I never imagined how different it would be to fall in love with my best friend. Besides better sex than I could dream of, you've given me your trust, both with your fears and your body." I stiffen with my admission of love, but he doesn't take it seriously.

"So, you're saying my dick has magical powers?" he teases.

"Magical healing, you've cured me of the darkness. I don't think it will be a problem anymore," I say with confidence and hope.

His face becomes serious, and my heart flip-flops with anticipation.

"Tinny..." His fingertips graze my cheek. "I've loved you almost all my life, and I've fallen hopelessly in love with you."

My face splits into a grin so wide my skin tightens. "I love you too." I say the words, and my heart is so full it could burst. But then it's hard to breathe, my vision gets blurry, and I hear my name echoing in my ears.

CHAPTER 28

GRAYSON

Austin has a panic attack as soon as he tells me he loves me, and at first I think he is being a smartass. I'm trained for this, but the sight of my big hockey player boyfriend struggling for air is unnerving. I rub his sternum and speak calmly to restore normal breathing.

The seconds pass as long as hours as his anxiety decreases.

"I'm here. You're fine." I hold him down as he tries to leave the bed.

"It's here. Everywhere." His eyes are wild with panic.

"Will King be all right to walk out on the ice for Pride Night?" I blurt out the first thing that pops in my head that will redirect his brain. My man puts himself last, and I can use it to my advantage.

"W-w-what?" he sputters, but he's able to take a full breath in.

"I'm worried about King. Are you?" I model deep breathing, holding his hand above my heart with my other one on his.

He automatically syncs with me, then falls on his side laughing.

"I think I'm dying, and you...you ask me about King?" he huffs.

"It worked, didn't it." I take a fistful of his short hair and yank his head back to kiss him. "You scared the hell out of me. Tell me what happened."

His eyes skate away, and his jaw tightens.

"Hey." I tuck my head under his chin so he's not self-conscious. "I love you, and I'm not going to judge you. All I want is to figure out how to avoid what happened."

"It was so fast," he croaks. "Pure joy telling you the words I've been holding back, and then there was no air."

I'm nodding into his neck. "That must've been terrifying." I leave the sentence hanging as if it's a question.

"Godfuckingdamnit." He goes limp.

"What?" I surge up to check his pupils.

"The answer is shame. Victoria asked me to connect the similarities in my episodes of darkness, and it's shame. I'm sorry I scared you."

"That makes sense." I curl back into his chest. "It's a hugely powerful emotion. If it were anyone else, it wouldn't have been scary, but it's hard to watch the man I love have a panic attack." I cradle his head.

"Say it again."

"Tinny, I love you." My voice is loud in the quiet of his room, happy to chase all remnants of shame away.

"Again."

"Tinny, I love you so much it scares me." I breathe out.

"Me too," he says in a small voice.

"At least we can be scared together." I roll so he's on top of me. My head swims with theories I'm afraid to verbalize. Pushing him to face something he's not ready for won't make it better. I could make it worse, and I would do anything to ensure he doesn't suffer.

"Sunshine?"

"Yeah?" I look up into his sky-blue eyes.

"I don't ever want to be without you. Ever. I love you."

"Good." I pinch his ass to lighten the moment, hiding my relief that he can say the words without passing out again. "Now you're stuck with me. No takesies-backsies."

Austin's laugh fills the room, but his face crinkles with anxiety. "You haven't pulled that since middle school."

"That's how serious I am," I deadpan. His features relax, and my concern bleeds away too.

"Don't have a note handy with an appropriate quote to express my love." His fingers tenderly glide through my hair. "How we got here is unbelievable, but my life is so much better because of it."

"Your words are better than a quote because they're real. You were solidly in the friend zone because I wouldn't have fucked up our friendship for a..." I wave my hand, trying to conjure words. We've crossed so many friendship boundaries, but I don't regret it.

"For sex," he finishes for me.

"Right," I agree, with a hug. The only significant time I spent away from him was the year he got pulled up to the NHL and I stayed in Michigan to finish my undergrad degree. He convinced me to live with him in New York to do my grad work. I can't imagine life without him.

"This—us—was never about sex." Austin sounds unsure, and I hope to turn the tables on him.

"We are so much more than that, but don't even try to tell me after you planted the best kiss of my life on me that you didn't have sex on the brain." My light tone teases him as I lick into his mouth.

"Maybe ten-percent about sex."

"See. Muah." I exaggerate a kiss on his cheek. "Talk more or eat?" Today has been momentous, and my goal is to give him what he needs.

"Eat. And listen to another audio recording on your app."

"Deal." I remind myself to breathe.

We'll be okay.

The practice facility is quiet, and no one has come to see me before the afternoon skate. It makes me nervous instead of grateful. And I'd be lying to myself if I didn't admit to worrying about Austin.

He loves me, but saying it caused him to be so overwhelmed that he almost passed out. He grew up with well-meaning parents who discouraged any emotions, so he never learned how to process his feelings. I'm not a professional in mental health, but I'm an expert on him. If he continues to put the team and other people first before dealing with his own emotions, it could cause a breakdown in public. I'll do anything to protect him from that.

He has an appointment later with the sports psychologist, and I encouraged him to talk to her about what happened even though it doesn't relate to hockey.

The black-and-purple logos, along with the layout, are so familiar I could find my way to the locker room blindfolded. I wander into the team's space to put eyes on the players who need a stretch or a taping.

As I walk in, Benzy leaps over the bench and yells, "Freeze." No one takes him seriously, but everyone turns his way. "The boys are back!" He fist-pumps while twerking.

Liska grunts as if to say "What the hell are you talking about."

"Look, the twins are twinning again." Benz points to me and Austin. "Let's see your socks," he demands.

Austin's pale skin is bright pink, and this is the type of situation I fear might guilt him into telling the truth he's not ready for.

I cross my ankles and pretend to be scandalized. "A gentleman never shows his socks in public. Mine are black, like your heart." I toss my hair back with indignation.

"They say goalies are weird. Trainers are unhinged," Benzy complains. "All I'm saying is I want things to go back to normal. Newsflash: we've noticed the tension between our captain and caretaker." He slumps down on the bench.

My face must show as much shock as Austin's. "You think we're fighting?" he croaks.

The room is silent, and the team glances at each other nervously, hoping someone will speak up.

"It's us. We're fine, don't worry," I say to take the heat off Austin.

"You don't go out with us anymore," Lucky accuses me, and I'm so taken aback, I remain silent.

"Here's the thing. You two were like Velcro, and now you avoid each other. It's not our business. We're not doing an intervention—"

"Thank you," Austin cuts King off. "Really, you guys are amazing, and I... we appreciate you all. Gray and I are fine. We're trying new things, but we'll always be friends."

"New things?" Drake raises a suspicious eyebrow.

"Yes, we're splitting up at team functions to spy on all of you and report back to Coach. Now you've foiled our plan." I hang my head and snap my fingers as if to say "Oh shoot."

Benz says, "Liars," at the same time as Lucky says, "Dickheads."

"Fine, don't tell us. You're acting like a snow leopard hiding in plain sight by blending in. But we see you." Lucky points two fingers at his eyes and then at mine. "I'm watching you."

Coach steps into the locker room and frowns at his team, who are still in their street clothes. "Get your asses on the ice. Now!" Everyone scrambles to get dressed, and I snag a few players to come with me to the treatment room.

As I'm walking out, my eyes find Austin's, and as expected, he's concerned, and the wheels are turning in his head. He should talk to a professional before making the decision to come out. I don't want him to feel pressured into it.

During practice, Benz gets a puck stuck in his pads, and I help him fish it out. "Austin and I are fine. I promise you don't have to worry." I give him a reassuring pat.

"You're so important to this team. We couldn't do it without you," he says, and I laugh. "It's not funny, it's true."

His hurt sobers me. "Thank you. I appreciate it, but I'm doing my job, and any other trainer would keep you guys healthy."

Benz shakes his head. "You're delulu. That's horseshit." He skates away, but I don't have a response.

His compliment sits in my chest like a strange itch I can't scratch. He clearly believes it, so maybe I should too. Slowly, I'd let my intrusive thoughts become reality, ignoring the actions of others that disproved my thoughts. Austin isn't the only one with lots of work to do on himself.

King comes in after practice for a hamstring stretch. "Had a little spasm."

"Let's go to the mats. It'll be easier for me." We cross the hall, and he lies down. "Did it bother you during practice, or was it only one spasm?" I ask him several other questions while I massage and manipulate his legs.

He can handle pressure on it, and there aren't any sore spots. "It's probably dehydration. Make sure you drink extra water and electrolytes."

"Didn't mean to interrupt," Austin says with amusement from the doorway as I'm standing over King with my chest against his leg in the air. "Come find me when you're done."

"I won't take up too much of your man's time," King calls after him.

Austin freezes for a second but doesn't turn around and walks away stiffly.

"Oops, my bad," King mumbles.

"What are you sorry for?" I turn his leg out to stretch his inner thigh.

He stares at me with apprehension. "Grayson, how many Black men are on the team?"

"Only you." I have no idea where this is going or if it was a trick question.

"And how many Black players in the league total?"

"Four or five?" I ask because I'm not totally sure.

"People who gatekeep my Blackness would say four, but most white people would say five," he says, as if that explains his point, but I'm more lost than ever.

"I learned to read the room to survive, and I can tell who tolerates me because they have to, who not to walk down a dark alley with, and who genuinely cares. I'm an expert at reading people because my safety depends on it." He holds up his hand when I try to argue. "That is a totally different discussion. But you and our captain aren't avoiding each other because of a fight, but because you're afraid of outing yourselves."

I've sunk down onto the mat next to him with my mouth hanging open. My first instinct is to deny it, but I don't.

"Don't worry. I'd never out anyone. I have mad respect for both of you." He uses my shoulder to stand up. "We good?"

"Sure thing," I say automatically, and he leaves.

We weren't as careful as we thought. Austin finds me still sitting on the floor and rushes over.

"Are you okay?" His eyes scan me as he reaches for me.

The truth is a double-edged sword that I can't protect him from because it always comes out in the end, so I take a deep breath. "King knows about us. I didn't tell him," I add.

Austin's knees give out, and he collapses next to me, grasping my hand.

"King won't out you." His palm is clammy in mine.

"I know. He's a true teammate." He rubs the back of his neck.

"Listen." I pause, gathering my thoughts and courage. "You might have the urge to tell everyone right away, but it's probably best to talk to Victoria before doing anything."

Austin's blue eyes cloud with confusion, and he tilts his head to the side in an unasked question.

"The practice facility isn't private enough for this conversation," I say, patting the mat with my free hand.

"What aren't you saying?" He tries to draw his hand away, but I won't let him.

"I would do anything for you. Take a bullet. Whatever it takes." I take his other hand, and he softens. "But there are things out of my control and yours."

"Go ahead and say it." He momentarily takes his hand out of mine to swipe his sweaty forehead.

I ground myself in the acidic scent.

"You want to tell the team about us so they don't worry, but I'm concerned about what happens to you afterward." My fingers grip his so hard they turn white.

"I'll be fine."

"Eventually, you will be. I'm positive of that. But." When I pause, he makes an impatient sound. "Have you ever considered that the darkness you've identified as shame is overriding your nervous system?" I let the question sit between us.

"I don't understand." His brow scrunches, and there isn't any anger in his voice.

"You can disagree with me, but I've noticed a pattern since you told me about it. It takes over when you experience extreme emotions. Good and bad. Self-loathing and"—I wince as I say—"love. It would be completely normal to initially have feelings of shame about loving a man."

"No," he disagrees.

Instead of arguing, I let him process what I've said.

"That's...sad." His head drops to his chin.

"Managing feelings is a skill most adults struggle with, and your family didn't tolerate big emotions. As someone who has known you for years, you have a hard time with that." He lets me hug him, and relief courses through me.

"It makes me sound self-deluded."

"Nah, most people don't share their true feelings. And you were able to identify it as the correct emotion after a few sessions. It takes some people years and *years*." I get the laugh I was aiming for. "My main concern is that you choose your mental health over prioritizing the team." I hold him close as if that will convince him.

Austin pulls away but keeps an arm around me. "I'm reeling right now."

"Are you upset with me?" I ask, sucking in a breath.

"No, you should be able to tell me your fears. I'm no relationship guru, but that's basic stuff." He pulls me back into a bear hug. "If I'm honest, you're probably right. I've dealt with repressing things for so long, I never considered the problems it could cause. I promise to talk to Victoria about everything before I make any big decisions."

The air leaves my lungs in a slow exhale, expelling my anxiety with it. The truth has weighed me down, but now I'm relieved and lighter. "As long as we have each other, we'll be fine."

"Better than fine." He kisses me on the mat in the practice facility, unconcerned that someone could see us. It both elates and terrifies me with the taste of cinnamon in my mouth.

CHAPTER 29

AUSTIN

My appointment with Victoria is in person, and I wish I had my computer to hide behind. Gray offered to come with me, but I feel stupid, like there's something so wrong with me that I don't have control over myself. Coming alone is one step toward regaining control.

Her office has beige walls with a few colorful, abstract paintings. There's her desk, desk chair, couch, and a club chair.

I plant my ass in the club chair, word-vomit my love for Grayson, my intense panic attack, my shame epiphany, and his theory about why it happened.

I explain how I tempted fate, and it kicked my ass. The darkness reared up and took me down without warning after I was sure it was gone.

She doesn't show any outward signs of surprise. "You've been holding in a lot, and I appreciate your trust in me. What are your thoughts on Grayson's opinion?"

"I don't know," I confess.

"Let's take a step back and talk about shame."

It doesn't take me long to go over my experiences, and she asks a few follow-up questions.

"You said he fears you coming out might negatively affect your mental health?" she asks kindly.

"Other people on my team have done it. I won't be the first, and I want the team to know I support them," I say, but my tone is sharper than I intended.

"You can only support your team if you come out?" she challenges.

"No, but they'll trust me more," I say, and she taps her steepled fingers together.

"You mentioned your parents won't appreciate the scandal of strangers talking about your sex life if you come out. What would've happened if you had come out while you still lived in their house?"

"I wouldn't have," I say without hesitation.

"Why not?"

"They wouldn't have believed me and would have taken me to the church for redirection. Shamed me." The truth of the statement physically hurts.

"How often were you told to quiet down or behave?"

"Daily." I swear they wanted a silent son, and hockey saved my sanity.

"Tell me how you expressed your joy or anger at home."

Memories flash through my mind of my father's reproachful look and my mother shaking her head. All the air leaves my lungs. "I didn't. I learned to hold everything in." My mind finally makes the connection. "Grayson's probably right." I shift uncomfortably in my seat.

"Your opinion is more important. Before you leave, let's talk through your reasons for coming out and the possible consequences."

By the time my appointment is over, I have more questions than answers.

Gray has a late dinner ready when I get home. He hugs me and sticks one of the notes he found to my chest. It says *I can't remember anything without you.* He doesn't push me to talk, and we eat in silence at the counter.

When we're done, he takes my empty plate and kisses my head. "I love you."

"How come you were never mad at me about your knee injury?" I blurt out. It might be projection, but he could harbor anger toward me.

"What?" He stops short in the kitchen with our plates in his hand.

"It was me and Smith who hit you." I brace for his reaction, never understanding his willingness to forgive me.

He sets the plates on the counter and rounds the island. "If you tell me these last ten years have been based on your guilt..." He trails off and chews the inside of his mouth. "Please tell me that isn't the case."

"No!" I shout in horror and per Victoria's instructions, I don't mute my response. "You were my best friend for years before that happened."

He closes his eyes and sighs. "Did you ever watch the hit? I have it on video."

"You do?" I'm shocked, and unsure if I can watch it.

"It's somewhere in the cloud." Gray digs his phone out of his pocket and scrolls and scrolls. It takes him forever to find it. "I'm casting it to the TV so you can see it on the big screen." He stands next to the TV mounted on the wall and uses the remote to slow the video down.

"Here it comes. You hit me, I'm fine. Smith smashes into my other side...and watch my feet... There, that's where I felt it." He stops the tape. "But I made it far worse." He starts the tape, and on it he tries to stand, collapses but keeps trying to get up. "If I had stayed down—like everyone told me to—I probably would've been able to play again. I panicked and thought if I could stand up, everything would be fine. I did so much damage to my knee putting my full weight on it. Have you felt guilty all these years?"

"For lots of reasons," I admit.

"There's a punching bag in the building gym. If I can find my old gloves, we're going to beat it to a pulp." He doesn't wait for my answer and retreats to his room for his gloves. He comes out holding them in triumph. "Me and punching bags go way back. They don't talk back when you get angry and yell at them."

I change into sweats and hand him some of my workout gear even though his clothes are available. Sue me for wanting to watch him in my joggers as I follow him down to the gym. It's a reprieve from prying eyes since it's empty. I couldn't vent in front of anyone else.

"Watch and learn." Gray pulls the gloves on and squares off with the punching bag. "I hate feeling helpless when Tinny's darkness overtakes him." He punches and sends the bag swinging. "I hate causing him stress." He pounds it again as it swings back.

I catch it and hold it steady for him as he yells his frustrations at the top of his lungs. When he's done, he wipes the sweat off his brow with his forearm.

"Your turn." Gray strips off the gloves and hands them to me.

Part of me maintains that this is ridiculous, but I punch the bag. "I hate being clueless about my own mind."

"Good start but I want you to send the bag flying, with or without a declaration. Focus your fear on the bag and get angry."

He steps back, and I dig deep to find the box I keep locked inside me and fling it open as I hit the bag.

My mind wants to go blank, but I sit with all the things I've kept pent up. My throat gets tight, and I'm burning up from the release I've never allowed myself.

I yell at the top of my lungs and punch with all my might, pouring out my anguish until I'm ready to collapse.

"I hate that I got to live our dream and you didn't." The gloves thump his back as my arms wrap around him. His familiar smell immediately slows my heart rate.

"I know." He holds the back of my head and hugs me to him. "The dream had to change, but we're still together, and look at us now. Neither of us would've predicted this."

"Teenage Austin would've run far, far away from you. He was a coward." I wipe my cheek on his shirt.

"Nope. You did the best you could, and so did I. Trying to rewrite the past will only drive us crazy. Now we're a team. You and me."

"Forever." I let go to kiss him.

"Forever," he agrees.

CHAPTER 30

GRAYSON

The forced smile I flash Austin is meant to be encouraging. We're sitting on opposite sides of the couch, and he's mentally psyching himself up to make the call.

"You can wait. There's no rush," I say for the billionth time.

"I won't hide you. You mean everything to me." He inhales for five seconds, holds his breath, then lets it out. "I'm fully aware that my parents won't approve, but they deserve the truth. It'll be worse if they're blindsided. This way, they can seek refuge in the church before it becomes public." He tries to smile but gives up.

Reaching across the cushion, I hold my hand out for him to take. "We're in this together. No matter what, I'm here."

He squeezes my hand and hits his dad's cell number. It rings a few times and goes to voicemail.

"Hey Dad, hoping to catch up. Call me when you get this." He hangs up and runs a hand through his short blond hair. "Of course, now I have to wait. Ugh."

His phone rings, and he jumps, fumbling it so it lands on the floor.

I pick it up. "It's him," I say, placing it in his palm.

Austin clears his throat and answers. "Hey, Dad."

"Austin, great to hear from you. I heard the team is doing well this season." His dad's voice booms from the speaker, and I rein in my irritation. Most fathers would watch their son's games or at least follow the highlights. Austin's sister, Lori, keeps his parents informed.

They make small talk for a few minutes, and anxiety slithers over Austin's face. I shift next to him so our legs touch and grip his knee.

"Dad, will you grab Mom? Gotta to talk to you guys about something."

"Sure." He calls for Austin's mom.

Austin's hand clutches mine on his knee.

"Hi, sweetie." His mom joins the call.

"What's going on?" His dad's voice is tense.

Austin's terrified eyes lock on mine. "Mom, Dad, I recently realized that I'm bisexual."

I throw my arm around him as his eyes close, anticipating the censure. He's shaking but leans into me.

His mom and dad speak at the same time.

"Did you pray about it?" Austin's mom's voice is high and stressed while his dad says, "Have you spoken to anyone at our church?"

Tinny opens his eyes and steadies himself. "There isn't anything to pray about. You've known for years my stance on sexuality."

"This is all Grayson's influence, isn't it?" his father spits out.

Before Austin can formulate an answer, there is a lot of background noise.

"In here, dear," his mom calls, and we hear Lori enter and greet her parents.

"We'll talk later, Austin," his dad says.

"Hey, big bro. What's up?" Lori says.

"We can't talk, we're going to lunch," his mom says in a rush to get off the phone.

"Lori," Austin yells. "I was telling Mom and Dad that I'm bisexual."

"Oooh." She draws the word out as if understanding all the tension in the room. "Cool. Who are you dating?" We hear a smack. "What? He wouldn't tell us if he wasn't serious about someone. Is it Grayson? Tell me it's Grayson, or I'm disowning you. That man is *fine*!"

Leave it to Lori to embarrass Austin while giving him a sense of acceptance.

"I'll pass that along," he says, leaning into me.

"If you're not dating him, I'll fly in to tell him in person and watch a game. He makes a killer brunch with potatoes *and* Canadian bacon."

"Thanks, sis." Those two words hold so much feeling.

"Love ya. Gotta run." The line goes dead.

I pull Austin into my arms. "All in all, that went well," I murmur into his hair.

"It could've gone worse," he admits. "Should I punch Lori or give her a huge hug?"

"Don't worry, there's only one Lapointe I'm interested in." He scoffs and lifts his head so I can press my lips to his. "And you know she was trying to irritate you, but she made the next call with your parents easier. She'll set them right."

"It wasn't bad, but it's infuriating that they view it as a sin and blame you." He rests his head against mine. The conversation clarifies the shame I've associated with my sexuality.

"I'll take all the blame in the world. I'm keeping you, and your parents are part of the package deal. We don't see them that often." We sit in silence for a few minutes, but I can't stand not knowing. "What are you thinking?"

"You're too good to me, and I can't show my appreciation because I'm meeting Kenney," he grumbles.

"I'm here whenever you're ready." I try to sound sexy but laugh. Even though we've talked about this at length, I have a niggling sense of unease that his emotions will sabotage his mind. "I mean, is everything okay up here?" I tap my head.

"You can use that voice later in the bedroom." He sits up, untangling us and I frown. "Sorry." He sighs. "I'm happy I told them and that part is over. Part of me was terrified they'd disown me over the phone. They love me, but I'm not the son they wanted: a straight preacher or doctor." He coughs. "We all have to live with their disappointment. I'm trying to identify my core emotion. And it ain't fun." He rolls his shoulders.

That's something he's talked about with the therapist that Victoria referred him to. It sucked diving into my emotions, and I assume it's the same for him. I've been putting off going back to my therapist for no reason. "And?" I ask.

"I'm sad even though the conversation went better than I expected. I held out a sliver of hope that they would surprise me. Instead, Lori surprised me by saying you're hot." He uses his weight to flatten me on the couch.

"I'm sorry your parents let you down. If things get to be too much—"

"I'll tell you or talk to someone. I promise." He brushes my hair back off my forehead.

To change the subject, I throw a quote at him. "*The greatest thing you'll ever learn is just to love and be loved in return.* Moulin Rouge."

"Profoundly perfect, like you." Austin kisses me softly. "Even if you're stealing my movie quotes."

I laugh and ask, "Is everything all right with Kenney?"

"He's having issues with his roommate or mates. Not exactly sure, but he doesn't like his living situation."

"You're not a realtor." I lean in for one more kiss.

"The least I can do is listen and try to help problem-solve." He stands and pats his pockets, checking for his wallet, which sits on the island.

I point to his wallet. "No, most people would respond with a text of sympathy or advice. He could put in the group chat that he's looking to move. More people, more connections."

"This is why I love you. You keep track of my shit and have great ideas."

"I thought it was for my magical cock," I deadpan.

"It's an enormous bonus." He holds his hands out shoulder-width apart.

"My dick isn't a fish tale." I adjust my hard-on as he walks to the door.

"I can make it bigger any time I want," he says over his shoulder with smoldering eyes.

CHAPTER 31

AUSTIN

The fans chant loudly along with the music at our first home game after an extended road trip. They're happy to see us in person, and we're happy to have the crowd behind us.

The thing I like the least is spending the night in the hotel away from Grayson. It's been weeks since the call with my parents, and the more time I spend with Gray, the more our love grows stronger and stronger. I worry I'm being a clingy mess, but Benz is cranky when he doesn't get to sleep with Leo, and I suspect Lucky and Drake sneak into each other's rooms. I've also seen Trevor leave the hotel late at night with Liska's driver.

If I can't set a good example, I shouldn't be captain.

Which is why I'm hunting Gray down before I change and we do our pregame ritual.

He's sitting on the edge of Doc's desk, looking over a report.

I knock on the open door. "Can I get a hamstring stretch before warm-ups?"

Doc waves Gray out, and I lead him to an empty workout room with mats.

"Since when has your hammy needed attention?"

"Not my hamstring." I pin him to the wall next to the door where no one can see us if they look in. "I missed you, Sunshine." I keep our lower halves separate as I kiss him deeply, inhaling the coconut oil clinging to him.

"Missed you too." His tongue runs along my bottom lip. "But you don't want to spoil your perfect image, so go get your skates on." He smacks my ass.

"That's not an incentive to stop. It's a keep-going love tap." I push off the wall and put distance between us. "My hammy's much better thanks to your magic," I tease.

"Go," he orders with a grin.

I haul ass to the locker room to find Lucky and Benz arguing over the dance party music. They both claim to have the perfect song.

The room gets rowdy, and King breaks out a dance sequence that should be on video because he's on fire. My insides glow with pride at how far he's come this season from the shy rookie who barely spoke to the center of attention during the dance party.

Lucky twerks against Drake, who smiles and spanks his ass. Lucky swears he's going to get Drake to lead a dance before a game. I don't see that happening.

My jealousy takes me by surprise as I watch them. They're stronger since coming out and ignore the online hate and rumors.

I could choose the same path. Victoria referred me to another therapist, one whose specialty will help me work through my issues. I've had an easy life compared to most people, and it's difficult to fully accept that the darkness I've felt inside me results from guilt and repressed emotions.

But my therapist insists that if I minimize my past, it will adversely affect my present. It's hard not to care about other people's opinions of me.

My parents and I have spoken again, and they've assured me they love me but have also encouraged me to stay silent until I retire. They will never understand how hard that is for me.

During warm-ups, we skate onto the ice to a standing ovation. The crowd's excitement and thirst for a win reverberate in my chest. Their support, or lack of, can be a game changer. Their spirit lifts us up when we're tiring.

I love my job and appreciate our fans. Not many people get to experience the force of fan admiration on a weekly basis. I'm so grateful.

We've got some downtime to get treatments and strategize before Coach comes in and does the pregame speech.

Liska tosses me a jersey. "Give that to Grayson." It's for Pride Night, and his name is embroidered on the back. I trace it with my finger, but I don't experience the guilt that he's not a player. He absolved me of any lingering responsibility, and I wouldn't trade our current situation for all the fame and fortune in the world.

I'd quit hockey before I let Gray go. None of this means anything without him. This team has given me my dream, but Gray is my Sunshine. The love of my life.

If anything, I wish he would wear a jersey with my name on it. I love seeing him in my clothes.

I scan the room, realizing these men are my family. They have my back, no questions asked.

"Hey," I yell, and clear my throat. "I've got something to say." I internally kick myself for stating the obvious. All eyes are on me as I keep talking. "It's been a weird couple of months for me. I learned some things about myself that were a surprise, the biggest thing: I'm bisexual." The room is eerily still for a moment, when the door bangs open.

"Kenney, time to tape your leg. Let's go," Gray hollers, then takes in the room. "What's up?" he asks cautiously.

"No big deal, but our captain came out to us," Benz sings.

"We're like a gay herd of rams," Lucky chimes in with a provocative hip swivel.

"Congratulations." Gray's eyes light up, and he turns pink, but he doesn't move.

I cross the room and kiss him. "Have you met my boyfriend, Gray?" I hug him tightly as he pulls back, wide-eyed. He once said I'd never kiss him in the locker room, and now I second-guess this. I whisper, "Is this okay with you?"

His grin takes over his entire face as he devours my mouth again, but then he ends the kiss with a laugh. "Benzy's gonna yell at us for kissy-face."

"Don't worry about that guy." I'm smiling so wide my cheeks hurt. "Liska brought you this." I shove the Pride jersey at him.

"Vho knew the shirt could turn people?" Liska's gruff voice is full of amusement.

"And if I see any of you fuckers exchanging money because you bet for or against Gray and I," I pause, thinking of a substantial threat. "I'll throw you out of the group chat." I ignore their grumbles.

Gray said he'd never push me, but he's so happy it's as if rays of sunshine are coming out of his pores. I made the right decision.

"I'm proud of you," he whispers in my ear, then gives me a peck and turns away. "Kenney, time's a-wasting." He points in the direction of the training room.

The game's a blur, but we win decisively. It's like I've been freed from a cage, and I fly around the ice. I score an all-time high of three goals with one assist.

Drake slaps my shoulder. "You should come out before every game." He walks past me as if I could actually do that every game.

Coach moves practice to tomorrow afternoon, and the team decides on a place to celebrate tonight.

We have a private room, so I'm able to touch Grayson, and it's liberating. I get to kiss him in the second place he never thought I would, so for the first time, I'm exceeding expectations. And my lips are constantly on him, warming me like a soft flame.

Almost everyone has come up to congratulate us on our relationship, and my heart soars. The ability to be ourselves is cathartic, almost like salvation. I'm not worried about touching or talking too close for too long or glances that give away my feelings.

It's an entirely new level of understanding of coming out. I thought I knew, but I had no idea. I want to shout from the rooftops how much I love my man. There will be no way of hiding my love for him.

"Do we have to tell management?" I ask Gray.

His brown eyes widen. "Technically, we're breaking the rules, but we signed releases when they hired me because of our friendship. They won't let me treat you anymore." He threads his fingers through mine. "We're really doing this."

"Nothing could stop me," I vow. "We can talk specifics, but by the end of the season, the world will know you're mine."

His smile tells me everything. "You're the one who needs a 'keep off' sign. No one cares about me."

To celebrate, I have an extra drink as the team toasts us. By the time we leave, the restaurant is closing down and the streets are quiet for New York, which means there's light traffic and only a few horns blowing.

We huddle against the building, waiting for our rideshare. He thought I ordered one, and I thought he did.

The team reluctantly leaves us when Grayson taunts them. "What, you think two petite little things like us can't make it home in the big bad city?" A few guys shout out to text them when we get home.

"Bunch of worriers." I wave at the last departing car.

Gray checks his phone again. "It says two minutes, but it said three minutes five minutes ago." He pockets his phone and blows on his fingers. "If it weren't so windy, or if we had on toques, I'd say we should walk."

"Yeah, hats would've been good, but I'll keep you warm." I rub against his shoulder.

"Get a room," a guy in his late teens or early twenties sneers as he passes by with a friend.

My temper flares, and Gray subtly grips my coat sleeve, muttering, "Let it go."

"Hey, that's Ace Lapointe. Great game, man." The very drunk friend of the sneerer stumbles toward us.

"Thanks." I plaster on a friendly smile.

He trips again, and Gray reaches out to prevent him from falling on me.

"You need a bodyguard?" the surly guy asks.

"Does he?" Gray growls as if daring the guy to get closer.

"Your team is full of—"

"Shut it." His friend cuts him off and attempts to pull him away, but he resists.

"Listen to your friend," Gray says, stepping between me and the guys.

"Excuse me. Do you have any idea who I am? You're a nobody!" The guy yells and lunges. I'll never know if he was posturing or meant harm because I hit him.

As I'm mid-swing, we hear a voice holler, "Hey, is everything all right?"

Another guy in a hoodie race-walks toward us with his hands in his pockets. My fist connects with the guy's face, and he goes down.

"He hit me," he cries. "Ace Lapointe hit me."

"No, he didn't, you idiot. I did. Are you so delirious you can't even tell who hit you?" Gray stands over him with a menacing glare.

"Let's go." His friend tugs him up, and they back away as the stranger reaches us.

Gray turns to him, ready for a fight.

"Those guys give you any trouble?" he asks, and the wind exposes his bright red hair.

I instantly recognize him as a rookie for the New York Nationals, our rival hockey team. "Hey, Rhys." I relax and explain. "One of them was obnoxious and I—"

"He was too polite to them, so I punched him," Gray interrupts me. "Do you know them?"

Rhys grimaces. "Unfortunately. I played in high school with the one with attitude. He's entering the draft this summer. I followed them because they were harassing a few women and I…" He waves his hand as if to explain. "It never occurred to me they'd bother two big guys."

"He was a cocky little shit and basically pulled the do-you-know-who-I-am card." Gray has visibly relaxed, but I can tell he's still tense.

"His father rides his ass, and they are politically connected. The asshat's sure he's immune to consequences," Rhys says.

"I'm glad I put him in his place." Gray quips as our rideshare pulls up. "Can we drop you somewhere?"

"Nah, I live close." He turns to me. "Not to be a total fan, but it was nice meeting you when you're not trying to kick my ass, Ace." Rhys holds out his hand and I shake it.

"You don't make it easy," I say honestly, and he reddens.

"Night." Rhys waves and continues down the street.

The small car is a haven from the cold, bringing the smell of warmth and cumin. Its size makes it totally normal for my leg to rest along Gray's.

"Why did you—"

"Will he go home or follow those idiots, looking out for innocent by-standers?" Gray interrupts me for the second time.

Gray only interrupts people when he's trying to protect them. I don't need his protection, but I'll wait until we get home to call him out. "Rhys seems like a good guy. I hope he doesn't end up needing help. Should we go back?" It would suck if something bad happened to him if we could prevent it.

Gray twists in his seat to see out the back window. "He's gone." He's distracted on his phone for the rest of the ride, and I'm fuming that he's ignoring me.

When we're alone in the elevator, he holds up his screen. "Here's Rhys Brant's number if you want to text him and make sure he's home safe." All the fight leaves me and he shrugs. "You can pretend you weren't worried, or you can reach out."

As the elevator doors open, I drag him out and into our apartment without a word.

The door shuts behind us, and my lips fuse with his. I'm intent on getting him naked as soon as I get an explanation.

He surprises me by leaning back, cupping my face, and searching my eyes. "Are you okay? Did the darkness take you over?"

"I'm fine, and we can stop calling it the darkness unless we want it to be a code word. Thanks to therapy, we can call it what it is: my repressed feelings overwhelming me." I press a chaste kiss to his lips. "But, G, I'm not some young kid who needs protection. As a grown-ass man, I can handle the consequences of my actions." My hand curves around his hip.

He sighs into my mouth. "You never resort to physical violence, so it shocked me. Can you understand why I'm concerned? It's so out of character."

"I've never had someone insult the man I love before, and I had to shut his entitled mouth. It wasn't a blackout or a rage surge. Instead, an old-fashioned protect-my-man punch. Thank you for your concern." I hug him tighter. "One more thing to work on in therapy." A humorless laugh escapes me. "I'm not backing away from my actions. I'll take responsibility."

"That kid is trouble, and I'm doubly sure after what Rhys said. You heard him yelling your full name. He's liable to sue for attention or clout. No one gives a shit if the Enforcers trainer knocks out an aspiring hockey player."

"I don't like it," I complain.

"Didn't think you would. Text Rhys and come to bed." His fingers skim my back as he walks away.

CHAPTER 32

GRAYSON

Ace's phone has gone off three times, and I can't believe he's ignoring it. Groaning, I reach for him and find his side of the bed empty. I'm immediately awake but relax when I hear the shower running. It's way too early for someone to harass him, and I snatch his phone to silence it, but my heart stops when I see Finn's name.

Finn never calls, and when he does, it's not good news.

"Tinny." I leap out of bed. "Finn has called three times." The steam obscures my view of him in the glass shower.

"Finn? Google me." He rinses himself off and grabs a towel.

"I told you that little shit was bad news."

Trending on social media is the headline *Ace Lapointe attacks a fan*. Austin clutches his phone in disbelief.

"You aren't getting involved. Please, please let me take the fall. What's the worst that can happen?" I plead.

"No. I did it, and I'm taking responsibility." The phone rings in his hand, and I take it and run. Not mature but effective.

"Finn," I answer as I close myself in my bedroom with my back against the door so Austin can't get in. "There's been a huge misunderstanding. I hit that guy last night because I'd been drinking and he called me a nobody. It's my fault."

"You should know enough to text me if something like that happens," he huffs. "You're not a rookie, Ward. I expect more from you."

"I know. The dude was an ass, and he thought Ace hit him, but I told him it was me. He's lying," I say without remorse.

"Can anyone back you up?"

"Umm, maybe. Rhys Brant was walking down the street, but I don't know if he saw anything." I'm praying to a higher power that Rhys is smart enough to keep his mouth shut if he saw what really happened.

"Both of you need to come in. I'll work on a statement for your approval." He hangs up without saying goodbye.

"What. Did. You. Do?" Austin seethes on the other side of the door.

I open it. "Good, you're dressed. We need to be in Finn's office for damage control ASAP. I told him the kid lied, and I hit him. If you change our story, I'll be the liar." This fact takes him aback, and his mouth snaps shut.

"You did that on purpose."

"Yup." I pat his cheek. If I take the blame, it will be yesterday's news instead of a media circus around him. "I'll change; there are protein muffins on the counter for breakfast."

He drags me back to his room and insists I wear his clothes. "We're not leaving until you put those on," he says, pointing at the clothes on the bed, including his clean underwear. He seems to need this so I comply.

Austin's quiet on the ride over, and I'm afraid he'll tell the truth to be noble and honorable and all the things he is.

"Hey." I take his hand. "This is a small thing I can do for you. Without you, I'd be living in my parents' basement, crying about what could've been. You single-handedly dragged me out of my misery and helped me find a purpose. I love my job. Don't paint me as a liar."

"You fight dirty, and I'm not making any promises." His blue eyes are clouded with conflict.

The elevator opens, and Finn's waiting for us and starts talking as if we're mid-conversation. "Rhys Brant put out a statement confirming Ward's story that Ward punched"—he scans the paper— "Blaine Dumas after a verbal assault by Dumas."

"Dumbass is more like it," I mutter.

"I didn't hear that. We only have positive things to say in this office. Unless it's outstanding gossip," Finn says over his shoulder as he walks toward the nearest conference room, expecting us to follow him.

"Ward, you're very sorry for the altercation. It's not like you, and you don't condone violence to solve problems. The statement will be along those lines. Got it?" he asks and doesn't wait for a response before he says, "Good."

Austin is agitated and hates the situation I put him in. His need to tell the truth weighs on him, but it's too late unless he paints both Rhys and me as liars, which I remind him of when he looks ready to burst.

I agree to a written apology, which needs to be approved by management before it's sent out to news organizations. As Austin drives us to practice, I smugly read comment after comment that Dumas probably deserved it. He's attacked for being a fame-seeking dickhead who can't tell the truth.

"Look who's here. The newest contender for light-weight boxing championship," Benz teases.

"Nobody say a word," Austin barks, and no one questions him. My smugness vanishes, and regret for making him lie settles in its place.

Halfway through practice, Mr. Dimon's assistant, Wes, texts me to leave practice and come straight to Mr. Dimon's office. The only thing that comes to my mind is that no good deed goes unpunished, but I'll gladly suffer the consequences to spare Austin.

I text the group chat that an emergency came up and ask them to give Ace a ride home. I'm purposely cryptic so I don't create any unnecessary panic.

Wes stands as if he's nervous as I approach his desk. "He's in a meeting, but he should be out soon." He stares at me and doesn't offer me the usual drinks or direct me to take a seat.

I wasn't worried until now. Wes is unflappable.

A few minutes later, the mayor and another man exit Mr. Dimon's office, glaring at me. I'm underdressed for this type of meeting.

Wes waves me into Mr. Dimon's office and follows with an apologetic glance. He stands off to the side by the windows as Ari greets me from behind his desk.

"Thank you for coming so quickly." He gestures for me to sit.

The air, thick with tension, becomes hard to swallow. I should respond or say something, but my words are stuck in my dry throat.

"I asked Wes to stay as a witness." He frowns and sits in his chair. "Do you know who left my office before you?"

"The mayor?" I respond, unsure.

"The mayor and the police chief." He steeples his fingers on the desk. "It seems young Dumas is well connected and wants me to fire you."

I stare without saying a word. Austin's fame might have protected him from such pettiness, but as a nobody, I don't have any clout. The silence drags on, but I don't defend myself because it's too late.

After my brain has discarded a million responses, I find my voice. "I'm sorry to hear that."

"Why?" he asks without anger or judgment.

"I love my job and this organization. I'm sorry about causing trouble." My voice shakes, but it's totally sincere.

Mr. Dimon's eyes cut to Wes. "I promised the mayor and the chief that I would explain Mr. Dumas's position regarding the altercation. Thank you for witnessing that." With a nod, he dismisses Wes from the room.

"Help me understand your thought process." He reclines in his chair.

"Sir, there wasn't much thinking. I'd been drinking, and Dumas called me a nobody, which, pardon my language, pissed me off, and I hit him. I deeply regret my actions and any harm they might cause the team." Only one word in my explanation was a lie.

"I don't appreciate the mayor and chief of police trying to tell me how to run my organization." He leans forward on his elbows. "I also need one hundred percent honesty to back my employees. Do you see how this leaves me in a bind, Mr. Ward?"

I shake my head. Mr. Dimon has a reputation for being a fair hard-ass, and I won't break at the first sign of pressure from him. He can't possibly know I'm lying.

"Did you know I'm the youngest GM in the NHL?" My head bobs in acknowledgment. "Many people underestimate me because of it or try to intimidate me. I don't argue with people's perceptions. One thing that sets me apart from my competitors is my thoroughness. Blaine Dumas is the nephew of the mayor, and his father plays golf with the chief of police."

"Oh," I say stupidly.

"Always know who you're dealing with when you enter a fight, Mr. Ward. You didn't know who you were dealing with, did you?"

"No," I admit.

"I'm friends with the owner of the restaurant you were at last night. I asked him for the security camera footage. Would you like to change your story?"

"No, sir." I'm not letting an entitled brat fuck up Austin's career. "Camera angles can be misleading. Dumas insulted me and lunged forward. I thought he was going to attack me or Ace, so I hit him. Ace threw his hands up to block Dumas. I'm sure it must be hard to see it accurately at night when everyone was wearing a black coat." I use Austin's team nickname to downplay our relationship.

Mr. Dimon thrums his fingers on his desk, not breaking eye contact with me. Security camera footage is grainy, so with the wind blowing snow around, there's no way any video could be decisive.

"It was self-defense on your part. How fortunate for you that Mr. Brant was there to back up your side of the story." His shrewd eyes never leave mine. There's a surprising underlying venom when he says Brant's name.

"It wasn't a coincidence. Rhys said he followed the guys because they'd been hitting on some women and he feared for their safety." I blow out a breath and mentally calculate how long before my savings will run out if I can't find another job right away. Austin will never throw me out, but I need to pay my own way.

"Interesting. Would you be opposed to my looking through your phone?" He holds his hand out, assuming I'll comply, and I do after I unlock it.

He quickly scrolls through several things on my home page. "In the team group chat, you asked for Mr. Brant's number." He raises his gaze, waiting for me to explain.

"Yes. After we left, we were afraid Rhys might keep following those guys and run into trouble. You know Ace would blame himself if something bad happened, so I asked for Rhys's number so Ace could text him."

"And you did not text Rhys Brant yourself," he says sharply, more like a challenge than a question.

"No, sir. Ace had his number from the group chat so there wasn't a need for me to contact Brant. Ace is Tinny in my contacts. A nickname from middle school," I add at his raised eyebrow and glance at the logo on my shirt. Players have slightly different gear than the staff.

"What social media do you have?" he asks, and I list the apps I have on my phone.

He scrolls and when he seems satisfied, he returns my phone.

"I won't let outsiders dictate who I employ, but I am going to follow company policy. This situation has been blown out of proportion, and I'll do everything I can to minimize the impact on you. But Dumas is pressing charges, and per your contract, I have to suspend you until the issue is resolved. You'll have to go down to the station to make a statement of self-defense, and I'll send a lawyer with you." He stands and reaches across his desk to shake my hand. "I'm sorry I can't do more."

"I'm not fired?" I ask. My head swims with questions that I'm terrified to ask.

"No, wait by Wes's desk for the attorney to escort you to the police station. Here's the card of the detective you'll be speaking to. He's expecting you." He offers me the business card.

"Will I be arrested?" The insanity of the situation is beyond words. That little prick Dumas figures he can do whatever he wants.

"Not if I can help it."

I walk out in a daze and stop short when I see half the team waiting outside his office.

CHAPTER 33

AUSTIN

The locker room erupts with mayhem as our phones ding and ring simultaneously. My heart literally stops as I read the headline "Enforcers fire trainer for violent outburst."

It can't be true, but Wes confirms Grayson is in a meeting with Mr. Dimon, and we race to his office, forty minutes away.

He can't get fired for something I did. I won't take away his life for the second time. He says he doesn't blame me for the hit that ended his hockey career, but he'll hate me for this. My head is in my hands, and my teammates pat my shoulder and head to console me while we sit in Mr. Dimon's waiting area.

They don't suspect I'm the one responsible, only that I'm upset over Gray losing his job.

The door opens, and Gray stands frozen in the doorway. Behind him, Mr. Dimon rounds his desk to greet us.

"What's going on?" Mr. Dimon asks.

"Don't fire Grayson!" Benz shouts, clutching the crystal around his neck.

"We're protesting," King says.

I stand ready to confess. "You can't fire him for something I—"

"What gave you the impression I fired him?" Ari asks, genuinely confused.

"It's being reported on social media." Lucky strides over and shows him his phone.

"This is highly inconvenient, yet it could work to our advantage. Wes, get Finn in my office." The elevator dings, and a woman in an expensively tailored suit stalks over with her eyes solely focused on Mr. Dimon. "Grayson Ward, this is your lawyer. Please take the conference room for a consultation before you leave." He rounds on me. "Mr. Lapointe, in my office. Wes, let me know when Finn arrives."

As he speaks, a breathless Finn barrels around the corner. "I'm here."

"While I'm speaking with Mr. Lapointe, please review the rumors of Mr. Ward's firing and formulate a list of pros and cons of denying his employment status. Do not issue his previous apology. It could be construed as an admission of guilt." He waves me into his office, and I dutifully enter, taking a seat across from his desk.

Mr. Dimon says, "I'm speaking first. You should know I have surveillance video that shows the altercation and matches Mr. Ward's and Mr. Brant's accounts. If you were to dispute their statements, it would cause more harm than good for yourself and them."

I deflate, utterly helpless to solve this.

"This isn't right. There must be something I can do." My fame and money are useless unless I can help my man. But Mr. Dimon basically told me not to confess. Either because he knows the truth or presumes it's something I would do to help my friend. My boyfriend.

"Mr. Ward said you texted Mr. Brant last night. Can I see your text?"

"Of course." I slide my phone across his desk. It's the strangest thing, but Mr. Dimon says Rhys's name weirdly, similar to a curse, but with longing. Maybe I'm imagining it.

My text to Rhys is completely innocuous. I asked him if he got home safe or if he followed trouble and needed help.

"Do you have a personal relationship with Brant?" He scrolls through my phone.

"No. Last night was the first time I spoke to him outside of the rink." I shift uncomfortably in my chair.

"Does Mr. Ward have a personal relationship with him?" His questions are sharp, bordering on accusatory.

"No, why?"

"It strikes me as odd that Mr. Brant happened to be there and you became concerned over his well-being."

"Rhys thought the guys were harassing women and followed to ensure their safety. He's a good guy, and I had to make sure he didn't get jumped by two assholes for being a good Samaritan."

"So, you never asked him to corroborate your version of events?"

I lean forward and stare him in the eye, choosing my words carefully. "Grayson Ward is my best friend. I'll do anything for him, but I absolutely did not ask anyone to lie or hide the truth. I hope you know me well enough to take my word on that."

"I admire your candor and trust your word, but you might have guessed with the appearance of a lawyer that Dumas is pressing charges." He holds his palms up so I don't interrupt him. "Based on your account, Brant's corroboration, and the videotape, the charges will be dropped, eventually. The video shows Dumas as the aggressor. However, he's the mayor's nephew, so that complicates things."

I scrub my hand over my face. "I'll do whatever it takes to make this go away."

Mr. Dimon narrows his eyes, and I swear he reads my mind. "As you said, you'd do anything for Ward. Will he do the same for you? He had an interesting wardrobe choice today."

I get the impression we are no longer talking about the incident but life in general. He knows Gray is wearing my clothes or at least my shirt. It could be a laundry mix-up, but I'll never deny my feelings for Gray.

"Yes, it's very mutual." I give him a pointed stare. "We're a package deal. If he goes, I go. I won't allow this to take him down." Gray had no idea it would get this bad. We'll talk when he gets home. There might be a way for me to take responsibility without contradicting him. Maybe he'll agree to saying we both hit Dumas.

I expect Dimon to be angry, but he seems to approve with a dip of his chin. "Forward the text you sent Brant to Ward's lawyer and keep your mouth shut for now. If asked, your only, and I mean only, answer is 'No comment.' Finn should have a strategy, and I'll keep you in the loop." He stands and so do I.

Ari steps around his desk and places a hand on my shoulder. "Ward's a good man, and we'll take care of him." He hands me a business card for the lawyer.

"Are you sure another version of events won't fix things?" I choke out. This has gotten so far out of control.

"A late confession by anyone will be seen as a lie or cover-up. You can't fix everything, and we need you here. Let the lawyers deal with Dumas."

Gray doesn't come home for hours.

"Sunshine." As he walks in, I wrap him in my arms. "I'm so sorry, it's my fault."

"It's not. If you hadn't hit him, I would've. He's a smarmy little prick." Gray leads me over to the couch and crawls into my lap. "He reminds me of Richardson."

"That asshole?" I plunge my fingers into his hair and massage his scalp.

"My lawyer said if Dumas wasn't the mayor's nephew, no charges would be filed. But the kid has a black eye, and someone has to pay." He nuzzles my cheek.

"The team is behind you a hundred percent. They made it their mission to 'storm the castle,' as Benz said to show support for you. Everyone said to tell you they're ready to testify on your behalf if necessary." My stomach rumbles so loudly it changes the subject.

"Did you eat?" He doesn't say it, but his intake of breath and mouth falling open show his astonishment at the team's support. Gray has no idea how much the guys love him.

"Umm." I can't admit I was too worried to eat. "Have you eaten?"

"Yeah, the lawyer took me to dinner so we could conference call with Mr. Dimon and she could explain all the procedural shit." Gray pushes up and drags me with him to the kitchen. "You have to eat no matter how upset you get."

Gray props me up between the fridge and the stove to make me food.

"You don't have to do that. I can order something."

"We both know this will be healthier." He taps my nose like I'm a child.

"I should be cooking for you," I grumble.

"That's not as appealing as you think." Gray's grin causes my stomach to flip. "Besides, I can cook and tell you every dirty detail."

The smell of food makes my stomach rumble, and I rummage in the fridge to find a bag of baby carrots to munch on. It's well established that I don't excel at cooking.

"I'll give you the basic gist, then go into detail. I'm suspended per my contract until the investigation reaches a conclusion." He blows me a kiss when I make a strangled sound of disapproval. "Mr. Dimon has hired me as a freelance consultant as a workaround, while appearing to agree to Dumas's demands. I'll be in the booth watching the games, but I can't be near the team or anywhere the cameras are. Road games are a no-go, but he's hoping this gets settled quickly."

"Why didn't you let me take responsibility? They can't fire me," I lament. "I'll say we both hit him, and we don't know who gave him the black eye."

"Dumas could drag you through the mud and try to tarnish your reputation. He's a child throwing a tantrum."

"But I have a reputation as a peacemaker, not a fighter. That'll help," I argue.

"He's using his social media power to his advantage. It's amazing how a pretty face allows people to get away with shitty behavior." Gray stirs delicious-smelling chicken and spices.

"All the more reason it should be me," I say, moving out of his way.

"Because it's me, it will die out much quicker. No one cares if a random dude employed by the Enforcers decks someone. I will endure my fifteen minutes of fame and shrink back into the shadows. This could follow you for the rest of your career, especially if the douche canoe gets drafted. A rivalry every time you play. Never-ending headlines for years."

"I didn't consider that. Is he good enough to get picked?"

Gray's face scrunches up. "Yup. Unless teams suspect he won't fit in with their culture, but assholes like him and Richardson always seem to find a home."

He gives me the long version of meeting with the lawyer, talking to the detective, and the ordeal at the police station as I eat his delish food at the island. "I've never been the star of a video." A laugh escapes him. "I've always been the secondary player in hockey videos, and I gotta say, I don't mind the anonymity."

"Do you want to keep talking or take a break?" I lean over to stroke his back.

"Honestly, let's curl up in your bed and you can have your way with me."

Leaving my dishes behind, I heft him off the stool and into my arms. Tonight is the perfect night to manhandle him and make him forget about Dumas the dumbass.

CHAPTER 34

GRAYSON

The apartment is so quiet I can hear my heartbeat.

The team is on a string of away games, and I'm stuck here. But as a consolation prize, I have brand-new state-of-the-art computers and monitors to watch the team's live stream. It's not the same. We turned my room into a temporary office with the remote equipment required so I can do my freelance job. It depresses me because I hate the reminder of what I've lost, and Austin's room is lonely without him.

He's worried, and the more time goes by, the more my anxiety increases.

It's been weeks, and the charges against me haven't been dropped. My lawyer says it's Dumas's team's way of financially pressuring me to take a plea deal. I'd have to plead guilty to battery, which my lawyer said is out of the question because based on the video. I had reason to fear his aggressive behavior and should only consider plea offers of third-degree assault. I've learned so much concerning the differences between assault and battery and the degrees. Time wasted.

If I didn't have a lawyer, I would've caved and pled guilty to make it go away, but it's a risk since I could go to jail and be unemployable.

If Mr. Dimon weren't paying me a consultant fee as an independent contractor, I'd be living off of Austin.

The string of unhelpful what-ifs won't do me any good, and I unlock my phone to use my app to refocus.

The separation is harder than I thought. I miss Austin. I miss the guys. There's no way to check their pain levels without looking them in the eyes.

It all got so fucked up.

I watch the game in real time, and my assistant uses a video link for me to talk to the players between periods. When Austin's face appears, my eyes drink in his sweat, but he's too close to see any problems.

"I miss you," I blurt out totally unprofessionally.

In the background, Lucky yells, "Aww."

Austin mouths, "I miss you too." We stare at each other for a full minute without speaking. It's been years since we've been away from each other this long.

"Your right ankle turned in when you shot on goal in minute five." My eyes flick down as if I can see his leg.

"I didn't notice a twinge or pain." He grins at me.

"You favored your left leg after that so get some ice on it, and track it to make sure it was a fluke and not a developing ache." I've learned not to say problem or injury to the players. For them, it's inviting trouble. They live with constant aches and pains, so it's not upsetting to them.

"Will do, Sunshine." Austin touches the screen, and I do the same. "Only three more days," he whispers.

"Okay, my turn." Lucky plops onto Austin's lap and Drake growls. "Don't get upset, Daddy Drake, my Gray's gonna give me the breakdown of my body movements."

"Nothing looked out of the ordinary. Does everything feel okay?" I lean closer to the screen to see his eyes.

"All good, Sunshine." He smirks and Austin whacks the side of his head.

"Do. Not. Call. Him. That." Everyone in earshot is startled by Austin's venom.

My assistant takes the phone away so I can talk to more of the guys, which is good to take the focus off the way his anger is turning me on at being claimed like that.

The team scrapes by, winning two to one. It will be the first time Austin will be in the pressroom since charges were filed against me. Finn kept him out to give the story time to die.

The team's official response has been noncommittal, and the Enforcers have not confirmed nor denied my firing. Finn has fielded questions but maintains the team is cooperating fully with the investigation and following the proper procedures and guidelines until the truth is disclosed.

It implies the team believes I'm telling the truth regarding my self-defense, but this way they have plausible deniability.

Austin's got his interview face on, a polite but detached smile. Even though the team won, he's most likely beating himself up over a few blown plays.

The interview starts fine with hockey questions, but one reporter asks him about me. "Is it true that Grayson Ward, the accused assailant, is your longtime friend?"

"That description of him is false, but our friendship is well documented." Austin's jaw ticks.

The reporter yells another question without being called on. "Do you fear for your safety around him?"

Finn steps up to the mic. "No more questions regarding an ongoing investigation." He calls on someone else to ask a question.

Austin's fuming and after a few more questions, Finn announces time is up. Austin stands abruptly, knocking over the chair he's sitting in.

"I'd like to state for the record, Grayson Ward is one of the best men I know. I'm proud to be his...friend, and I've never feared him." He storms off camera, and it's a toss-up whether to kiss him or kill him.

My phone rings two minutes later.

"Tinny," I breathe.

"No shot you missed my presser, huh." He sounds defeated.

"I love you for it, but you shouldn't have given them any leverage." I wish I could see his face, but he's in the locker room, and it's common courtesy not to video while the team changes and showers.

"Ugh, I hate being so helpless. And the press dude looked smug as fuck."

"And you gave him what he wanted—a reaction." I lean back in my chair. "Someone is knocking on our door."

"Take me with you."

"You're cute when you worry," I tease, knowing he won't argue with me with the team there.

"It's an officer," I whisper. I'm frozen with the phone to my ear, one hand on the door, and looking out of the peephole.

"I'm right here. Hopefully, it's good news that the criminal case has been dropped." His voice is so excited that I don't bother telling him that's not how it works.

I open the door. "Can I help you, officer?"

"It's sheriff," he says indignantly.

"My apologies." I wait for him to state his business as he glares at me.

"Are you Grayson Ward?"

"I am."

"You've been served." He hands me an official envelope and walks away.

"What? What happened?" Austin shouts into the phone, and I'm glad the sheriff is down the hall.

"Hang on, let me open the envelope," I say, blindly walking over to the island to set it down and sit before my knees give out.

Carefully tearing the seal, I scan the papers, but my brain glitches, and I can't speak.

"Talk to me, Sunshine."

I let out a grunt, forcing my brain back online.

"Dumas is suing me. Lost playing time. Damages. Emotional distress. Five million dollars." My voice cracks on the last word.

"I will end that motherfucker."

"No, don't do anything. Promise me, Tinny." The quartz countertop cools my overheated forehead.

"I'll fix this," he vows.

"You can't take action without permission from my lawyer and Finn. Please don't accidentally make it worse." I'm not sure that's possible, but I won't tempt fate.

"Don't worry. He doesn't have a case."

"Yeah," I say, unconvinced. A civil case has a lower threshold for the burden of proof. "Let me call my lawyer, and I'll call you back." I hang up while he whispers he loves me, and guilt stabs me through the heart.

My lawyer has me scan the documents on my phone to send to her.

"This is very stressful, but it's not terrible news. My sources say the criminal charges are going to be dropped, so I assume this is a last-ditch scare tactic on their part. We're going to countersue for ten million," my lawyer says.

I smother a gasp. "What?"

"Trust me, it's not going anywhere. It's about optics and paperwork."

I bite back a rude comment about the lawyers winning with their paychecks. But Mr. Dimon is paying her, and it's not my business. My sole role is to do what she tells me.

After hanging up, I lie on Austin's bed and inhale his scent. I've never felt so alone, but I don't answer when he calls back.

CHAPTER 35

AUSTIN

I skate off the ice with my head down. Drake, the last person I expect, throws his arm around me.

"He'll be fine. We will make sure of it," he says in a low voice.

It's understood that 'he' is Gray. I'm playing like shit. If this were a tryout, I wouldn't make an AHL team. I grab my water bottle and focus on the game. My problem is that my mind wanders to Gray and the fact that he barely answers my calls and hardly texts back. He's spiraling, and I'm thousands of miles away.

The second period ends, and we're behind by one. Drake steers me into an empty video room instead of the locker room.

"I've watched my man self-destruct. The best thing you can do is keep your head in the game. If he sees you stumble, he's going to blame himself, and it will make everything worse." Drake speaks with the sincerity of a man who has lived it. Lucky's addiction tore him apart.

"I'm trying." My voice sounds weak and pathetic.

"The team is here for both of you. Lean on us." He up-nods to the door, and we enter the quiet locker room. Normally, I would give an inspirational pep talk, but Liska bangs his stick and does it for me. If goalies could be captains, he would be ours. That thought hurts more than it should.

The team rallies, but I'm a detriment instead of a help. I miss a pass from Drake, trip before a shot on goal, and lose the puck three times. I have zero points in this game, and although the team fights back, we lose by a goal.

As soon as we get back to the locker room, I dial Gray. No answer. It's possible he's talking to the coaches or Doc, but he doesn't send a text stating he'll call me back.

The only good thing is we're heading home in the morning. I need to see Gray in person and hold him in my arms.

No one argues with me when I say I'm skipping the team dinner. My stomach rumbles in protest, but I'm not in any condition to be around people. I spoke to my therapist earlier today, and she gave me some coping techniques to stop my perseverating thoughts.

Instead of using the strategies, I call Gray for the fifth time. My chest tightens when I get his voicemail. My thoughts get darker, and I imagine the worst. He's alone in our apartment and hurting.

The lawsuit is weighing on him. If it would help, I'd pay it so he wouldn't have to worry, but neither he nor his lawyer will agree to it. It's eating him alive.

Gray's in survival mode, and I'm not with him. The insane thought he might be hurt rears up and takes over my mind.

My head swims, and it's hard to breathe. There's a knock at my door along with the low voices of my friends. But I'm paralyzed and can't even call out to them. My survival instinct kicks in, and I drag myself to the door.

Suddenly, I'm surrounded by people. Benz and King guide me back to the bed. Benz's fingers dig into my jaw, and I'm staring at King's concerned aqua eyes.

"Breathe with us. There is plenty of oxygen in the room. Inhale." Everyone in the room takes an audible breath in. "Hold, one, two, three, four, five, and exhale." It sounds like a bunch of balloons losing their air. "You're doing good. Let's do it again." King leads me through the exercise five more times, as if it's a team participation activity.

"There's our captain." Benz flops next to me when my breathing becomes normal.

"You're always here for us, and now it's our turn," King says.

"We brought dinner." Lucky holds several bags in the air. "Nothing fancy, just subs." He and Drake pass them out.

I didn't think I could eat, but my stomach insists. "Thank you," I say lamely.

"Ve are here for you," Liska announces as if it's a decree of law.

My phone rings with Gray's song, and I lunge for it. "Hey. How are you? Everything okay? Where were you?" I ask without taking a breath.

My teammates, my friends, pack up their subs and quietly leave my room before I can protest.

"Yeah. Sorry to worry you. I took a long shower after watching the game." His voice is small, and I want to protect him from the world. "Are you okay?" His question heavily implies I'm not okay.

"Had a bad night for sure," I admit. "I'll bounce back," I say with false cheer.

"Tinny," he whispers. "I need honesty, not a press answer."

The silence stretches between us as long as the miles.

"Can't wait to be home. It's hard when you're not here. I'm worried about you." That's as honest as I'm willing to be. It won't do either of us any good to replay my panic attack.

"I miss you too. Don't let my situation hurt your game." He moves and there's a creaking sound from the couch.

"Get in bed, and I'm video calling you so we can fall asleep together. Plug your phone in so it doesn't die." I intend to watch him sleep and hear him breathe until morning.

His warm brown eyes hold so much uncertainty I wish I could crawl through the phone. We prop our phones up so it's like looking at each other from the next pillow.

"Hi, Sunshine." I focus on his face and block out all the negativity.

"Tinny," he murmurs, and sweeps his hair back. I like it spilling all over his face as if he were here and I could touch him.

"I'm coming home to you," I say, and a smile brightens his face. I exhale and give him a rundown of the locker room antics to entertain him.

My eyes get heavy, but so do his. I talk so much that he falls asleep first. His lashes rest on his cheeks, and he's so peaceful. I'm determined to give him that while he's awake.

I barrel through the apartment door, yelling for Gray. He stands from the couch, and even with the dark circles under his eyes and matted hair, he is so beautiful. Dropping my bag, I throw my arms around him and bury my face in his neck, inhaling his warm sweetness.

"I stink. Thought you'd be another hour." He sags into me.

"Skipped the crap and came straight to you." I'm usually the last one to leave, making sure everyone has their miscellaneous belongings and answering questions. Today, I bolted.

He palms the back of my head with a shaky hand. "We should talk."

We should, but first I'm reminding him of why we're so good together. "After a shower." I lead him to our bathroom. It's no longer mine; it's ours. Everything is ours.

"Sorry the place is a mess," he mumbles as I start the shower.

"The neat police are giving you a pass," I say, but he winces. He had to go back to the police station for questioning again, and I should shut the hell up.

We've said sorry to each other so many times that I don't say it again. I strip off the shirt he's been wearing for three days and get him naked and under the warm water. After taking off my clothes, I join him in a full-body hug.

"Tinny." His voice cracks as I hold him tighter.

"I'm not letting go," I assure him.

"But—"

"Shhh." I press my mouth to his. "Let me wash you, and then we'll talk."

Gray agrees and I wash every inch of his body with my mouth trailing along his newly clean parts. Water runs over his head, turning his hair into a dripping curtain.

"If you keep that up, you'll make me a mess again," he says as I kneel in front of him and tongue the head of his cock.

"Is that a challenge?" I ask and get a genuine grin that I haven't seen in weeks.

"I know better than to challenge you." He runs his fingers through my hair.

"I accept anyway." I swallow him down, and his moan helps me relax.

He tastes incredible, and I devour him as if I'll never get my mouth on him again. My fingers tease his balls and hole. When I press his rim, he shouts my name and comes down my throat.

Gray goes weak in the knees, and I support him. He tries to reciprocate, but the water is getting chilly, and I tug him onto the bathmat to dry him off.

He seems like he wants to protest, but I speak first. "I've wanted to lie next to you naked in bed the entire week. Get your sexy ass in bed and make my dreams come true." I smack his ass and ignore the haunted expression on his face.

We have to talk, but if I know him, he's going to want to leave me, and I have to convince him not to.

Once I'm wrapped around him, he speaks. "Tinny, this isn't going away. My lawyer predicts they're going to drag it out to bankrupt me into an admission of guilt."

"But that won't happen because you're working, and even if you weren't, I won't allow it. I love you." His pride won't allow him to live with me rent free, but I'm not letting him go. We have to find a compromise.

"It's affecting your game, your career. I can't weigh you down." He snuggles closer, clutching me, and his desperation scares me. "Dumas is a trust-fund baby and will do anything to save face. It wasn't a coincidence I got served while you were away. My lawyer thinks they are trying to build a case against me and have hired private detectives."

"That's insane. Your lawyer is exaggerating." This is not the plot of some crazy book.

"It's worst-case scenario, but Dumas wants to be drafted and can't afford the label of false accuser."

"I'm not trying to argue, but teams have drafted guys with way worse pasts." The league is improving its image, but this is less than a bar fight. "You promised not to leave me." I'm afraid of where this conversation is going.

"What if I took a vacation and went to see my family? I won't leave you, but maybe if Dumas assumes he ran me out of the city, he'll back off." He lifts his face, and I hate the pain in his bottomless eyes.

"I don't want you to go," I whisper. "It's selfish, but I need you with me."

"Two weeks. I'm paranoid and going crazy in this apartment. I'll go see my family and bring you back maple cookies." His forefinger smooths out my eyebrows.

"You have to answer my calls and texts. No avoiding me."

"Tinny, I'll talk to you so much you'll be sick of hearing my voice."

"Never," I say and he falls asleep. I have to get off the bench and into the action of our life. I won't sit back and watch the man I love destroyed by a child having a tantrum in the press. A plan forms and it gives me a sliver of hope.

CHAPTER 36

GRAYSON

"Are you icing it?" I ask Benz while I stare out the window of my parents' house into the blanket of snow. I forgot how much more snow we get in Canada compared to New York City.

"Leo's love bite? No. Are you listening to me or blocking me out until your man gets out of the shower?"

"Sorry, I zoned out." Benzy is a great guy, but when he talks, he changes subjects abruptly. I swear he was talking about his knee. Finn also sent me a video file that's burning a hole in my mind and phone. He never sends me things.

"I'm doing all the talking so you're not sad, but it's not working," he says.

"Thanks for helping Ace. He needs you guys." The phone rests on the arm of the leather recliner.

"I'm not doing this for Ace, I'm doing it for my friend." He huffs, and after a beat, he says, "You, ya idiot, you're my friend."

"Oh, yeah." I cringe at my response.

"Gray doesn't know how much we love him," Benz yells to the rest of the team. "But we can't do hug therapy because he's in a blizzard."

"Listen, Finn sent me something urgent, so I'll call back." I hang up before Benz can argue and take a deep breath. Three days here feels like a lifetime. Austin warned me that staying with my parents wouldn't be fun.

He didn't have to worry because they left the day after I got here.

That day was enough of them to last me for the next couple of years. My mom acting like I'm a convicted criminal on the run and my dad trying to get me alone to tell him the real story was exhausting. But then my dear older brother needed help with his kids, and they got in the car and drove the hour to him without a backward glance. My brother is a lazy fuck-up and their favorite child. His wife is divorcing him, and he's incapable of taking care of his kids on his own.

There's bitterness under my relief that they left. They see him and the grand-kids once a week, but they don't visit me or even show support. It's childishly ridiculous because I'd lose my shit if they were up my ass like they are with my brother.

Finn attaches a puzzling note to the email. "Don't say I never gave you anything, my little muffin. FYI, the meatballs were told to say 'no comment.'"

From the looks of the file, he's strung together a bunch of media clips. The first is Liska, who responds to a question about my lawsuit. "Grayson vas instrumental in getting me back on the ice after my concussion."

Lucky responds with his trademark cheeky smile. "I could've avoided a lot of pain and suffering if I had listened to Grayson. He's our owl and bear wrapped up in one."

My snort turns into a laughing fit. I'm sure that made sense in Lucky's mind. I guess he means I'm wise and fierce or protective. His bear reference isn't clear.

Benzy's baby face appears, and I brace myself for whatever will come out of his mouth. "Grayson's the man. He keeps us all in top shape. He's the best part of our team."

My eyes sting, and his words sink in.

King's aqua eyes go wide when he's asked about me. "Grayson's the real deal. We won't tolerate any trash talk about him."

There's video of most of the team giving me credit for helping them or hyping me up. It's too much to take in all at once.

Maybe it's the therapy session I had that kicks my insecurities in the teeth, but I'm overcome with gratitude and cursing myself for taking these men for granted.

I scroll through all the messages the team has sent me over the last month. Not addressing me in the group chat but sending me individual messages of support and encouragement.

My blood brother hasn't texted, and my parents express all their worry and concern but no empathy. The team and Austin care more about me than my family.

I'm foolish for thinking they only spoke with me as Austin's friend. They always include me, and my isolation is all in my head.

As if on cue, my phone rings.

"Hey, Sunshine," Austin says.

"Hey. You did much better in the presser," I say.

"I've mastered the 'no comment' response." There's a commotion, and he sounds muffled. "Hang on. I dropped the phone trying to put my shirt on." I hear more movement, and he says, "I'm back. The phone's on the bench where it should be stable, but you're on speaker."

"No kissy-face," Benzy teases.

"Meanwhile, he was telling me about the marks Leo left on him," I shout to ensure Benz hears me.

"Don't we have doctor-patient confidentiality?" Benz pouts.

"Dude's not a doctor," King responds, and I can hear the exasperation in his voice.

"Gray, we need you to cheer our captain up and give him some loving," Lucky chimes in.

"I'm fine," Austin growls. "I'm going somewhere else to video call you." His face appears on my phone, and I accept the call.

"Sunshine," he murmurs, and pets my cheek on the phone.

"You aren't fine," I blurt.

"If you let me tell the truth, I can make it better for both of us." His face twists in frustration.

"It's too late. Dumas is petty and won't let it go. At the very least, they'll prosecute me for lying to the police and charge you to make it worth their while.

And they'll dissect our relationship. We can't let the team lie for us." We've been over this, but the guilt is killing him, and it shows in his playing.

He got the nickname Ace for being a sharpshooter. He hasn't had a goal or an assist in three games.

"We should come out now with a statement about us," he says defiantly.

"I love you." His face lights up at my words. "I love how much you love me...but...don't do anything without running it by Finn, who will probably talk to Mr. Dimon."

"You're always so logical," he grumbles with a grin. "You don't want the world to assume my playing sucks because I miss my boyfriend," he says sarcastically.

My face goes all soft and mushy in the camera. "I like it when you call me that. But don't make me the most hated man in New York City. Enforcer fans will blame me for everything that goes wrong. Sports gossip sites already say the team—aka me—is withholding you have a serious ankle injury."

"Fine. It's completely fabricated, and we aren't living in fear of Dumas or the fans forever. I'll retire before I let that happen. This year if I have to."

There's a gasp behind Austin, and he turns, but I can't see around him.

"Benzy," Austin calls. "Shit." He's jogging, and all I see is the ceiling bouncing up and down.

"Ace said the R word," Benz moans. From the little I can see, they're in the locker room.

Austin remembers I'm on video and holds the phone so I can see Benz collapse on the bench as the team turns sullen with understanding.

Liska strides to the rarely used whiteboard. "This vord?" He writes "retire" in black marker and Benz nods. "Because of the lawsuit?" He stares at me and Ace like he's looking into our souls. "I vill take care of it," he announces, and leaves the locker room.

Lucky makes a call with his phone to his ear. "Hey, Trevor, quick question. Is your fiancé in the mob?" We hear a roar of laughter on the line. Lucky shrugs and hangs up. "Had to ask."

We talk as he goes to dinner with the team until his phone dies mid-sentence. I get up and wander into the kitchen to find something for myself to eat.

My phone lights up with a text from Finn.

> **Finn: I heard a rumor Ace said retire**

> **Finn: Is he serious?**

I'm unsurprised Finn already knows. He hears ev-er-y-thing.

> **Me: We can't let him retire**

> **Finn: Don't tell me the obvious, sugar britches. Give me solutions**

> **Me: I got nothing**

> **Finn: *middle finger emoji***

This is not the time to view myself as an anchor around his neck. Neither of us will be happy apart, and I promised not to cut him loose. It's exhausting fighting the lawsuit and my mental chaos. I owe it to him to get my shit together.

My phone rings and it's him. Austin is the best medicine I have.

The team is fighting for me the only way they can, with positive statements in the press. My lawyer is doing everything she can to protect me. I have to steel my backbone and stand up for myself.

I muster a smile and answer. "Hey."

CHAPTER 37

Austin

I'm nothing but a lying fucking liar. I've spent my entire life trying to live up to other people's expectations of me, and now all I can do is lie.

Brant promised me he'd ask around and we'd find the women Dumas was harassing the night I hit him. He asked me to be patient, but my boyfriend has fled the country and I'm out of fucks to give. I'll hire a private investigator if I have to.

My game suffers and speeds by me as if I'm playing underwater. The team has rallied around me to pick up the slack, but it's not enough. Coach assumes I'm in a slump and gives me more ice time than I deserve.

Lying has become a sickness I can't stop. Doing the right thing will cause damage and harm, but doing the wrong thing is killing my soul. The team is better when I'm not on the ice, and for the first time in my career, I fake an injury to remove myself from the game.

It's surprisingly easy, given that there are already rumors. I've seen how Gray evaluates players' bodies and know what to say. When a defender slashes my ankle, I turn it inward and go down. I tell the assistant trainer I'm fine but yelp when he takes my skate off. I sigh with relief when Coach tells me I'm not going in again.

My teammates vow to win for me, and they come from behind to avenge me. Drake and Lucky combine to score, and King finds the back of the net. Benz makes incredible saves.

We win. And there's no joy.

I'm not the man I thought I was.

Ari Dimon intercepts me on the way to the locker room. "Can I have a word with you?" He asks politely but doesn't wait for an answer as he ushers me into the nearest office. "How serious is your ankle injury?"

"I haven't had a full eval, but from experience it's not serious." I lean against the wall to stand on my "good" foot.

"Glad to hear it." Mr. Dimon clears his throat. "Are you doing okay?" The weight of his stare and tone nearly breaks me.

I open my mouth to tell him I'm fine, but I shake my head instead. "Everything is wrong, and it has gone on for too long. I'm done." I say defiantly.

"The lawyers are pressing to close the case. How is Mr. Ward holding up?"

I shrug. I'm saved from answering when Wes, his assistant, knocks on the door.

"Sorry to interrupt, but I thought you'd want to hear this right away. Rhys Brant is at the police station, and the press is there."

Mr. Dimon's body convulses before he closes his eyes and locks his emotions down. "What does that have to do with me?" he snaps.

"He went to make a statement about the night Ward hit Dumas, and he took two women with him." I'm out the door, running to my phone before Wes finishes his statement.

There are missed calls and messages from Brant. I listen to his last one. "Hey, I hate to do this without you, but tomorrow I've got a road trip, and one of our friends is a server and works later. I'm taking them to the police station, and we'll all make statements. I'm an eyewitness so it won't be weird. I hope. Anyway, call me. Later."

There's a hush in the room, and I hear Rhys's voice on someone else's phone. I'm surrounded by media personnel and bombarded with questions about the video. I'm thankful I already listened to his message, but I can honestly say I never saw Rhys's statement. There's talk about a second video from that night from a different vantage point and I ask to watch it. Without a doubt, it looks like self-defense, and, more importantly, in the audio, Dumas is the aggressor.

It's the only positive news I've had in weeks. A reputable reporter uses her phone to cue up the video of Rhys standing outside the police station.

"When I heard the charges were still pending despite the video evidence, I felt it was my civic duty as a witness to come forward. The police hadn't interviewed me yet in their investigation, and my friends"—he gestures to two beautiful women beside him—"provided their account with Mr. Dumas that night."

My phone goes off with Gray's ringtone, and I rush to answer it, unofficially dismissing the reporter.

"What did the trainer say about your ankle?" he asks before I can say "hello."

"Haven't seen him yet. Do you know what's going on?" I'm purposely vague.

"Austin, go see the trainer!" he huffs, unintentionally answering my question.

"Listen, search Rhys Brant and call me back." I hang up and dial Rhys.

"I owe you one," I say instead of hello. "The press was a nice touch."

"That part was pure luck and a hockey fan." He chuckles. "I hope it puts pressure on the lawyers to drop the charges against Ward. Not gonna lie, the police are mad about it."

"Thanks again, I gotta roll." I hang up to answer Gray's call.

"When are you coming back?" I blurt out. In my bones, I know Rhys's statement along with the two women will be the tipping point to end this nightmare.

He hesitates and dread poisons my mind. My finger hovers over the video button as I rush out of the locker room and find an empty room.

His tired face has a small smile when he answers my video call. "Tinny," he rumbles, and his use of my nickname eases my tension. "How's your ankle?"

Of course he's worried more about me. "Totally fine. A strange phantom pain that's gone." I beg, "Come home. It's not over, but I miss you and need you."

His eyes get glassy, but he shakes his head on the pillow. "It's not that simple."

The darkness rises, but it's my fear of rejection. Of loving Grayson with my whole heart and not being loved back. It's not darkness, it's despair.

"Sunshine, you're not here to lift me up. I need you." My entire world crumbles as I realize I'm begging him to love me. "I give zero fucks about headlines," I snarl. I regret my tone as his face crumples and decide to switch tactics. "All this means nothing if you're not by my side. I'd rather never score another goal than score a hundred more without you."

He covers his face with his hand. "I love you, but there's a snowstorm and I'm stuck.

CHAPTER 38

GRAYSON

I sit in the recliner and watch the snow continue to fall. My parents were right; if they hadn't left when they did, they might not have made it to my brother's house. It's been snowing for days, and the schools are closed. All the flights are delayed or canceled.

Not being able to leave is killing me. Austin thought I was giving up on us, and that is not acceptable. His doubt, even for a second, crushes me because I should be the one he can count on.

The bottle of whiskey is heavy in my hand, and I rub my heart with the other.

I'm to blame for him not being in the right headspace to play hockey. I made the wrong decision by coming here, and now I'm trapped in the snow. We're both unraveling, and it's too dangerous to go back to him. I take another sip of whiskey.

I'm hurting the man I love because I'm scared that someday in the future he might change his mind.

I

Am

An

Asshole.

He begged me to come home, but I stubbornly thought I knew better. My reasons for waiting were based in fear, not reality. And I made it so much worse.

Austin has worked hard for his career, and he can't retire for me. It will be the kill shot to our relationship.

He'll be happy at first. But I've felt the shock of not playing hockey. Little things will sneak up on him. He won't be on the All-Star team, and that day will be a gut punch. If the team makes a run for The Cup without him, the FOMO will eat at him. He'll be lost on draft day and during rookie training camp because he won't be taking new players under his wing.

A hundred little moments will add up to a gaping hole in him. He'll resent me because of his retirement. Austin might not do it purposefully, but the bitterness will grow, creating distance between us.

I should've gone home yesterday when I had the chance. Missing him is a physical ache.

The thought of him making a statement about his sexuality while I'm away haunts me. I need to be there for him. He doesn't fully understand that he won't come out once. It'll be necessary to come out every time he meets someone new. He'll have to come out hundreds of times. His parents were easy compared to the hate he'll receive from anonymous people hiding behind their screen names.

I bring the bottle to my lips and take another swig, wallowing like a child. Austin's been clear he wants us and for me to be with him. I've given him a reason to doubt my love and commitment.

I'll call him first thing in the morning. There's too much whiskey in me to talk again tonight, and even with one eye closed, I can't see my phone to send a text.

My phone rings on my chest, and I jerk awake in the recliner. I fumble to answer it in the muted light of early morning.

"Tinny?" I rasp.

"Mr. Ward?" Mr. Dimon asks, and I pull the lever on the recliner, sitting up with a gasping grunt. "Are you drunk?"

"Uh, no? Maybe?" I slap my face to get my brain cells working. "How can I help you, sir?"

"I want my trainer back," he says bluntly. There's a pause, and I should speak, but I don't know what he's saying. "Did you speak to your lawyer?"

"Umm." I search my phone and see two missed calls. "She called, but I was asleep."

"Ah, let me be the one to give you the good news that the criminal charges against you have been dropped. You're free to come back to work."

I shut my eyes, daring to hope. "What about the civil case?"

"Based on the evidence, it shouldn't be a problem. Will you be in today?"

"I'm, uh, I'm in Canada, and there's a snowstorm." There's a blanket of white with no distinction of the roads. "I'll be back as soon as possible. Thank you."

Since it's early, I text Austin to call me when he wakes up. My phone rings immediately.

"I'm so sorry, I pushed you away when I should've pulled you closer. I love you. Please forgive me," I rush all the words out.

"You're coming home." The certainty in his voice brings me to my knees.

"Yes, but there's that inconvenient snowstorm still standing in my way. I spent last night trying to get any flight out here but there's nothing," I ramble.

"We'll figure out a way." I hear the smile in his voice.

"Oh, the criminal charges were dropped." Getting home to fix things with Austin is crucial, and everything else can wait.

"Wait. Did you say the charges were dropped? Why aren't you happy?"

"Because I'm coming home for you, not my job." I punch my thigh at my stupidity at not leaving yesterday.

"Sunshine, if you say you love me and you're coming home, I believe you. I'm texting you a quote since you're not here for sticky notes." My phone beeps, and I read *You have bewitched me, body and soul, and I love, I love, I love you*. Pride and Prejudice.

"I don't deserve you."

He switches to a video call, and he's breathtaking. His short hair is sticking up, and he looks like he hasn't slept, but he's the reason my heart beats.

I let out a slow breath. "I love you so much it hurts."

"Same. How can I help you get home?"

"You got any pull with Mother Nature?" I might have to rent a car instead of waiting for a plane.

The storm swept through Canada and then barreled down the East Coast, knocking out power and closing airports.

"Our game is postponed," Austin says, staring at me through the phone from our bed.

"It's the damn apocalypse. Maybe I'll find a polar bear to ride down on." I refresh the airline page, then shut my laptop. "The airlines are all grounded, but of course rich people can use their private jets." I snort at the hypocrisy. "If the airports don't clear flights in the next few hours, I'll drive back."

Austin's face scrunches up and brightens, not matching his words. "Ugh. Team business. I gotta go. I'll call you back." He blows me a kiss and hangs up the phone.

In the past, his needing to get off the phone for team business would've brought on a strong bout of otherness. Now I'm secure enough to tell my destructive inner voice to go kick rocks.

The plow clears the road, and I snow-blow the driveway so I can leave quickly when the time comes. I dwell on the fact that I didn't solve anything by coming here, and now I can't go home.

There's been no new snow since this morning, but a few highways are closed due to large snowdrifts and dangerous ice. Hopefully, I can fly out tomorrow. As long as the weather holds, everything should be clear.

The mindless physical activity gave me a chance to register the relief of the criminal charges being dropped. The threat of jail no longer looms over me, and the weight of anticipation has disappeared. I've been granted a reset on my dream life to appreciate every precious minute with the love of my life.

Austin and I play phone tag for a couple of hours. Finally, we're able to talk around dinnertime.

Austin can't stop smiling, but I can't place his background. "I have a surprise. It's a good one, but don't book a flight until you talk to me."

"What, you need extra time to pull this off?" I tease and he turns pink.

"Something like that. I gotta go."

"Call me when you go to sleep so we can stay on the phone all night."

"I can't wait to see you." His blue eyes crinkle with happiness.

"Don't get your hopes up. They have to get all the stranded people to their destinations before I can book a flight. It could be another day," I say softly, not wanting to disappoint him.

"Right. All positive thoughts." He snorts. "Do I sound like Benz?"

"Almost." I laugh. "I love you."

"I love you more."

***

I've worn a path in the carpet from pacing. I'm not worried, but I'm far from stress free. He promised me a good surprise, but it doesn't make sense in a snowstorm.

Suddenly, I hear a horn beeping repeatedly. Out the picture window, I see a van pulling into my parents' dark driveway. I smirk, thinking it has the wrong house, when the door slides open and Austin pops out, followed by Liska, Drake, Lucky, Benz, Griff, King, and Kenney.

"How?" I fling the door open and run out in my socks.

"Hi, Sunshine." Austin picks me up, and I wrap my legs around his waist.

"Six out of ten," Lucky declares, and we all turn to him. "The classic run and jump got off to a slow start with a small leap, but you finished strong with the leg wrap." He grins as if he makes perfect sense.

I hook my legs tighter and take Austin's mouth.

"No—" Benz starts.

"Back off, they're allowed kissy-face," King cuts Benz off.

"What are you all doing here?" I allow Austin to carry me back to the house since I don't have shoes on.

"You said rich people could fly, so I thought of the team jet and called Mr. Dimon. He's at the airport waiting for us, so hustle and get your crap. I'm taking you home." Austin pecks my lips and sets me on my feet. "Go." He smacks my ass.

"But why is everyone here?" I call over my shoulder as I run up the stairs.

My bag is packed, so I'm back in seconds.

"We weren't going to miss Operation Retrieve Sunshine," Drake drawls in his Swedish accent.

"He's *my* Sunshine," Austin growls fiercely, as if they've already had this disagreement.

"But why? You were going to see me soon." I'm confused.

"We did this wrong." Benz throws his head back and groans.

"We weren't doing a choreographed dance," King admonishes him.

Lucky holds his hands up and wiggles his fingers. "Congrats on not being a criminal."

I sink down on the bottom step. "Thank you?" I'm not sure how else to respond.

Liska pats my head. "I told you I'd fix it. And we did." He gestures to Austin.

"What did you do?" Austin jolts in surprise.

"You have friends. I have friends. Friends help friends." Liska shrugs with a smug smile.

"Friends?" I parrot like an idiot.

"The hardest part of this surprise was making sure no one texted in the friend group chat," Drake says.

My gaze travels over the men in my parents' house. I took their loyalty for granted because I'd been oblivious. It was as if I couldn't accept their friendship at face value; I put limitations on it that were all in my head.

These men are the best friends I've ever had. I can count on them to have my back. My eyes sting as I take them in and feel like today, my nickname should be Lucky.

King taps my head. "Low-key, he's having a moment. Let's wait for him outside."

They file out the front door as Austin picks up my bag and holds out his hand. "Come home where you belong, Sunshine. Our friends are waiting."

"Our friends." I grin like an idiot and follow him out. After the team spoke up for me, I knew they had my back, but this is on an entirely new level.

In the middle of hockey season, when they have almost no time to spend with the people they love, they chose to get on a plane to come get me. That's ride-or-die friendship right there, and I've never been so grateful.

My life reset is off to a spectacular start.

CHAPTER 39

AUSTIN

I'm a full-blown addict because I can't stop touching Gray, or inhaling him, on the drive to the airport. The guys notice but, for once, are keeping their mouths shut.

"There's one thing you have to promise me," Gray murmurs.

I sit up straight, removing my nose from the crook of his neck to look at him. "Anything."

"No matter what happens, with us or the civil suit or coming out, you can't retire from hockey." He's serious.

I scoff, but he silences me with a kiss.

"In terms of hockey, you have way more experience than I do, except in how it feels to lose it. Some mornings I walk into the arena and smell the ice, ready to lace up my skates, and it's still a shock to remember that playing is in the past. It will sneak up on you when you see a headline about your teammate. The loss will steal your breath with a sharp pain in your gut. Don't lose hockey because of me. It will tear us apart." He cups the side of my neck, and my pulse hammers under his hand.

"I won't be able to live with the guilt. It will ruin us. Promise me." His eyes bore into mine as if he could extract the promise by sheer will.

"But if I have to choose between you and hockey, I choose you." There is no choice. Grayson is my future, and hockey is a job. I've lived the dream, and although it will be hard to quit, being away from Grayson tears me apart.

"I will never make you choose. Even if we're separated by distance, we'll make it work. Any obstacles will be temporary, but your legacy is forever. Don't cut it short and regret it."

"I'll do what's best for both of us," I assure him. I won't lie and make a ridiculous promise.

"No, we'll talk it out, and you'll play hockey until it isn't fun or your body gives out."

I cover his mouth with my hand. "Do not speak that into existence," I hiss. I'm not the most superstitious hockey player, but I'm not tempting fate. I won't want to play if it becomes a job, so I'll convince him whenever I decide to leave hockey behind.

"I have a demand as well." I fist my hand in his silky hair so he can't look away.

"Reeeally?" His mouth quirks up.

"Really. From now on, for the rest of your life, I'm your New Year's Eve kiss. It's how we started and a tradition from now on." My decree turns his big brown eyes glassy.

"That's the easiest promise to make. You're the only one I want to ever kiss." He seals his pledge with his lips on mine.

Our van rolls up to the tarmac at the airport, and we board the team jet. Mr. Dimon is on board, working in the back.

We all take our regular seats even though the jet is almost empty.

A flight attendant announces the plane needs to be de-iced before takeoff, so there will be a delay.

"Thanks for coming to get me." Gray pulls up the armrest so he can snuggle close.

"I wasn't going to spend another night without you." I drag him into my lap and rub my cheek on the top of his head. My eyes drift shut, and I'm close to drifting off since I haven't slept well in days.

My body jolts from a tap on my shoulder, and Mr. Dimon stands over us. "I'd like a word with you two in the back, if you don't mind."

Grayson scrambles up, and I drag a hand over my face, following them. We sit in luxury chairs facing each other with a table between us.

"First, I'm happy you're back, Mr. Ward." Mr. Dimon's tone is formal, setting me on edge.

"Thank you, sir."

"I won't waste your time with small talk. We'll need to make a few changes based on your current relationship, specifically, Mr. Ward, you cannot treat Mr. Lapointe."

I'm ready to argue, but Gray lays his hand on my thigh. "Of course, it would be a conflict of interest, and I won't risk him or the team. But as of now, we don't have a plan to announce our relationship publicly."

A growl escapes my throat, and Mr. Dimon raises an eyebrow.

"Austin, don't bend under pressure to come out. You're already under scrutiny because of me, and we shouldn't add to it."

"What difference will it make?" I'm not proud of my childish question.

"If I may interject, you have two choices." Mr. Dimon folds his hands on the table. "You can wait for a better time to make an announcement, such as the off-season. The advantage is you'll be out of the spotlight. The disadvantage is that it prolongs the time you're the source of gossip and speculation. Or you could get it all out at once. Make a statement about the altercation and both criminal and civil charges and your relationship. Include anything I left out." He chuckles. "You will be hounded, but we're experienced at protecting our players from mobs. Liska is a hard man to disguise, but with Trevor's help, we kept photographers away from him. Take your time to discuss it, but I've set up a meeting for you with Finn. Do you have any questions?"

"What specific changes do I need to make to keep my job even though we're in a relationship?" Gray asks.

"The lines were blurred regarding our policy since you two had a personal relationship before Mr. Ward began his job, and the organization overlooked it. I won't stand in the way of your relationship or Mr. Ward's livelihood," Mr. Dimon states matter-of-factly.

"Shit." My mind races with all Grayson could have lost because of me.

"You will both sign new waivers, and Mr. Ward will agree not to treat you, Mr. Lapointe."

"But he's the best," I blurt out.

"It's a power imbalance if my treatments and assessment of your fitness affect your playing time. If you're hurt, I'll make sure your treatment is appropriate." Gray nudges my shoulder.

"I didn't hear that." Mr. Dimon shakes his head. "No one told me running a hockey team would be so similar to facilitating a dating app." His smile contradicts his stern tone.

We return to our seats for the short flight. Sleep will have to wait.

"I can hear you thinking." Gray's lips move against my neck.

It's embarrassing to admit he's right. "Should I come out now instead of later?"

"Are you ready for it? Did you change your mind?" He throws a leg over mine as if to comfort me.

"I don't want to hide you or sneak around." It's hard to put into words all the things I want at the same time that are in direct conflict. Like telling the world I love him and keeping our relationship out of the public eye.

"We don't have to decide today. Once you're ready, we'll do it."

"It's that simple, huh?" I rub his thigh, bringing him closer.

"It's never going to be simple, but we're in it together." He ducks his head and curls into my chest.

"I like the sound of that." I wrap my arms around him.

CHAPTER 40

GRAYSON

I leave the flogger on the edge of the bed as a hint when I go to prep myself.

When I return naked, Austin stands next to the bed fully dressed.

"Where do you want me?" I ask, not giving him time to back out.

He points to the bed, and I climb up onto all fours. My hard dick bobs, hitting my stomach. Austin slaps the inside of my legs, so I widen my stance. My full balls hang on display for him.

"I've been obsessed with your ass since Vegas." He trails the falls over my cheeks and lets them gather in my crease, then moves them lower to my sack.

I let out a low moan.

"I could eat your sounds." He continues to tease me with the flogger and light touches.

There's already a shift in our dynamic. I'm usually the dirty talker to keep him out of his head, but I love hearing his breathless words.

"Your cock is leaking. Is it for me?"

"Yes, for you," I groan.

"Tonight, I'm proving to you who you belong to." He strikes the back of my thigh and I squeak.

"Green, green, green," I ramble, loving his confidence.

"When you beg me, I'll take my cock out of my pants and fuck you until you can't walk."

"Yessss." I drop to my forearms.

He peppers my backside with hits, and I moan like a slut.

"When I smack your hole, there's a stream of precum. Gather it up for me," he orders.

I capture the string and shove my hand between my legs, offering it to him. He bends and sucks it from my fingers.

"My favorite snack."

The flogger snaps through the air.

"Harder," I cry. It's so much lighter than his hand.

The only warning I get is the swish before he spanks me. "My hand was getting jealous and wants in on the fun."

He's reduced me to grunts and groans. The weight of his hand and the thud bring me to the edge. All my nerves are on fire. It almost makes me laugh how worried he was to use the flogger, and I like his hand better.

My skin becomes hot and tight. He massages it and soothes it with his tongue. I push my ass back, trying to get my balls and dick closer to his face.

Austin tsks me and resumes his play. "Should I keep your skin bright pink or turn it red?"

"Turn it red. Green light," I gasp.

It's his turn to groan, and he pulls my cheeks apart to lick my hole. "I can't hold out." He buries his face in my ass while spanking me.

"More," I beg.

Austin pushes my chest down on the bed, and I hear the rustle of his pants behind me. I glance over my shoulder to watch him lube my favorite toy—his dick.

I rest the top of my head on the bed so I can see him between my legs.

"Sunshine, you're sucking my fingers right in." He works me open, and I curse him for taking so long. "Hang on." He slams in, balls deep.

My face smashes deeper into the mattress, and I chant his name. He pulls out an inch at a time and snaps his hips, returning all the way in with a single thrust. Austin does it over and over. I'm mindlessly babbling and begging for more.

He rotates his hips and pegs my prostate. "So close," I pant.

"Not yet." He pulls out and flips me over. "I'm going to watch you come all over my cock and get yourself all dirty." Austin pushes back in, and I grab his face to kiss him.

Our tongues twine, but the pleasure builds so high, I'm only capable of sharing air with him.

"You're all mine." He bites my neck, and I scream his name. "Louder," he commands.

Every cell in my body explodes with searing pleasure that I feel from the top of my head to the bottom of my toes. I twitch and spasm with each new wave as he fucks me through my orgasm. It's too much and not nearly enough.

I lock my ankles around his back, pinning him to me.

"Mine," I say, and he chuckles in my ear.

"Yours," he agrees. "I love you." He circles his hips and loosens my hold on him. "Now I'm gonna fill you up."

"I need it." I arch toward him to fuck myself on his cock.

"I'll always give you what you need." He fucks me so hard I have to brace my legs on the bed so I don't go flying.

"Sunshine," he gasps as his stroke falters and he empties himself in my ass. The warmth of his cum coats me as he collapses on my chest. "Welcome home."

"I hate being away from you, but I'm so into welcome-home sex. Let's make it a habit."

"Deal." We lie half on and half off the bed. Eventually, we straighten out and get under the covers.

"I love you, Tinny," I mumble into his chest, but he's already asleep.

◆◇◆

I wake up feeling his stare. "What?" I ask without opening my eyes. It's too early to get out of this bed, and let the real world close in because I'm not ready for reality.

"I was thinking." Austin pushes my hair back and traces my widow's peak.

My eyes blink open. "Mr. Talkative is at a loss for words. Should I be worried?"

"I'm unsure when I'll be ready to come out." His blue eyes fill with pain. "There will never be a right time, and the longer I wait, the worse my stress is going to get."

His confession doesn't end the same as it began. "What are you saying?"

"Pride Night is next week. What if we don't make a statement? We could walk out holding hands and not confirm or deny anything. Drake and Lucky sort of did that when they kissed on camera, and Leo and Benzy have never admitted to being in a relationship. We can be like them and just be together and act like it's not a big deal. Because it's not."

"I disagree. Being your partner is a very big deal. It's the best deal of my life." His heartbeat increases under my palm. "Teasing," I say, and peck his lips. "I know what you mean, and I'll do whatever you want. I've come out, and I'm not famous like you are, so I'll follow your lead."

"Is it a good idea?" He sounds unsure.

"Holding your hand on Pride Night in front of the fans? Priceless." I roll him under me. "How much time do we have?"

CHAPTER 41

AUSTIN

We scheduled Pride Night for our last home game of the regular season. In a perfect world, we'd schedule it in June for Pride Month. But it's not a guarantee we'll have a home game, *and* it's taunting the hockey gods.

The team is aware of our plan, and Finn met with us to discuss our statement. It was trickier than I thought because of the league's stance on player/trainer relationships.

I crane my neck. "Do you see Brant?" Since we're playing the New York Nationals, Rhys Brant wants to join us on the ice for Pride Night. His team doesn't involve LGBTQ members in their celebration.

It seems like all of New York showed up to support us.

Sunshine laces our fingers together. "He might have a hard time getting permission to leave his team for enemy territory." Gray appears calm, but he's eager to thank Rhys in person. His statement to the press and at the police station brought a public outcry to the case and ultimately forced Dumas's attorney to drop both the civil and criminal charges. From what Gray's lawyer said, Dumas's father was the force behind pressing the lawsuits.

"True." The visiting team's locker room and entry to the ice are on the opposite side of the arena. "I gave security a heads-up, and Finn said he'd escort him if he comes over." Brant is half out. His team, friends, and family know, but he hasn't discussed his sexuality publicly. We've texted a bunch of times since the altercation with Dumas, and he's a great guy.

The crowd is fired up because we're in the playoffs and playing great hockey. Earlier, I saw the sea of Pride jerseys, and it brought tears to my eyes.

"Look alive, my stud muffins. The show's about to start." Finn rolls up with authority and deposits Brant behind us.

"Hey, man, good to see you." I let go of Gray and give him a buddy hug.

"I'd give my left nut to play for a team like this." He grins, peering down the tunnel.

"I'm so grateful to you, man." Gray wraps him in a two-arm bear hug. "Thank you."

Mr. Dimon exits an office, and I wave him over. "Mr. Dimon, have you met—" He abruptly turns and stalks away before I can introduce him to Rhys. "That was weird."

The music blares, and the announcer gives his cue for us to walk onto the ice. There's a rainbow carpet for us, and the players have their skate guards on.

We walk forward with Jayce McKenna, our Director of Player Development, his wife Madyson, and fiancé Emmet, at the front of the procession. The cheers are deafening as we reach the end of the tunnel.

"This is the greeting I imagine we'll get when we win The Cup," I mutter in Gray's ear.

My chest fills with a surreal pride as we walk forward. In addition to a sea of Pride jerseys, there are Pride flags and banners waving. The song "Pink Pony Club" works the crowd into a frenzy.

My sister, Lori, is in the crowd tonight for support. She's been an amazing ally and has kept our parents from spouting homophobic rhetoric. I can't see her yet.

King stumbles, his ankles turning in. He glances over his shoulder with wide, terrified eyes.

Grayson lunges forward, calling my name, snaking an arm around King's waist. We flank him to keep him upright. The one word I would use to describe King is smooth. Ten months make a world of difference. He arrived shy and cautious, but as he became comfortable with us, he's shown his strength and unflappable demeanor.

He handles insults on the ice better than most veterans and moves with grace and ease. To see him stumble is more than disconcerting.

"They'll all know," he whispers, shrinking into himself.

"We've got you." Gray tightens his arm around him. "They don't know shit."

"You're an ally," I declare, giving him an out if he's not ready for this. Some members of the organization are walking out to represent their loved ones and aren't technically a part of the LGBTQ community.

My fears about people's perception of me have vanished as I concentrate on King.

"Smile for your parents," Grayson urges him.

"I'm ruining your moment." King tries to break away from us but trips.

"We're good," I assure him.

"This could be hilarious." Brant steps up even with us. "The rumors of you guys in a poly relationship like McKenna are going to be delicious. I want in on this." He drapes an arm over Grayson's shoulder, and I fight the urge to snarl at him since he's helping King.

King stifles a laugh and smiles.

My insides are ready to burst with the acceptance and love the crowd is giving us. "I wish I could bottle this," I say in awe.

"This matters," Gray agrees. "For all the scared kids who think no one will understand or love them, this is life-changing."

With that, King steels himself and steps forward, out of our arms, to wave at the crowd.

"You did good," I praise Grayson for helping King find his strength. Spontaneously, I kiss the side of his head, and there's an audible gasp from the crowd.

"Cat's out of the bag." Brant whoops and throws his arms around both of us. "I should kiss you both." He laughs and ruffles our hair before going to stand next to King on the rainbow carpet. His energy reminds me a little of Benz, but he's got a redheaded temper for sure. Playing on the same team as him would be a privilege.

I'm floating on air, ready to fight for every goal to bring The Cup to this city. Of course, I'm getting ahead of myself and tempting the hockey gods.

We start off on a high, and Drake scores in the first three minutes. But then Kenney gets his stick on the puck by our goal and gets tangled up with their winger. He goes down and doesn't get back up.

Gray vaults over the boards to tend to him.

"I heard a pop," Kenney groans. Gray and I carry him off the ice, and they disappear into the treatment room.

Benz is hyping up the bench, and I join in. "We've got this, team. Make Kenney proud."

The Nationals are a young team that didn't make the playoffs this year, and they're resorting to violence. I can hear Brant's voice telling his teammates to chill out.

In between periods, the team doctor informs us that Kenney has an ACL tear and Grayson has taken him to the hospital.

I give a speech about rising above adversity, and Lucky loosens us up with a two-minute dance party for extra good luck.

During the third period, I take a hit from the back that pitches me forward on the ice, and my helmet hits first. It makes me woozy, but I stumble over to the bench unassisted, grateful I wasn't hurt worse.

Next thing I know, I'm opening my eyes to King and Brant kneeling over me, yelling my name.

King and I are never on the ice at the same time because we play the same position.

And I don't remember taking the ice for my next shift.

The arena is too quiet.

"Sunshine," I call for Grayson. "I need Sunshine." He'll know what to do.

The doctor and assistant trainer help me off the ice and won't let me sit on the bench. I'm taken straight to the treatment room.

Everything is hazy, and I don't understand why Gray isn't with me. He's always there when I need him.

The doctor says "concussion" as if it's not the first time. That's when I notice the team gathering in the doorway.

"Did we win?" I ask.

"We did." Drake takes a step into the room. "We can take him home," he says to the doctor.

"Sunshine will take me," I insist, looking around for him. "Hey, Lori, when did you get here?"

"I was in the neighborhood and showed up for Pride Night." She's wearing a Pride T-shirt we sell for fans.

"Cool. Where's G?" I have a killer headache, and my eyes won't focus.

"He's with Kenney. He'll meet us there," Lucky says softly.

"You're all being weird," I mutter.

***

I wake up with a start, and hands push me back on my couch, but they're the hands I want.

"Sunshine?" My voice sounds distant as I keep my eyes shut and fumble around for him.

"I'm here." Gray kneels beside me, cradling my face.

"Don't take my sunshine away," I sing and giggle.

"Is he going to be okay?" Lori asks.

"Lori? You came to visit?" I squint at her but can't fully open my eyes.

"You betcha, big bro."

"Can you swallow these pills?" Gray asks, and his smile lights up the room when I do.

The next time I wake up, we're in bed.

"Hey, what's the date?" he asks. The question throws me off, and I stare at him. "Okay, sleepyhead, I'll start easy. What's your name?"

"Austin Powers Lapointe," I answer.

"Close enough." He laughs. "What's my name?"

"G Sunshine Ward." I pat his face. "Why are you asking me?"

"Sorry, Tinny, but you have a concussion."

"No, I don't."

I wake again to bright lights and Doc talking to Grayson. "What's going on?" I ask.

"How much do you remember about last night?" Doc asks.

I sit up, thankful I'm not naked. Gray wouldn't call Doc if one of us suffered a sex injury. "Umm."

"It was Pride Night," Grayson prompts.

"My head hurts." I rub my temples.

"It's only been three hours," Gray says to Doc.

"His pupils look good, so if he stays awake for an hour, give him more acetaminophen; otherwise, promptly when he wakes up again." Doc turns to me. "You had us worried. It's good to see you awake."

I tilt my head; my brain has a hard time processing his words.

I am literally on the sites that make fun of people coming out of anesthesia, but my actions weren't from a drug but confusion. Gray blames himself for not being there, but he was doing his job. Despite my protests, I apparently have a severe concussion. Grayson panicked when my symptoms didn't get better the next day and took me to the hospital for an MRI. No brain bleeds or swelling, just me acting like a moron.

Lori stayed the night with us but had to leave for work. Gray assured her I'd be fine. Fine is relative, if you ask me.

"He's seen it," Gray whispers to King as he lets him into our apartment.

"I'm not deaf," I grumble. After I took the hit in the game, I got up and skated to the bench, and no one noticed anything was wrong until I started yelling "Sunshine" and toppled over the wall onto the ice.

The reputable news outlets are using the incident to warn of the dangers of concussions, but social media has turned me into a meme. To make matters worse, neither Kenney nor I will recover in time for the playoffs.

"I'm gonna take a quick shower," Gray announces, and leaves the room.

"I don't need a babysitter while he's in the shower." I fold my arms across my chest like a child.

"Actually, I came to thank you. We talked on the phone yesterday, but I'm not sure if you remember our conversation." King sits on the other end of the couch.

"Thank me?" I snort.

"For holding me up on Pride Night. I sorta lost it." He stares at his hands. "I thought I was good...but I was out there raw with all those eyes on me."

"Oh, I'm sorry," I reply, still having a hard time putting thoughts together.

"The upside is all the fun speculation." He meets my eyes with a small smile.

"Huh?"

"I thought Gray said you saw it." King turns around with panic in his voice.

"I saw me stumble over the wall and pass out on the ice. What else did I do?" I ask suspiciously.

"You didn't do anything else," he assures me. "I'm glad the MRI looks good." He changes the subject.

I stare at him for a beat before Grayson rushes back into the room with wet hair, wearing my clothes after taking a three-second shower. It's cute he knows it makes me happy to see him in my sweats but annoying he's afraid to leave my side.

"I'm going to go." King shoots up.

"Sit," I order, and my eyes swing between them. "What don't I know yet?"

Gray approaches slowly and sits next to me on the couch. "Doc advised me to limit the information I give until your brain is ready to handle it. I'll tell you one thing, and if your head hurts or you're confused, I'm waiting to tell you the rest."

My head bobs in agreement because I can feign understanding and project being fine.

In my peripheral vision, King sits in the recliner.

Gray takes my hand. "King had some anxiety after we walked out on the carpet, and the two of us supported him so he didn't trip or fall." My hand motions for him to continue. "Do you remember, before you left the carpet to be with the team, you kissed the side of my head. It's on camera and everyone noticed."

"Understatement," King mutters.

"Is that your polite way of telling me I outed myself?" My face breaks into a wide grin.

"That and we're internet memes. So we're trending on all social media platforms with some creative captions."

My head swims a little, but it's funny. "And you released the prepared statement?"

Gray shakes his head. "It was something we agreed to do together, and you couldn't make any decisions. I'd never out you unless I knew for sure without a doubt it's what you wanted."

"You doubt me?" My voice cracks, and King fidgets uncomfortably.

"Can I bounce?" King asks.

"Not until I know how this involves you," I say.

King minds his own business and never gossips, so even though his presence seems irrelevant, he must be involved.

King hangs his head, and Grayson assures him none of this is his fault.

"Finn fell back on the standard statement, saying the team doesn't comment on players' personal lives and we've been friends for years. But some social media felt the need to dig deeper and have insinuated that the three of us are in a relationship or possibly us with Brant too. I'm not joking when I say you're trending. Your name is searched more than Taylor Swift."

My back hits the couch as I howl with laughter, but that hurts my head, and I have to stop. "Are you okay?" I ask King.

He glances away and rubs his hands on his jeans. "It's nice to have the focus off my relationship with my bio dad and stepbro. Also, peak comedy." His smile is tentative.

"How about Brant?" I ask Gray, not wanting to make light of a situation that devastates someone else.

Gray rolls his eyes with a relieved laugh. "He's playing into it, and it's hilarious." Grayson explains Brant's post-game press conference after my concussion. Brant got angry at a reporter for asking about my sexuality after my injury. I'm confused how that relates.

"That was for context. Here's the short clip getting attention." He pulls out his phone to cue up a video showing Rhys Brant surrounded by paparazzi, trying to enter his building.

He tells them he'll answer one question, and the pap asks if he's my Sunshine. Brant's face gets serious, and he says with honest innocence, "I don't know." He's silent for a beat, then says, "But wouldn't that be cool as fuck? I'd be so honored to be his Sunshine or Ward's or King's. If any of you are looking for a man…" He puts his hand up to his ear like he's holding a phone and whispers *Call me* while staring straight at the camera. He shoots finger guns and turns around. Over his shoulder, he says, "Have a good night," then disappears into his building.

I blink several times after the video stops. "He's eating that shit up." I chuckle. "What's the fallout from that video?"

Without pausing, King chimes in. "For real, I called him, and we're together now."

My mouth drops open. "What?"

G Call me waves his hand. "He's kidding. You're kidding, right?"

King stands and shrugs. "Real ones move in silence." He strides to the door. "I got your back."

"He's messing with us?" I say as a question.

"I think so." Sunshine bites his lip.

"We're totally showing these memes to our future kids." I pounce on him.

"We are not showing our kids memes about fucking other people." His mouth twists with indignation.

"Fine." I use other methods to put a smile on his face.

CHAPTER 42

GRAYSON

By the time the horn blows, signaling the game's end in Boston, my team is defeated literally and emotionally.

The Enforcers' playoff run has ended, and I'm nervous about Austin's reaction. He hasn't taken his restrictions well, and I'm grateful I'm not allowed to treat him. I love him, but he's a terrible patient. Luckily, I don't have to argue with him about protocols. Officially not my job. I assumed that I'd always be on Austin's side for treatment, but brain injuries are tricky. Most of the time, you don't know if something is too much until it's too late.

He has pushed himself too far a few times, and it's slowed his recovery down. His solution for forgiveness is to leave me massive amounts of sticky notes. I woke up with one on my forehead that said "Mine." Did it melt me like a holiday candle? Yes. Did I still lecture him? Also, yes. But I was naked so it probably wasn't effective.

With the playoffs and celebrities behaving badly, our memes are old news. I saved them on our phones in case we need a good laugh. Austin has never been afraid to make fun of himself, so I worried needlessly.

The Boston series has been a mindfuck, to say the least. Their top defender, Theo O'Keefe, couldn't play for shit. He's King's stepbrother and usually plays like King and the rest of the team have insulted his entire lineage. O'Keefe didn't get into one fight or try to get away with any shady plays.

In Boston, all the players exit and enter the ice from the same tunnel but turn opposite ways at the end.

I've treated all the minor injuries, and the guys won't come for my help to stretch out until after they shower. Austin and Kenney are coming down from Ari Dimon's suite, and I'm waiting for them by the elevator in the tunnel nearest to Boston's side. Part of me wants to give Austin a big hug, and the other part wants to assess him. I wouldn't have let him come if I was in charge of his treatment.

He doesn't need this stress combined with guilt, noise, and bright lights. If I had my way, I'd strap him to the bed and not let him up until he was fully recovered. Probably overcautious.

Down at the end of the tunnel, King's still on the ice, talking to his parents in the stands.

He's handling coming out with grace and determination. Because of all the outrageous rumors, he's having fun with innocent yet suggestive comments with Brant and me. Austin's head hurts when he tries to read his phone, so he hasn't joined in on the jokes yet.

King makes his way down the tunnel, and when he gets close enough, I offer my comfort. "Tough game. You looked good out there."

He scoffs, but he had a goal and an assist. Our trouble was that without Kenney, our defense fell apart.

"Hey, Jamal, do you have a minute?" O'Keefe steps out of a doorway, still in his uniform but missing his stick.

"Not the time to gloat," King bites out.

"No, it's not that." O'Keefe's face is pink, and King jerks with surprise. "Can we talk for a minute?" His eyes cut to mine. "Privately?" They are opposites in looks. King has dark skin and black braided hair, and O'Keefe could give a ghost a run for his money, except he has green eyes. Eyes that are so intent on King, he makes me nervous.

"I'm not going anywhere with you, but we can talk right there." King points to a spot a few feet away. I give an up-nod to confirm I'm here if he needs me. Hopefully, O'Keefe isn't dumb enough to start a fight with me as a witness.

"What?" King snaps when they pause.

O'Keefe's demeanor is nonthreatening, almost apologetic, looking at King anxiously.

I turn my back to give them some privacy, but I can hear O'Keefe whisper.

"Listen, I saw you on Pride Night, and—" he cuts off with a strangled sound.

"Is that your problem?" King sneers, and I whirl around to see him pin O'Keefe to the wall with his forearm to his throat. "You didn't play us because you're afraid you'll catch gay. You really are a piece of shit." King shoves him and stalks away.

O'Keefe rubs his throat and slumps dejectedly against the wall as he watches King's back. When King disappears out of sight, he faces me. "That's not it. I'm not homophobic," he says with a tortured expression.

The elevator dings, and the door opens to reveal Austin, Kenney, and Mr. Dimon.

"What's going on?" Mr. Dimon's eyes sweep between the two of us.

"Nothing. Just asking if he needs help finding something." O'Keefe turns and walks away.

They look at me, and I notice the security cameras. O'Keefe could be setting King up.

"Can we talk and walk?" I ask, sweeping my hand toward the locker room to explain everything, although both O'Keefe and King would want it to stay private. Mr. Dimon alerts Finn of the altercation and goes to speak to King.

Austin leans against a locker frame and closes his eyes.

"You okay?" I ask, moving to his side.

"Other than sitting idly by and watching our Cup dreams die, I'm fine."

<hr />

I wake to Austin's incredulous voice. "Holy shit."

"What's wrong?" I roll to face him and see his eyes wide.

"Check me out." He opens his eyes as wide as possible. "The light doesn't bother me. It's like the fog has lifted. I know it should come gradually, but I'm a new man."

My first instinct is to grill him with cognitive questions, but that's not my job. My job is to be his supportive boyfriend. "Best news of the day." I kiss his jaw.

"Let's make the news even better for today. I'm dying to be inside you. I need to fuck my boyfriend." Austin stretches his neck to give me access to his Adam's apple.

"Yes, but we need to take it slow." I pin him with my leg and grind on him.

"Not slow." Austin gathers my hands and pins them over my head.

"Such a bad patient," I murmur in his ear, and watch him shudder. "We're fucking but no pounding my ass like the sex-deprived maniac you are. We can be gentle and have incredible orgasms. Trust me?"

"With my life." He bites my bottom lip.

Austin pulls me back when I reach for the side table. "Lube." I wriggle out of his hold, and he lets me go. The cap snapping open echoes in our quiet room. "You can have the pleasure of opening me up, or I can do it. I'll be faster." I hold the bottle out of his reach.

"You are not depriving me of any part of your ass." He snatches the lube from me and positions me flat on the bed. "It's been torture. You back this ass up against me while we sleep but declare it off-limits." Austin settles between my legs and kisses the tip of my leaking cock.

His slick fingers rim me, and I angle my hips, spreading my legs wider.

"I'm not the only sex-deprived maniac in the room." Tinny sucks my inner thigh and leaves a mark.

"Hurry," I groan, fucking myself on his thick fingers. "We'll do it on our sides."

He pushes a third finger inside me and sucks my cock down.

"Tinny," I cry, already close to the edge.

"Don't you dare come until I'm inside you." He yanks his fingers out as my dick falls from his mouth. A chuckle escapes him as I growl in protest. "On your side. Tell me how we're doing this."

I sink into the bed and pull my top leg up to my chest. "Fuck me like this, and I'll show you a trick." My hand comes into contact with his hip, and I pull him toward me.

"Trick sex, huh? Interesting." He lines himself up, and the stretch of his entry is the most welcome burn. My body has been hungry for him. Each stroke is slow, and I feel every inch of him.

I reach one arm back behind my head to thread my fingers in his short hair. He circles his pelvis and hits my gland, sending sparks of pleasure throughout my body.

"I never want to live without you," he pants in my ear. "You are the most important person in my life."

"I'm here, Tinny. I'm yours," I declare, and his fingers dig into me. His thrusts get harder and wilder, which we need to avoid. It could prolong his recovery or worsen his symptoms even though he seems symptom-free.

"Get ready. We're turning so you're on your back." I palm his ass cheek to keep our bodies connected and rise up so when he's lying down, I'm riding him reverse cowboy.

"Holy fuck." His hands wrap around my hips and pull me down onto his cock. "In my life, I've never seen such a beautiful sight as your ass swallowing my cock. You're sucking me in. Sunshine, I won't last long."

"Thought I was the dirty talker." My words come out breathy. "Fill me up so you're inside me all day." I increase my pace, slamming onto him.

"I want everyone to know you're mine and I'm yours. So they know we chose each other and no one else can have you. Ever."

His words light up all my senses. The privilege of being claimed by my Tinny, my Austin, known as the famous Ace Lapointe, is monumental.

"No one else. Ever." My hands are on his shins as we work in tandem to fuck me on his cock. Tinny moans and his legs spasm. He's close, and I don't want to miss watching his face while he orgasms. "Hold on, cowboy." Even with my best effort, I can't swing around and keep him inside me.

It's worth it to see his eyes roll back in his head as I impale myself on his rock-hard length.

"I'm so close." His hands circle my waist, thumbs stroking my stomach.

"Don't hold back. Give me your cum." My fingers splay across his chest, giving me leverage as I grind harder and faster, sweating with the effort.

I lean forward, and the change in angle creates a delicious drag against my prostate. My orgasm goes from a building pressure to a detonation of all of my cells. I'm scattered everywhere.

Tinny gathers me in his arms, buries his face in my neck, and pumps his cum into my ass. His embrace, whispers of love, and a flood of cum, bring me back together piece by piece. I'm disconnected, but he's here to catch me and make me whole.

We're clinging to each other as if afraid something will rip us apart. The only sounds are our harsh breaths and racing hearts.

With tremendous effort, I ease back. "Look at me, Tinny."

Gorgeous blue eyes, filled with love, meet my gaze. His pupils are a normal size, and I move a finger for him to track.

He bursts out laughing. "No one else could blow my mind and then examine me for a head injury. I love you more than words."

"We can't be too careful." I smack his ass. "Your brain is a vital part of you and, dare I say, one of your most important organs. We need to treat it with reverence and vigilance."

"We should take a vacation, and I'll let you pamper me and my brain in luxury."

"Don't tempt me." I lay him down while he's still lodged inside me.

"I'm serious. As soon as Doc clears me, we should go somewhere. It will take my mind off not being in the playoffs." He pushes my damp hair back and cups my face. "With my concussion, the team isn't counting on me for anything. It's a rare time with no expectations."

"You're serious." My heart rate kicks up. Tinny hasn't taken more than a long weekend off in years. So long I can't even remember.

"Let me take you away. Pick anywhere and we'll go."

My brain turns to mush as if I'm the one with the concussion. I love traveling with the team, but we don't get to sightsee. The world suddenly seems too big, and the possibilities endless. It's impossible to choose one place.

"Think about it and let me know." He kisses me tenderly.

"I've always wanted to go to Greece. I fantasized about going to Camp Half-Blood with Percy Jackson as a kid and—"

"I'll book us tickets," Tinny interrupts me, reaching for his phone.

Joy bubbles inside me like a tangible thing. "Slow down, Ace," I tease. "One thing at a time. Make an appointment to see Doc tomorrow, and we'll plan from there."

"Whatever shall we do until then?"

"I dreamed of strapping you to this bed." I lace our fingers together and pull them above his head.

"I'm all yours, Sunshine."

EPILOGUE

AUSTIN

The sun's bright, and I slip my shades on outside the arena. "That went better than I expected," I admit.

"Yeah?" Gray reaches for my hand but stops himself.

"I could tell my head was better, but Doc is a stickler, and I was afraid he wouldn't agree." I'm not cleared yet, but in Doc's opinion, I should be able to fly in a few weeks, which gives us plenty of time for a vacation.

"It gives us time to really plan it out and make a stop along the way so the flight is shorter." He's always one step ahead. Long flights could increase my chances of headaches, dizziness, or even a seizure, and Athens is a ten-hour flight.

"What should we do today?" I grasp his hand and won't let go when he tries to pull out of my iron grip.

"Tinny, what are you doing?" he asks softly.

"I'm spending the day with my boyfriend and not worrying about things that don't matter." My grip loosens because I won't force him into a public display of affection.

"It matters." His thumb strokes my hand, and my anxiety melts away.

"Not as much as you." I change the subject so he can't argue with me. "I want a normal day like a normal person. Why don't we stop at the grocery store on the way home? We can get steaks, junk food, and dessert." Sometimes I wish Finn and Gray had made the statement about our relationship without me.

Like, if the decision was out of my hands, I could separate myself from anything negative afterward. It doesn't make sense, but I just want it done.

He stops to face me and places the back of his hand on my forehead. "You don't have a fever, so the only explanation is you're an alien in my boyfriend's body."

I tug him along. "Funny." I've never suggested buying junk food, but life is for living.

We don't live far, and there's a grocery store only a couple of blocks away.

"I know you're not always recognized out in the wild"—He waves his hand around the store as we step inside—"but someone will notice." His gaze drifts to our linked hands. "If you're ready to do this, we can talk about how you want to do it."

"Do you ever get tired of having to plan things with me?" I wheel a cart around and head to the produce section. "I mean, people dissect and analyze everything we do and say. Honestly, it's not that serious."

"Since when?" Gray stops in the middle of the aisle with his hands on his hips, challenging me.

"It's all about perspective and not letting the negative in." I continue as he frowns in disbelief. "When I was drafted, bloggers said I was a mistake the Enforcers would regret. When I made the All-Star team, a lot of people said I didn't deserve it. I had a severe concussion diagnosis from both the team doctor and an emergency room doctor, and there are rumors that I faked it because I knew our playoff chances were over with Kenney out."

Gray's arms drop to his sides, and his face softens.

"Those things don't bother me. If they did, I wouldn't be able to go out on the ice and prove them wrong because I'd be stuck in my head with self-doubt. You mean more to me than hockey, and I don't care what people say. Maybe it doesn't have to be a big deal. Maybe it can just be real."

"What do you mean?" Gray's gentle doe eyes and smile take my breath away.

"It doesn't have to be an elaborate, scripted plan. We could do it now. Come here." I hold my hand out, and he takes it.

"Finn will murder you in your sleep," he says with a chuckle.

"I'll have you to protect me." I take my phone out of my pocket and hold it up for a selfie of us. Right before I click the button, I look at him. Gray gasps when he sees how I'm staring at him because it's obvious I'm in love with him. And we are wearing the same shirt. Twinning again.

"Tinny." He sucks in a breath as I open a social media app to post our picture.

I type the caption: *So grateful to be feeling better and out shopping with my boyfriend. My Sunshine. He's the biggest score of my life.*

"You ready for this?" I ask, searching his eyes.

"So ready." He rests his head on my shoulder as I post the pic to make us internet official.

"We can get some fruit for smoothies." I steer the cart up to the peaches.

"When's the last time you bought your own groceries?" Grayson scoffs.

He's not wrong. I've had groceries delivered for a few years. I pop into the store only if I need one or two things.

"I've been missing out." I hold up a big peach. "This looks so juicy." As I pretend to take a bite to tease him, he snatches it out of my hands.

"Do you know how many germs are on this? Not to mention it's stealing. I can see the headline: *Enforcers star forward steals fruit and blames concussion.*"

I back him up so his ass hits the crate of peaches. "Then you'd better let me lick your peach later."

"That can be arranged." He bumps my chest to move me. "Now let's get food so we can go home and eat." He says the word eat with so much innuendo I get hard. "Someone took a pic of us," he says out of the corner of his mouth.

My phone rings, and Finn's avatar takes over my screen.

"I warned you," Gray says smugly.

He could be calling about releasing info on my health status, so I answer.

"Would it kill you meatheads to give me a heads-up?" Finn fumes before I say a word. "I spend all my time trying to present the best version of you to the world, and you have the audacity to post a picture in some random store? The lighting was terrible. It's a beautiful, sunny day. You could've used the skyline to highlight actual sunshine as a visual cue to his nickname. But no, you—"

"Finn. Finn, are you there?"

"Don't you—"

"You're cutting out. Finn? I—" I hang up the phone and put it on silent. "Terrible reception in the grocery store." To see if anyone else has seen my post, I open my app. It's only been a few minutes, but it's been reposted hundreds of times. There are tons of likes, and the top comments are from my friends.

Lucky: Second cutest couple on the Enforcers *eggplant emoji*
Benzy: Hey, @Lucky, not funny. Glad you're doing better @ace
Drake: @ace is in the scoring zone *fire emoji*
Brant: My heart is shattered *broken heart emoji*
Brant: Call me @King
King: @ace rest up for next season, bro
King: @brant show me what you got. I'm not that easy
Liska: @ace now I'll teach you the handshake

"Handshake?" Gray asks as he takes out his phone and types.

"The gay handshake?" I laugh, unsure if they're all fucking with me. Even though I'm watching him, I'm surprised he's added to the comments.

Ward: @ace you had me at hello. Jerry Maguire

He puts his hand over my phone. "That was an answer to your note that you complete me. Now, we could laugh at these guys all day, or we can go home and practice what you *peach*." His brown eyes smolder with his pun.

"Have I told you lately that I love you?" I abandon the cart and yell over my shoulder. "I'll get steaks, and you get dessert, and I'll meet you at the checkout." We need to get home as quickly as possible.

"Race you," he calls after me.

I hope you loved Austin and Grayson because they stole my heart. I send them to Greece and use my vacation as inspiration. There's a chapel on the hotel grounds, find out if I wrote a vacation or a honeymoon! Bonus Epilogue: https://dl.bookf unnel.com/n87c7fl775for Scoring Zone Greece trip

BONUS – END OF JUNE

JAMAL KING

I'd be lying if I said I wasn't stressed about this meeting with Mr. Dimon. To distract myself, I open my social media app. I've peeped at Wes, his assistant's body language, but he's giving nothing away.

Brant's responses on our socials have me rolling. No one can tell whether we're flirting or being sarcastic. It's eased some of the pressure of coming out, as people speculate about our non-relationship. I'm learning how to let false rumors fly. It's so easy when everything is untrue, but it's good practice for when I actually decide to date somebody.

Dating hasn't been my priority. But watching my teammates find love has been inspiring. I've never known a same-sex couple who are openly out and engage in PDAs. There've been guys I suspected of being involved with other men but not confirmed.

"Mr. King, thank you for waiting." Ari Dimon stands in his doorway, as intimidating as ever. The fact that he called me to his office right before July 1, free agency has messed with my head.

I had a great season, but players get traded all the time. We're deep on offense and short on defense, so I could be on the chopping block.

Mr. Dimon leads me into his office, across the purple Enforcers logo on the carpet. I wonder if I'll wear it next season.

"Have a seat. Sorry for the short notice, but as you know, trades are worked out behind the scenes before they're made public." His brow is creased, which is a sign of stress for him.

This is not going to be a good meeting.

"It's not a secret that we need qualified defenders." He leans back in his chair, but his body is tight with tension.

I sit in the type of silence where you know some shit is bout to drop.

"We drafted a couple of great players, but they aren't ready to step up and play immediately. My goal is to win The Cup next year. Do you understand what I'm saying?" He steeples his fingers, waiting for an answer.

My mind races for an answer. "That's the plan for me too," spills out of my mouth, and I about punch myself in the face. He's about to trade me, and I tell him I want to win The Cup too.

"That's what I like to hear." He smiles and I didn't see that coming. I'm tripping.

I expect Lucky to jump out laughing. Mr. Dimon isn't the type for practical jokes.

"Our best strategy is to trade for current qualified defenders. This team is my chief priority, which means I take your physical and mental health seriously. We can't win if we don't stand together."

My head nods in agreement as if on autopilot.

"If this is going to be a problem, you need to tell me now, not after the season starts." Mr. Dimon flexes his hands, and I brace for the bad news.

"Theo O'Keefe will be a free agent. Can you play with him?"

Nothing in this world could've prepared me for his question. Memories of meeting him when we were seven pop into my head. He'd wanted to be my friend until his mother dragged him away.

Every single time we played each other, he came at me like I'd held him back. As if he was the poor Black kid and I was the rich white dude born with a silver spoon. He taunted me and took shots at me as if I'd disrespected him. If anyone should hold a grudge, it should be me.

I had to fight poverty, racism, and homophobia to get where I am. He just had to show up and skate.

"Mr. King?" Mr. Dimon raises his eyebrows.

"He's the one with beef. I'm not the one you need to worry about," I say with my chin held high.

Mr. Dimon studies me, and the silence is uncomfortable.

"If we trade for him, can you find a way to work together?" he asks.

"Yes," I answer, and wonder what I've done, so I add, "But I doubt he'll say the same."

"Thank you for your honesty, Mr. King." Mr. Dimon stands to shake my sweaty hand. "Nothing is final, but I will keep you informed so you don't have to find out on the news."

"Thank you, sir." My head spins and I'm shook.

Before I leave, he says, "One more question. I've heard your father is a difficult man. Is that true?"

"He's not my father." I turn back to face him fully, with my feet shoulder-width apart and my hands linked in front of me. "He's nothing more than a sperm donor. He was never in my life until it looked like my hockey career would blow up. That relationship only exists in his mind."

I wait for backlash or admonishment, but Mr. Dimon nods, dismissing me.

Theo O'Keefe sits in Mr. Dimon's waiting area. To prove I'm the bigger person, I give him an up-nod and leave.

He can be the one to trash-talk me and blow his shot on my team. His sorry ass can go somewhere else.

But two days later, I get a call from Mr. Dimon. Now I gotta rock with the same man who tried to tear me down: Theo O'Keefe.

I regret telling Mr. Dimon I can play with him.

Enemies to teammates. You can't make this shit up.

This season is fucked, and it hasn't even started.

Enemy Zone will be Jamal and Theo's romance set to release in April 2026. Pre-order here!

BOOKS BY HEATHER LEIGHSON

ALL BOOKS HAVE A GUARANTEED HAPPILY EVER
AFTER & QR CODES ON LAST PAGE

UNFRAMED ART MM ROMANCE NOVELS

The Truth of Loving You Book 1 – Cole and Shane MM

He's the worst mistake I'm dying to make

Cole is on dick-hiatus so a relationship is out of the question. Shane has one
focus—his career until he's sidetracked by an unexpected attraction to Cole.
They are complete opposites, with 100 reasons why they shouldn't get involved.
But walking away isn't an option. Not when forever is at risk.

The Truth of Our PastBook 2- Alec and Von MM

He's a contradiction I can't resist

Alec wants what he can't have—Von. Von's obsessed with Alec's dimples and craves his comforting, quirky charm after enduring a tragedy. Knowing their relationship is doomed doesn't change their explosive chemistry. Alec suggestions a sexuation, since love isn't an option. Spoiler alert: love wins.

The Truth of Our Secrets Book 3 – Emmet, Jayce and Madyson MMF

Three hearts. Two secrets. One Epic Romance

Jayce does everything in his power to prevent Emmet from rekindling a relationship with his wife. Madyson's desperate to reconnect with her former student Emmet, since he ghosted her four years ago. Emmet wars with his desire for the man who took away the one person who believed in him. Although their past is full of lies, their forbidden craving is undeniable. Emmet is exactly who Jayce needs if he can see beyond his jealousy to choose both of them. True love hinges on the truth and forgiveness.

ENFORCERS MM HOCKEY ROMANCE SERIES

Truth Zone

Prequel – FREE for newsletter subscribers – Patrik and Trevor

I can stop a puck but I can't stop falling for him

Patrik pines for Trevor from afar, afraid to get too close because Trevor could ruin his carefully constructed life. Trevor has zero interest in hockey, but the mountain of a man slips past his defenses and into his heart. Their forbidden attraction has disaster written all over it. But the more time they spend together, the harder they fall.

Misconduct Zone

Book 1 – Lars (Drake) Drakenberg and Dylon (Lucky) Felix

Two men. One team. Love changes the game.

Lars is determined not to ruin their friendship by falling for his sexy, straight teammate, but his heart believes Dylon is his. Lars will do ANYTHING to protect what's his even if it means hurting himself. Dylon owes Lars his life and his hockey career, but soon realizes he can't live without him. Dylon is terrified his past is too much for Lars and intrusive thoughts could ruin everything. Hockey's just a game—but Dylon and Lars are searching for forever.

Penalty Zone

Book 2 - Caleb Benz (Baby Benz) and Leo Griffin
The hardest thing to defend... is my heart
Caleb's obsession with his best friend's dad started years before they met, and he's kept it a secret. But now he's working with the object of his desire, feeling Leo's amber eyes like a physical caress. Leo Griffin's blindsided by his attraction to a submissive Caleb and the risks he's willing to take. But for the sake of his son, he can never truly possess Caleb. If miracles existed, Leo would gamble for one.

Scoring Zone

Book 3 – Austin (Ace) Lapointe and Grayson (Gray) Ward
Love was never the game plan
Austin wakes up after the best night of his life only to find his worst nightmare come true—he hurt the one person he can't live without: Grayson. Vegas unlocked Austin's craving for Gray, but something he fears alongside it. If Austin tells Gray the truth, he could lose him. But by staying silent, he already has.

Enemy ZoneComing April 2026

Book 4 – Jamal King and Theo O'Keefe
Rivals to teammates—with one shot a love
Jamal's father never wanted him until he became a hockey star. His stepbrother Theo got all the privileges that come with the King name and money. Jamal is the first black man in the league to come out, and he felt safe with his team...until his rival Theo gets traded to the Enforcers.

QR CODES
THE TRUTH OF LOVING YOU

THE TRUTH OF OUR PAST

THE TRUTH OF OUR SECRETS

TRUTH ZONE

MISCONDUCT ZONE

PENALTY ZONE

SCORING ZONE

Enemy Zone

ACKNOWLEDGEMENTS

Some days I can't believe I'm able to live my life as a published author. It's been just under two years, and it still feels surreal. I have all of you to thank for this gift you've given me.

To peel back the layers of help I need to be successful, I have to thank the people who get me out of bed in the morning: the 9am Inkers Sprint – part of my Inkers Mastermind group: https://inkerscon.com/mastermind-fall-2025/

I don't know where I'd be without all of you to keep me on track.

Huge thanks to my irreplaceable beta readers, who always help make my books better! TG and Dee also double as my sensitivity readers and keep my books away from my unconscious bias. Kate is my hockey expert and instrumental in fine-tuning the hockey plots. CM, CZ, Monroe and TG provide the feedback I need to hear to grow as a writer. I couldn't have published without all of you.

TG Ramsey:

https://www.facebook.com/t.g.ramsey.writer

C.M. Degen:

https://www.instagram.com/c.m.degen/

CZ Reeves:

https://www.instagram.com/c.m.degen/

Monroe Beckett:

https://www.facebook.com/author.monroe.beckett.2024/

Kate Lucas:

https://www.instagram.com/pawsandbooks_kate/

Dee Lamarr:
https://www.instagram.com/thatswhatdeeread/

As authors, we get inspiration from everywhere. One of my favorite content creators inspired a grocery store scene in this book, and I hope it's everything she could ask for. Thank you, Christine: https://www.instagram.com/paperb ackintheday/

I wouldn't be here without readers who review and post about my books. I owe all of you a debt of thanks and gratitude. Thank you from the bottom of my heart.

My beta and sensitivity readers help me deliver not only a spicy, heartwarming romance but make sure the details are correct. If you think I didn't get something right, feel free to email me at heather@heatherleighsonwrites.com I'm happy to hear from you.

My family has been my rock and biggest cheerleaders. I'm lucky to be able to write and have their unwavering acceptance and encouragement. Thank you: Hubby, First born, and The boss xoxoxo

ABOUT THE AUTHOR

Heather Leighson has been a book addict since childhood. Books are her escape. Her TBR is always over 420 books, no matter how many she reads. A self-proclaimed book dragon. She pretends not to lose track of things but needs to be reminded to shower and eat when she's in a writing groove. Or reading a particularly long book, lol.

She has proudly passed this love along to her children. They are now adults and cheer on her dreams even though they are not allowed to read her books. Her and her husband call Central New York home.

Heather is in love with love and writes about finding the person who fills your soul and heals your hurt. Romances that unbreak hearts. She finds there is something satisfying about overcoming the obstacles and struggles to find true love. Of course, that journey involves lots of spice and a bit of kink.

When she's not writing or editing, she's reading and planning her next adventure.

Sign up for my newsletter for updates, releases and sales! Click hereor go to my website www.heatherleighsonwrites.com

Follow Me:

a https://amzn.to/3JfnhtM

f facebook.com/heather.leighson.writes.2023

⊙ instagram.com/heatherleighsonwrites/

BB bookbub.com/authors/heather-leighson